THE NEIGHBORS

K. LUCAS

THE NEIGHBORS

K. LUCAS

EBook ISBN: 979-8-9850093-4-7

Paperback ISBN: 979-8-9850093-5-4

Hardback ISBN: 979-8-9850093-6-1

Cover Design by Pretty In Ink Creations

Interior artwork by Pretty In Ink Creations

Formatting by K. Lucas

For my son

The pain is excruciating. I feel like I'm dying. All the birthing classes in the world can't prepare you for the actual, real-life agony of labor. No one ever mentioned what back labor was like, either. I feel like someone is trying to grab onto my spine, just between my hips, and yank it out of my body. Maybe they're not yanking; maybe they're just stabbing me with a dagger, over and over. This feeling consumes me as an invisible band tightens around my pelvic region, gripping me like a vice.

I scream, needing to find release anyway I can. "Charlie!" I call for my husband, forgetting he's not home. I'm all alone. As soon as this contraction passes, I move to find my phone, so I can call him. When I do, I feel something warm trickling down my leg. Now *this* is something they've told me about. My water broke; it's completely normal. But when I look down, it's blood I see, not clear fluid. Anxiety shoots through me in an instant. I can barely breathe from the fear that's creeping in. *Something is wrong.*

I wake up with a jolt. I'm in a cold sweat, panting, trying to catch my breath. Looking around, I remember that I'm not there. I'm here. I'm in my thirty-five-foot travel trailer. We've started a new life in Washington. To my right is my daughter, asleep beside me. I take a deep breath to calm my racing heart. The nightmares still come after all this time. Lately they've been less frequent, almost gone completely.

Checking the time on my phone, I see that it's two a.m. I send a quick text to Charlie. "Nightmare again. I'm fine. Love you." He knows about the recurring nightmares, of course, and worries about me. I could opt to not tell him about them, but I think he would know I have them even if I said nothing. He works most nights, but not every one. There are times he's next to me in bed to witness for himself what wakes me up at night.

The phone flashes with his response but I leave it laying on the bed. All I can do is roll over and hold my daughter as tight as I can without waking her. The sound of Bear, our German Shepherd, whimpering to be let out, wakes me up in the morning. I groan, knowing he doesn't give me much advanced warning. If I don't pop up now, there's a good chance he'll do his business on the floor.

As soon as I'm up, Bear gives me a wet kiss good morning, along with whining, telling me how much he's missed me while I've been sleeping. I open the door and he flies out.

"Morning, Mommy!" Looks like Bear woke up Ellie, too.

"Good morning, cupcake," I say, giving her a kiss.

"Is Daddy home, yet?"

"Not yet, baby. Another long night for Daddy." I fight the urge to clench my fists in frustration. She misses him so much. Ever since he's started this new job at our new home, his hours have almost doubled; It feels like we barely see him at all anymore. "Let's do something fun today," I say, trying to cheer her up.

"Okay. I want to go exploring!"

I chuckle. Somehow, I suspected that's what she was going to say. "Sounds good to me!"

Ready for the day, we open the RV door, stepping out

onto our forty acres of raw land. Our temporary home is set up in a clearing and we're surrounded by seemingly endless forest. My mind is still baffled that it's all ours. This is real. So much beautiful land, covered in enormous pine trees and what seems like endless life, all belongs to us. It's amazing and a little scary.

Before moving, the closest I'd been to this kind of nature was documentaries on Netflix. Our life before was an entire world of difference, compared to now. We lived in San Francisco, in a small studio apartment. Because I could walk everywhere I needed, we were a one car household. Charlie took the car to work, and it was fine. I didn't need one, or even want one. If I needed to go a little farther, there was always a taxi, or rideshare.

Now, it takes almost twenty minutes to get to the nearest grocery store. The only place I can reasonably walk is down the driveway to the mailbox. There are no sounds of cars honking, or people talking. There are no sounds of the trolley car, or a cruise ship coming into port. The only sounds I hear now are the birds chirping and the rustling of the leaves in the breeze. The quiet is deafening to a city girl. We've only been here for a month, but I'm getting used to it; I'm starting to even like it a little.

As Ellie and I start to explore our property, I realize Bear still hasn't come back from his morning potty break. "Bear!" I call, hoping he hasn't wondered too far. Ellie repeats after me, "Bear! Bear!"

"It's okay, cupcake. I'm sure he's just found something interesting to sniff," I say.

"I miss Bear," she frowns.

"Don't worry, he'll come back soon." Bear is one of the smartest dogs I've ever seen. He comes when he's called and knows not to wander off too far. He rarely *wants* to be that far from us anyway, but dogs will be dogs. When he finds something interesting, he'll sniff around for a bit.

We don't have a fence for him yet but aren't really concerned because of what a good boy he is and how much land we have. There's plenty of room for him to roam around without bothering anyone. He's not responding now, which is unusual for him. Normally, if he doesn't come running back to me, he at least barks so I know he's heard me.

"Come on, Mommy! Let's go." Ellie pulls me out of our little clearing, into the forest. She has a walking stick and I have a large branch clipper to help clear the way. Ellie and I have been trying to make some walking trails throughout the property, so we have a place to walk other than to the mailbox and back, but it's been a slow process.

Our goal is to have a trail that winds through the entire property so we can go on daily walks without having to fight the vegetation. After living in the city for so long, my legs have been aching for exercise. Ellie looks at it as our daily adventure and I love it.

After several minutes, a gunshot rings out. We stop in our tracks, and I pull Ellie tight against me. I've never heard a real gunshot before, but it's one of those sounds that you just know what it is when you hear it. I think it's close, but how am I supposed to know how close, close is? Fear seeps in. "Bear!" I call, but he still doesn't answer. *Shit!* "Ellie, let's head back to the camper, okay?"

"Why?" She looks scared too, but that's the last thing I wanted.

I try to hide my worry, "Let's just check if Bear came back to the door yet." This seems to make sense to her because she agrees without a fuss.

As soon as we're back to the trailer, we hear Bear's barking. Relief washes over me. *Thank God.* Bushes move in the distance before Bear leaps out. "Bear!" Ellie yells, running toward him. He meets her, licking her face, making her laugh from his tickles.

My relief is short-lived however, and is completely gone when I hear the roar of an engine on our driveway. Bear trots up to my side. A low growl comes from his throat as we hear a vehicle coming towards us. "Ellie, come here," I say. My tone is urgent, allowing no argument.

"Why?" she asks. She hasn't noticed the sound like Bear and I have.

"Listen to me, now Ellie. Please don't ask questions, cupcake." I'm trying to get my point across, without scaring her again. Her three-year-old little brain is so curious; it's an amazing thing, but right now, frustrating as hell.

"Why, Mommy!" She yells at me now. Bear's hairs are standing up on his back. He barks a single time. I've never heard him like this before. He looks like he's ready to rip someone into shreds. He's in a protective stance, watching for the vehicle to come around the bend in the driveway.

At his bark, Ellie stops asking questions. She finally realizes something important is happening and comes to my side. With one hand, her little fingers grip me. I put her behind my back, bending my arm so I can still hold on to her. With my other hand, I pet Bear's head gently, whispering, "Good boy, Bear."

Finally, an old rusty pickup truck appears. It stops about a hundred feet from us. Bear barks again. He stays by my side, waiting. No one has gotten out of the truck; we're all at a standstill. My hands are starting to sweat. *Why didn't I text Charlie when I had the chance?*

TWO

The engine on the old truck turns off. A lanky, middle-aged man steps out holding a shotgun. My eyes go wide. I'm frozen in place, unable to think or move. I feel like my lungs forgot how to work. What kind of person would show up at a stranger's home, holding a gun? Fear holds me in its grip, but one thought gets through. *Ellie.*

I turn around and kneel at her level. "Listen to me right now, Ellie Marie. Don't you ask me any questions. You do what I say, I mean it, baby girl." Her eyes are saucers; I can tell she's about to cry, but there's no time to baby her. "Take Mommy's phone and run inside. You go to the back of the trailer and hide under your bed. Then, you call 911, and tell the nice person what's happening." We've gone over what to do in an emergency before. She is already prepared and knows how to make a phone call.

Ellie nods. "Okay, Mommy."

"Which numbers are you going to push, Ellie?"

"9-1-1."

"Good girl, now run." I hand over my phone and watch her take off to the trailer door. I'm not the only one with my eye on her. The man in the driveway watches her run, too. I say a silent prayer that she'll be fast enough and will be *safe* from this lunatic.

The man is still walking toward me, now keeping his eyes on Bear. As he grows closer, bear's growls become louder. Now that Ellie is inside, I call out to him. "What makes you think you can bring a gun on *my* land? Who the hell are you?" I'm shaking, scared to death, and feel like I might pee myself, but I'm not about to cower.

He stops walking. *Thank God.* "That fuckin' dog!" he says, then points the shotgun at Bear.

My heart hammers in my chest. I feel light-headed. *Jesus, what the hell is happening?!* "Whoa! That's *my* fucking dog, asshole!"

He finally takes his eyes off Bear, who is still by my side and still growling. The man looks at me. I've seen no one look that angry in my entire life. The malice in his eyes sends chills through me. His face is so red it looks like it might explode. I say, "Look, lower the gun and let's talk like human beings." I don't want to make him angrier, but what am I supposed to say to someone who looks prepared for murder?

My words seem to get through to him because he lowers the shotgun. Now, he walks towards me again. I have a hand on Bear and can feel his tension. He's like a one-hundred-pound spring, with really sharp teeth, ready to launch as soon as I give the word. This guy in my driveway is an absolute idiot to think he can come here and threaten us this way.

At this moment, I'm so thankful for Bear. I'm terrified for all our lives, but at the same time, I feel so much love for this loyal dog, who's ready to protect me and Ellie until the end. He would lay down his life without question. The love I feel for him is overwhelming, almost bringing tears to my eyes. *I won't let it come to that,* I say to him in my head.

I can smell the stench of the man as he comes closer. When he's close enough to have an actual conversation with, I say, "Bear, stop," and Bear stops growling.

The man says, "Your dog is out of control!"

I look at Bear. *There's never been a dog more IN control*, I think. I ask, "What makes you say that?"

"He killed my fuckin' chickens. Every fuckin' one." He spits on the gravel.

I can't hide my grimace. Two things go through my mind. One, is that this man is my neighbor. Two, is that this doesn't sound like Bear. He's so gentle and I've never even seen him chase after a squirrel. "I'm sorry for your loss." *Is that the correct thing to say?* "Are you sure it was him?"

"You're goddamn right, I'm sure. Was out on the porch and seen him come trottin' up the road. Sure enough, fucker grabbed every one of my girls."

My brows furrow as I try to understand his accusation. "Were the chickens in the road? You don't have a fence for them?"

Apparently, that's the wrong thing to ask, because suddenly he's turned a frightening shade of purple and *really* looks like he's about to burst. "That don't fucking matter! They're free-range birds and that animal," he points at Bear, "needs to be in a fucking cage. Next time I'll shoot 'im dead, make no mistake. You're lucky I don't do it right now."

There's so much I want to say, but I'm still afraid of what he might do. How can he justify caging a dog but not chickens? He's dead serious and I'm baffled by his logic. This total stranger is over here waving around a shotgun, threatening us over some *chickens*! It sounds like Bear didn't even go onto the man's property, so it's not like he can claim trespassing.

"Look," I say, "I don't appreciate you coming onto my land, waving your gun in my face, and threatening the life of my dog. You scared the shit out of my daughter and myself.

It's uncalled for. I'm sorry about your chickens, but surely you see threatening us will solve nothing." I take a breath. "Can I compensate you for the chickens?"

I thought it was sort of an olive branch; at least I was offering to pay, even with no proof that Bear is the one who killed the damn birds. Instead of him calming down to a more rational level, the opposite happens. He explodes into a litany of curses and waves the shotgun around again. When he does this, Bear starts snarling and I'm more afraid now than ever that this is going to escalate to an ugly level.

"That dog is *dangerous!*" he screams. "I'm calling animal control. You're *fucking* done."

Bear isn't about to let this asshole mess with his mom. When the man raises his voice, Bear moves in front of me. His hackles are up, tail stiff as a board, and he's snarling so much that foam is dripping out the sides of his mouth. His two-inch long canines are ready to rip into the crazy man's flesh. I'm proud of him, but I don't want it to come to that. Bear's chances against a shotgun aren't good.

Then, there are sirens in the distance. *Thank Christ!* I want to breathe a sigh of relief, but I'm not out of the woods yet. My insane neighbor is still yelling at me. After another minute, the sound of the sirens seems to get through to him. He stops ranting and looks at me up and down. He looks a little confused, like he's trying to figure out how the hell I managed to call the cops. I want to cry. I want to scream, "That's right, motherfucker! Who's done now?" I want to tell Bear to eat his fucking face. I'm so angry and frightened and all the feelings in-between. I want to let it out, but I can't. Not yet.

The sirens are growing closer. I'm waiting to see what the man will do. He looks like he's weighing his options. *Is it that hard of a decision to make?* After what feels like an eternity, he says, "You're gonna pay, alright. Don't you worry about that. You don't know what sorry is yet, but don't you worry. You will." He turns around then and heads back to his truck. Bear is silent now, watching him leave. The engine starts, then he peels out of the driveway, his rear tires spitting rocks.

THREE

As soon as the neighbor's truck is out of earshot, I break down. I fall to the ground crying with relief. Bear whimpers and licks my face. "Good boy, Bear. Good boy. *Good boy*!" I cry, over and over. I can't tell him enough how much he's saved me. I have a feeling if he wasn't right there next to me, my lovely neighbor wouldn't have been so lovely. Bear was probably the only reason he didn't use that shotgun.

A shutter racks through me as I think about how ugly it really could've gotten. I'm so thankful for Bear. I grab him and hold on tight, sobbing into his fur. The sirens are still in the distance; they sound like they're nearly here. I try to pull myself together as best I can and run to the camper for Ellie.

Opening the door, I call for her. "Ellie, baby!" She's silent. *Good girl.* We've gone over this countless times. She's supposed to wait for the safe word. "Cheesecake, Ellie."

"Mommy?"

"It's okay, cupcake, he's gone."

She comes out, running to me with her arms open, crying. My heart breaks seeing her this afraid. "Shh. It's okay now. Shhh," I say, rubbing her hair the way she likes. "I'm so proud of you. You saved us, baby."

Ellie sniffles. "I did?"

"You sure did. You called 911, just like I asked."

"No, I didn't."

"Baby, those are police sirens. You didn't call 911?"

"No. I forgot numbers. I called daddy."

What a smart little girl. She didn't remember the numbers, but she knew she could call her daddy for help. I smile at her, then pull her in tighter. "Baby, you still saved us. I'm so proud of you."

Outside, a Sheriff's car comes up the driveway. The three of us: Ellie, Bear, and myself, all greet the officer. I explain what's happened and how frightened we all were.

"Do you know who he was? Did he give you his name?" he asks.

"No. We didn't get that far in the conversation."

Officer Adrian nods. "Sounds like your neighbor, alright. Tom Morgan. He's been known to have a temper and there's always one complaint or another regarding him. This is farther than he's ever gone, though."

"Well, he was pretty pissed." I shake my head. "What's going to happen now? I'm afraid of him coming back, officer. And he threatened to call animal control."

"There's not much I can do at this point. Animal control will come out to have a chat. He was in your driveway, which is technically a safe zone. Anyone can go there. He wasn't pointing the gun at you, so he wasn't threatening your life. It's the first time it's happened, so it's not an ongoing issue."

"You're just full of good news."

"I'm sorry. I wish there was more I could do, but my hands are tied. If I go over there and he decides he doesn't like the police, he could try suing the department for harassment."

"But animal control can come over here and harass me?"

Officer Adrian shrugs. "I'm sorry. That's the way things are in our county."

I'm disgusted. Nothing about this situation is right. "So, what do I do?"

"Lock your doors and try to ignore him. People like this will run out of steam, eventually. Try to keep your dog from getting out."

"This is insane. I'm supposed to lock myself inside a trailer twenty-four-seven? There's literally *nothing* that can be done?"

"From what I've heard about Tom, he's pretentious. He likes to make himself look like a tough guy, but that's it. He's all puff. I would lie low for now, let him run out of steam. I don't think he'll come back over here if you keep your dog locked up."

I'm not sure how much I can rely on that. I'm not putting my family's lives in danger just because this cop thinks it's *not in his nature.* "Maybe he won't be all puff this time."

Officer Adrian thinks for a second. "You could be right." He sighs. "I would be more worried that he'll go after the dog than anything else." He points to Bear.

"What can I do?"

"You might want to get a front gate, for starters. It might not do much to stop him from walking in, but at least it would slow him down and might keep him from driving in. I know it's not fair, but if you have a rope or chain, I'd keep Bear here, tied up for a while, at least until Tom can cool down, like I said."

I shake my head, frowning. There's no way I'm going to tie Bear up to a rope.

"I know," Officer Adrian says, "But this way, there's no doubt that Bear is staying at home. If he gets out again, there's no telling what Tom will get into his head."

A few hours later, Charlie comes home. He makes sure we're fine, then because he's exhausted from a fourteen-hour shift, he pecks me on the cheek and goes to bed. I want to cry. This morning's ordeal weighs on me, and I feel an urgent need to talk to Charlie about it. I want him to hold me and comfort me; I want him to do *anything* to make it better. But he can't. He has to go to bed so he can go back to work in ten hours.

Ellie, Bear, and I stay outside for most of the day. We wander into the woods, collecting rocks and exploring. I don't have the heart to lock Bear up. I still don't believe he could've done something like that unprovoked. No. I refuse to chain him. I make sure he doesn't leave my line of sight, though, just to be safe.

Sometimes being in the woods, how we are, feels more suffocating than the city ever did. Trees surround me as far as I can see. If I look up toward the sky, they loom over me, blocking the clouds and sunlight. Sometimes it's magnificent. Right now, it isn't.

I try to keep my mind off it, knowing that Ellie and Bear are having a great time. Every now and then Ellie tosses a stick and Bear runs to grab it and gnaws on it. Every movement in the trees, every sound, makes me flinch. I think it's *him* coming back. He wasn't done with me. I know it.

Soon, I'm sweating all over, despite the mild weather. I'm panting, trying to catch my breath. I look like I've just worked out, even though I've barely made any physical effort. The anxiety is getting to me, and I've had about all I can take for the day.

"Ellie, let's go in now," I say.

She's in the middle of examining a caterpillar. "No."

"Ellie Marie, what did you just say?" I have my mom voice on now.

"Whyyy?" Great, just what I need. A tantrum.

"Cupcake, I don't feel good. Please, let's go inside for a bit."

"Okay." My heart warms. Ellie always has empathy for me when I'm not feeling well, no matter what kind of temperament she's in.

As we make our way back to the clearing, I take deep breaths, trying to calm myself down. I tell myself everything is fine and as soon as I can, I'm going to figure this out with Charlie. We can get a front gate, like officer Adrian suggested. If there's a gate, no crazy neighbors will get through. These thoughts help me relax a little, until we get back.

Ellie screams. My breath catches and I'm frozen for a moment before I can reach to cover her eyes. Dead chickens are everywhere. They're mutilated, with guts hanging out and some of the heads severed. Feathers cover the yard along with their bodies and various parts. At our reaction, Bear barks and runs forward. He sniffs at a chicken, but he doesn't take any interest.

"It's okay Ellie, let's just go inside."

She's not screaming now, but I can tell she's terrified. "Are the chickies okay?"

"I don't think so, baby." I don't know what to say. I don't think I can explain to her what's happening, even if I wanted to. I'm still covering her eyes because I don't want her to be traumatized by this. We weave our way through the yard to the camper door. I hold back a cry when I see the spray paint on the side of the trailer. Tears stream down my cheeks as I read, "Fuck you!"

CHAPTER
FOUR

There's an animal control truck coming up the driveway. After speaking with Officer Adrian, I've been expecting them to show up, but didn't realize it would be so soon. The large cage on the back of the truck sends a sinking feeling to my stomach.

The animal control officer approaches with a grim look on his face. "I'm officer Gonzales with animal control," he says. "Your neighbor has issued a complaint against your dog for killing his chickens."

"Yes, I'm aware he believes that, but I don't believe my dog would do something like that."

"He says he witnessed the event. In this county, that's all that's required."

"I'm sorry, what? He may be confused. My dog wouldn't do this. Not unprovoked. There are other dogs in the neighborhood, I'm sure. He has no fence; the chickens walk in the road–"

"Stop trying to argue," he says. "Stop trying to blame the victim. *You* may not believe your dog is dangerous, but I'm going to believe this man if he says he saw this happen with his own eyes."

I can't believe what I'm hearing, and I'm growing more

agitated by the minute. "This man has it out for me. He came up my driveway, yelling and cussing at me. He threatened me in front of my child! I believe he'll say anything if he believes my dog was responsible. And he spread his dead chickens all over my yard and vandalized my property!"

"His chickens just died. He has a right to be upset."

"I don't deserve to be treated that way, no matter what happened to his damn chickens."

"Ok, well I'm here to inform you that your dog is under investigation for being dangerous."

This man's attitude towards me grates on my nerves more than anything he's saying. The look on his face tells me how biased he is. How unwilling to listen to both sides of an argument. I wonder what kind of *investigation* there might be, when he's basically already told me he's going to listen to Tom's side of the story, automatically, with no other proof. His attitude is pure snark. I want to tell him to get the hell off my property. There's nothing else to be said. He's obviously not willing to listen to me.

"What does that mean?" I ask.

"If he's declared dangerous, you may be required to surrender ownership."

"That's not going to happen." This is unbelievable. Over fucking *chickens*!

"There's a dangerous animal permit. The cost is two hundred and fifty dollars each year. You'll also be required to carry personal liability insurance in the amount of one hundred thousand dollars. There will be other requirements as well, like making sure he's sterilized and in a fenced location at all times. All the details are available on the county website."

"I can't believe this. This is insane." I'm so angry I could scream. I'm barely hanging onto my patience by a thread. "Look at him. Look at this dog. You're telling me he's dangerous?" I point at Bear, who's right next to me, sitting down, *not* barking.

Officer Gonzales ignores me. I realize he's just doing his job, but he's being an asshole about it. He could be more understanding. Bear is a *dog*, for Christ's sake. Even *if* it was him that killed the chickens, how can they blame a dog for doing what's in his nature? How can the county possibly think it's okay to hold that against him?

"Would you like to provide your contact information so I can call you when there's a decision made? Otherwise, you'll get a letter in the mail."

I feel so abandoned by the government right now. Not just abandoned, but attacked. Because of the words of one angry, insane individual, my dog might either be taken from me, or I might be fined to death. There's nothing I can do. There's no protection from psychos like this. How can they not realize there are people out there who will lie their asses off if it means they get to stick it to the neighbor they don't like?

Surely, they should know that people hold grudges. People aren't stupid, either. If they know they can accuse their neighbor's dogs of things like this, they're going to be doing it. If you want a neighbor out of your hair, this is a fine way to get it done quickly. This *officer* is supposed to be unbiased. He's supposed to gather all the *facts*. I'm not sure when opinions became facts, but it's clear that's how he sees things. It disgusts me to my core.

CHAPTER

FIVE

Melanie turned on the kitchen faucet to clean some dishes. When she did, water came from below the faucet body instead of flowing from the spout. She jerked back when it sprayed her face. "Shit!" she cried. She fumbled for the handle. It took her a moment to clear the water from her vision so she could shut it off.

When she got it, there was a lot more water than what had just sprayed her. Melanie opened the cabinet, peering down below the pipes. *Dammit*, she thought. There was a leak again, and it seemed to be more than just the pipe needing a little tightening.

She pulled out her phone and opened her social media app. In a community group, she asked, "Any recommendations on a great plumber? Having some issues with our kitchen sink!" Then she locked her phone. It looked like dishes weren't getting done today, so she moved on to some other household chores.

Later that day, Melanie checked the responses to her question online. Several people had recommended Dave's Plumbing. She googled the company, double checking reviews, then posted, "Looks like it's Dave's for the win.

Thanks all!" Melanie pulled up the phone number for Dave's Plumbing and scheduled an appointment.

The soonest they could squeeze her in was in three days. She begged for something sooner, but it was the best they could manage. It seemed they weren't the only company booked out, so she took what she could get.

The next day, Melanie received a phone call from a blocked number. She never answered unknown callers, but thinking it might be the plumber, made an exception. "Hello?" she answered.

"Hello. Is this Ms. Lewis?" A voice asked.

"Yes, it is. May I ask who's calling?"

"This is Taylor Dave, the owner of Dave's Plumbing."

"Oh, Taylor! Thank you for calling."

"My pleasure, ma'am. I just wanted to let you know I had a cancellation come in, and if you're available, I can squeeze you in earlier than planned."

"Yes! Absolutely! Anytime you can come out, I'll be here."

"Great. I'm right around the corner; I should be less than twenty minutes."

"Excellent! See you soon."

Melanie hung up, then rushed to tidy up the kitchen. She wanted to make sure the plumber had plenty of room to work. She peeked out her front window. From her living room, she could see down the gravel driveway, to the dirt road. Living in the country usually meant it took people a while to get there, and twenty minutes really was right around the corner for her.

She glanced at the clock. Plenty of time before she had to pick the kids up from school. She thought, *Nick is going to be so proud of me!* Her husband had just been complaining that she never made appointments, and always left them for him to take care of. It was mostly true, but only because any appointments they needed were for home maintenance, which she knew nothing about. Melanie was far more comfortable having her husband find the repairmen, but this would show him.

Right on time, twenty minutes later, a white van caked in mud pulled up the driveway. It was old and looked like it was barely running, which gave Melanie a moment's pause. She didn't want to be judgmental, but thought if Dave's ran a successful business, surely they would have the funds to upkeep a company vehicle. She noticed the van was also unmarked. She'd been expecting to see a company logo, but supposed it wasn't unusual to not have one.

Melanie made herself busy, giving Taylor a few minutes to get out of the van, grab the necessary tools, and come to the door. When the doorbell rang, Melanie opened the door to welcome Taylor inside. "Thank God you called," she said. "I don't know what I would've done waiting another two days."

"My pleasure," Taylor said, smiling. "I'm glad it all worked out."

THAT AFTERNOON, NICK RECEIVED A PHONE CALL FROM HIS children's school.

"Mr. Chadwick, Ben and Molly are here, waiting to be picked up," the school secretary said.

"What? My wife hasn't shown up?"

"No, sir. They've been waiting here for an hour now."

"Okay. Tell them I'm sorry and either Melanie or I will be there right away."

When he dialed Melanie, she didn't pick up. It was unlike her; she never forgot the kids. Nick was growing worried by the minute. He sent a text to Melanie on his way to the car. "Mel, getting worried! Please call!"

As soon as he picked up the kids, the three of them went straight home. Nick was the first through the door. What he saw paralyzed him with fear. He was too shocked to stop Ben or Molly from coming in.

At the sound of Molly's scream, Nick moved. He called 9-1-1, then herded his children back out the door. "9-1-1 what is your emergency?" the operator asked.

"My- my wife is hurt."

"How badly is your wife hurt? Can you identify the injury?"

"She's- she-" Nick gasped in air, trying to catch his breath. He choked on sour bile, trying not to vomit. "She's not moving."

"Okay sir, help is on the way."

Nick dropped his phone. There was nothing else he could say. The image of his wife was seared into his brain; he'd never be able to get rid of it.

The first thing he saw was "Fuck you," spray painted in black on the living room wall. Then his eyes dropped to Melanie. She was mutilated beyond recognition. Her blood was splattered on the walls, along with thick chunks of her flesh. It was hard to see through the blood, but Nick could tell that she was naked. She was tied up face down on her stomach. Her arms and legs were bent behind her, all bound with rope. She would've been completely helpless.

Without wanting to, Nick imagined the things that were done to her that would've brought so much blood. An image of a dark figure over her body came to mind. Nick shuttered to think of how much pain she must've gone through. He shook his head, hating himself for trying to picture it.

By the time the police and ambulance showed up, Nick was broken down, sobbing with both kids. He knew he was supposed to be strong for them, but *how?*

CHAPTER
SIX

I'm on a gurney, being rolled through the hospital. Nurses and doctors surround me. They're speaking to me, saying things, but none of their words are getting through. Everything is muffled. I can see everything I need to know in their eyes. Every single one of them has a look of pity. I look away, unable to meet any of their gazes.

When I look down at myself, I see the blood that's still gushing from between my legs. Pain rips through me again as another contraction holds me in its grip. "Charlie!" I cry out for my husband, but he's still not with me. Tears fall from my eyes. I can hardly breathe, but it's not from the pain. It's from anger.

Someone is shaking me. I wake up to see Charlie hovering over me. "Hey," he says.

"What's wrong?"

"You were yelling and grinding your teeth again. Did you have another nightmare?"

Still groggy, I rub my eyes and sigh. "Yes."

Charlie sits on the bed next to my legs. He has the same look that all the nurses and doctors had. I roll over, looking away. He says nothing then, just gets up and heads to work.

Charlie knows what my nightmares are about; he doesn't have to ask.

Unable to get back to sleep, I get up early and turn on the local news. Bear lies on the bed with me while I watch. The highlight of the day is a story about a woman who was murdered in the area. Her husband and kids had come home to find her brutally raped and murdered, and the police were still searching for suspects. Apparently, her uterus was cut out while she was still alive. *Poor woman.* It's too depressing to watch, so I turn it off and grab a book instead.

It's been a week since the visit from our neighbor. Charlie and I still haven't had a proper discussion about it. I've been too angry with him for sleeping the entire time someone was right outside, vandalizing our property. He blames me for being gone while it happened. I'm angry with him for blaming me. It's a vicious cycle.

Officer Adrian had come back to take my second statement for the day. He took pictures and filed a report, but again, there was not much else he could do. "Get a gate," he'd urged. I know we need one. It's another thing that Charlie and I argued about.

AFTER AN HOUR OF READING, I SWAP MY BOOK FOR MY laptop. My goal today is to do online hunting for a car. We've been a one-car family in this new home for too long; it's time we put an end to it. I'm so tired of waiting for Charlie for everything. I could throw up just thinking about it. Ellie starts preschool soon, and I'm tired of feeling so trapped and isolated. Especially with this neighbor incident, I need a car to feel safe and not so confined.

Bear starts to whimper when he hears Ellie stir. When she comes out of her room, she gives him love, laughing at his kisses, as always. "Morning cupcake," I say.

"Morning Mommy."

"How would you like to go on an adventure today?"

"Yeah!" She jumps from excitement, causing the trailer to rock back and forth.

I laugh at her enthusiasm. "Okay, okay. Ellie, stop jumping, please. Remember, not in the trailer, baby."

She stops, then comes to give me a big hug and kiss.

It was hard, but I was able to find a rideshare driver willing to chauffeur Ellie and I around for the morning. Because of our distance from the nearest town, no one really wants to come out this far. But money talks. For the right price, anyone will go anywhere, it seems. And Charlie is working enough; we can afford the extra expense. If I don't take matters into my own hands, I'll never get a car of my own.

I'm nervous about leaving Bear home alone. It's not because I don't trust him; it's because I don't trust our neighbor. What if he shows up again? What would he do to Bear if they were alone together? The idea terrifies me, and I almost decide to stay home. But I tell myself that Crazy hasn't shown up again since he left the dead chickens. If he was going to, surely he would've done so before now.

"WILL YOU TAKE NINE THOUSAND?" I ASK, STILL LOOKING over the Jeep and already in love. I have a terrible poker face and don't want the seller to see how much I want this Wrangler.

There's a moment of silence while he thinks about it. It's already a great deal, and he could get more. I'm sure he knows it, too. I hate to be a low baller, but I figure it doesn't hurt to ask. "Yeah. I guess I can do that," he says. He's eager to have the sale over and done with. I don't blame him.

Yes! I fight the grin that wants to spread. "Sounds great, thank you." We shake hands and I grab the bank envelope full of his money while he gets the title ready. This must be the happiest moment I've had in a long time- probably since the day that Charlie came home with Bear.

It was shortly after… well, it was while we were in San Francisco. I was in an awful place and Bear saved me. I know it's supposed to be your kids that save you. I'm supposed to say Ellie pulled me out of my darkness, and it's true, I *had* to be there for her. I know that, but with Bear, it's different. It's like he ate my demons. Not all of them; there are definitely still some lingering. But without Bear, I don't think I would be around today. He saved me from myself.

Ellie and I ride with the top off our new Jeep, wind whipping our hair. The feeling of freedom engulfs me, and I feel better than I've felt in ages. I don't think about how Charlie will react when he sees what I've done. Thinking of that will ruin my mood.

SEVEN

When we get home, there's an eerie silence. Normally, the crunch of the gravel under our tires has Bear barking and going berserk. He knows when it's me coming home and has a hard time containing his happiness. I can always hear him when he's inside the trailer. Now, though, there's nothing. A feeling of dread winds its way to the pit of my stomach. *Bear!* I run for the trailer door, hoping he's just taking a nap.

"Mommy, what's wrong?" Ellie is starting to be concerned now too, although she doesn't know what's going on. I don't answer her. I swing open the trailer door, lift her inside, and follow.

"Bear!" I call, looking everywhere. It's not that big of a space; there are few places a dog his size would be able to lay. "Bear!" I yell again, my voice wobbly now.

"Mommy?" Ellie is starting to cry now.

I'm too worried about Bear to comfort her, though. I pick her up and run back down the steps. Outside, I call for Bear again, over and over. I know it's pointless. *He's gone.*

I can feel the cold hands of panic starting to grip me. It grows harder to breathe; my lungs don't seem to be working right. I can see black spots in the corner of my vision, and I grow lightheaded as my heart is about to beat out of my chest. *Bear!* I set Ellie down and focus on breathing. She's still crying, yelling for me to stop. She wants to know what's happening. *I need her to stop!* Her noise is making my head pound too, on top of everything else. *I just need one minute to think!*

This has to be the neighbor. He's pissed about his goddamned chickens. I could scream at the idiocy of it. It had to be him, but how could he have done it? The trailer door was locked. I don't know. What else could've happened? Who else would be angry enough to take Bear from me? No. It's simple. There *is* no one else.

When I finally have myself a little under control, I say, "Ellie. Please give me a minute to think. Stop crying now, everything is going to be okay."

"Why?"

"Why what?"

"Why!" Still crying, and my head still pounding.

I sigh, picking her up and holding her. I rock her back and forth; the momentum calms both of us. Ellie finally stops crying and I'm able to breathe again. I think of texting Charlie about Bear, but then I think, *What will he do about it? Nothing. That's what.* I decide not to bother him. He'll find out soon enough.

TWO DAYS LATER, BEAR STILL ISN'T HOME. FOR THE LIFE OF me, I can't think how he got out of a locked trailer. I've thought again about the neighbor coming to snatch him, but the door was locked when I came home. How would he unlock it and lock it back again? *Why* would he do that? And if he did get in, I don't even know how he would get Bear out of the trailer without Bear eating him alive. I play the scenario over and over in my mind, thinking it was Tom, but questioning how it makes sense.

Charlie was upset about the Jeep. He knew I needed a car, but didn't expect me to spend so much money. "I can't believe you took that much out of savings. We're trying to build a house here, Paisley. Why would you do something like that without me being there?"

We argued about it, and about how I'm always waiting around for him to stop working. "I'm sorry," he said. "You want a nice house, don't you? When he says things like that, I feel so guilty. He's the one working his ass off, after all. At the same time, I want to hit his smug face with my fist. He has no idea.

He knows how much Bear means to me; Bear means a lot to Charlie too. After the initial fight about the Jeep, he hasn't brought it up again. We've both been anxious about Bear coming home. Ellie doesn't understand why Bear is gone; none of us do.

I'm frantic with worry. There isn't much we can do other than wait. Bear has a microchip and we've put out the missing posters, but we're in the middle of nowhere. It's so different from the environment I'm used to. At the apartment, we would've had neighbors helping us search. There would've been so many different eyes to help, so many people to care and lend a hand. Here, there's no one. We wanted to start a new life. We needed some place fresh and new. This is what we wanted. But it can still be lonely.

The longer Bear's gone, the more it gnaws at me. I know it was Tom Morgan who took him. I don't know how he did it, but there's no other alternative. He took Bear. My mind races as I try to think of what I can do. I can confront him, but I'm afraid. I would have Ellie with me too, and Tom has already shown himself to be a dangerous man.

What else is there to do? If I want Bear back, there *is* nothing else. I make my decision. I'm going to go over there. Worst case, I won't find Bear and that'll be the end of it. Tom will probably yell at me some more, but I'd rather take that than never know what happened to my Bear. Taking a deep breath, I get myself and Ellie ready for a quick trip down the road.

I know which house is his because I pulled up the county website and searched the online records for nearby parcels. Property ownership is public information, and it was just a process of elimination. It just so happens I'm lucky enough for him to live *right* next to us.

"Cupcake, we're going to go look for Bear. Okay?"

"Okay."

"We're going to look for him at the neighbor's house."

"Why?"

"It's the scary neighbor from the other day. I-"

"No!"

"Ellie-"

"No!" She's starting to freak out, remembering how crazy he'd been and how frightening. I don't blame her; I feel the same way. I bend down to her level and pull her close to me.

"Cupcake, you can't stay here alone. I need you to be brave. You are going to stay in the car and I'm just going to do a quick look around."

Ellie sniffles. "I don't want to."

"I don't want to either, but think about Bear. What if he's lost over there and can't find his way home?"

She thinks for a minute. "Okay. For Bear."

"That's my girl." I squeeze her next to me, then we get in the Jeep.

CHAPTER
EIGHT

S itting by the front window of our studio apartment, I watch people walk by on the sidewalk below. They're so casual, walking like they don't have a care in the world. Most are on their phones, oblivious to the world around them. One person is eating, another is riding a bike. *Life goes on.*

I haven't taken a shower in days. I'm wearing week old sweats, am greasy and probably stink, but I don't care. I don't care about much anymore. What's the point of it all?

As I sit alone, I hit my hand against my head over and over, trying to clear the memories that won't stop replaying. Each one brings raw pain with it. I don't want to remember; I don't want to *think* at all. Why can't my brain just shut off and *be?*

My phone vibrates; it's a text from Charlie. "How are you?" he asks. I laugh hysterically at the stupidity of it. How am I? Does he really not know? Of course he knows. The apartment is a disaster, I'm a mess; a blind man couldn't miss it. Charlie *knows* how I am. He's not a big talker, and I under-stand that. At least he's trying, I guess.

I text back. "Fine." I'm not fine though, and he knows that, too. It's just something to say.

Guilt clenches my stomach. I quit my job and Charlie is out there every day working himself to the bone. He supports me and although he doesn't know how to comfort me emotionally, he's still doing the best he can. We're living on half of our normal income and it's hard. He doesn't say anything though; he doesn't pressure me to go back to work. He recognizes I'm not ready. *Still.*

While he's driving his semi through the city, making deliveries, dealing with *people*, I'm at home feeling sorry for myself. I begin to cry, feeling hopeless and useless. Charlie must really hate me right about now. I'm sure he wishes he would've married someone else, someone who would actually pull her weight in the relationship.

Eventually I pull myself together and get into the shower. I have another breakdown there when I look down at the scar on my body. The one where they cut me open to take my child away from me. I rub my fingers over it slowly back and forth, feeling the texture of the raised scar tissue. Doing this makes me feel a little closer to her somehow. She was a part of me, connected to my body in this spot. My tears mix in with the water until there's none left for my body to shed.

Once I'm clean, I force myself to start picking up the apartment. All I want to do is curl up in a ball and sleep for the rest of my life, but it's not an option. "For Charlie," I say. If nothing else, I need to do it for him. He deserves better than what I've been giving him. I can try harder.

In the middle of picking up, I hear the key in the lock. I glance at the clock, noting that it's hours too early for Charlie to be home. I hear a "Yip, yip." *Is that a puppy?* The door swings open and Charlie walks in holding a baby German Shepherd.

With a black body, brown face, and big black ears that are flopped over, it has to be one of the cutest dogs I've ever seen. It's licking Charlie's face and wiggling all over the place. Charlie is laughing, trying to keep the dog from falling as he holds it with one arm and his lunch bag with the other.

I'm standing frozen. I'm shocked. Not only did he take off work early, but he was also standing there with a puppy. What was Charlie thinking? There's no way we can afford this. And besides the money, he's fully aware my mental state is fragile, to say the least. How can he think giving me a puppy to take care of could be a good idea at all?

"Hey," he says.

"Uh, hey. What's that?" I ask, pointing at the puppy. It's so adorable, I can hardly tear my eyes away from it.

"*He* is Bear." Charlie is grinning like a fool. When he brings the dog closer, it sniffs me and I can't hide a laugh when it sticks its wet nose in my neck.

I take him from Charlie. "Charlie, how can we have a puppy?"

"Don't worry. I already spoke with Larissa."

Our landlord has banned pets, so this comes as a surprise to me that she'd allow a dog, especially one of this size. "She's okay with it? She knows he's going to get big, right?"

"She knows. She's making an exception for us." He looks away, flushed. He knows better than to bring it up. He knows I can't bear talking about it. I think for a minute. There's nothing I hate more than pity. That being said, this dog is damn cute.

Charlie's gone through this trouble for me, that's obvious. He means well, but it's irritating that he wouldn't ask me if it's what I wanted. Something like this is a huge decision. It's a commitment. Charlie should know better than to sign me up for something like this without asking. Good intentions be damned.

Irritation fills my voice as I ask, "You're sure we can afford to take care of it?"

"Him. And yes. You let me worry about that part." Charlie kisses me then, and I don't turn away. I return his kiss. For a flicker of a moment, there's something warm in my chest. It's gone in the blink of an eye, but it was there long enough for me to notice.

I turn to look at Bear. He's snuggled up in my arms, already getting sleepy. *Like a baby.* Well, not quite, but kind of close. I can't believe how soft he is; he feels like velvet. His floppy ears are so big for his little body and his paws are huge. He's going to be big when he's full grown. I'm already falling in love with this stupid dog. I start to cry.

"Hey, no don't do that." Charlie pulls me in.

"I'm sorry," I say, sniffling.

"I wanted something to cheer you up. I thought Bear would do the trick." He looks so hopeful. It breaks my shattered heart even more. I'm something that needs fixing, and Charlie is looking for the right tool to do it.

"Why didn't you ask me first, Charlie?"

He shrugs. "I wanted to surprise you."

That's kind of obvious. "Thank you," I say, still partly annoyed but not wanting to fight. "I love him," I say, and I mean it.

I take Bear on our first walk when we go pick up Ellie from daycare. I'm happy that I made myself take a shower today. Our walk is mostly me holding him, because he doesn't have all of his shots yet, but I let him walk a little and sniff around the sidewalk for a bit before picking him back up.

Ellie is thrilled when she sees him. "Puppy!" she screams.

Her enthusiasm is contagious. We stop by the corner pet store and get Bear some puppy treats and toys on our way home. I love seeing her smile; it's like a balm for my soul. I feel the warmth starting to pull me out of the darkness. Instead of fighting it like I usually do, feeling too guilty to be anywhere else but in the black, I embrace the feeling. It's been so long since I've been able to smile.

CHAPTER

NINE

om's property has a gate out front, but it's open, so I drive through. If I hesitate, I'll be too afraid to go any farther, so I don't give myself the chance. His land is heavily forested, similar to ours. I wonder how he was able to see the road from his front porch, like he claimed.

He's got less land than us, only ten acres. I say *only* ten acres, like it's not that much, which is funny because six months ago, a half-acre was gigantic to me. Living on forty acres, though, I've become acclimated to how much space that kind of land really is. It's amazing what a person will get used to.

Our neighbor's yard looks more like a junkyard than anything else. I'm not trying to be judgmental, just observant. There's old, rusted car parts and tires everywhere. In one area, there's a heaping stack of trash bags. In another, a mountain of tires.

Everything appears to be in piles, ready to be burned. There are tools, oil bottles, old children's toys and even silverware, all scattered around the yard. I don't know how they can even walk without stepping on things. Maybe he's a hoarder.

I've been looking for Bear the whole time I've been

coming up the driveway, but there's so much stuff; it's so hard to see. He could be hidden anywhere. There are so many places to look.

The driveway takes me around the back of an old, beat-up manufactured home, to an enormous barn. I park and say to Ellie, "Okay, cupcake. Be back before you know it. Hang tight." I lean into the back seat to give her a quick kiss, then make my way into the yard.

"Hello?" I call out. I'm heading toward the barn, but I still want to make my presence known. Who knows what Tom will do if I surprise him? "Tom!" I call. Moments pass and there's still no answer. My intention is to confront him face to face, while at the same time taking everything in.

If I can spot Bear first, all the better. I'm not trying to go behind Tom's back, even though he scares the hell out of me. I try to be an open and honest person as much as I can, and besides, he *might* not have Bear. What if I start making accusations and I'm wrong? It would make a bad situation even worse.

I'm parked closest to the barn, so I start towards it, still calling for Tom. When I make it to the entrance, I hear the whimpering. "Bear?" It sounds just like him.

When I call his name, the whimpering gets louder. I hear a thwack, thwack, thwack. *His tail!* "Oh God, Bear! Where are you?" I run forward, frantically searching for him. In a horse stall, toward the back of the building, I find him.

Bear is chained to one of the support beams. There's no food or water to be seen, and he looks like he's lost weight. "Bear!" I cry, falling to my knees beside him. I hold him, crying into his fur. He looks so unwell, like he's been starving and alone for the past two days.

"Come on, boy. Time to go home," I say, setting him free. He's wobbly, but makes it up to follow me out. When I open the back door, he's too weak to jump up; I have to help him in.

Ellie cries, "Bear!" He licks her face; he misses her too.

"Found him, cupcake, now let's go home."

I turn the Jeep around, seeing Bear rest his head on Ellie's lap in my rear-view mirror. God, I can't believe how much I've missed him these past couple of days.

He's so frail; it breaks my heart. *That bastard is going to pay for this.* We come around a bend, almost to the road. That's when I see the old rusty pickup truck. He's blocking the gate, which is now closed. *Shit, shit, shit!*

Stopping so I don't ram into him, I honk my horn. Tom gets out of the truck, but there's no way I'm about to do the same. Instead, I roll down my window. "What the hell are you doing on my land?" he asks.

He's angrier now than he was when he visited, if that's possible. He's not holding his shotgun, which surprises me. Maybe I caught him off guard and he just didn't grab it yet, or maybe he doesn't have it with him. I'm hoping I don't find out.

"I was looking for my dog. Why did you take him?"

"If it's on my property, it's *mine.*"

What? "That doesn't even make sense!" My voice is rising. I'm about to lose control of what little calm I had. "You stole him from me!"

"I didn't steal nothin!" He takes a step closer. "That's payment for my girls he killed."

"Bullshit! You can't have him!" I'm heaving and my face is red. I glance back to check Ellie. She's pale, frightened, but quiet. "Open the gate. We're leaving," I say to Tom.

He doesn't move. He doesn't say anything else, either. I think he's thinking about his options again. *Shit!* I'm sweating now, thinking about my options too. Am I technically trespassing? I'm not sure what the requirements are to be considered that, but he *stole* my dog! Ugh, I can hear my mom's voice in my head saying, "Now, Paisley, two wrongs don't make a right."

I have to get us out of here. Analyzing the gate situation, I see there's a ditch on both sides. There's no fence; I'm assuming because he doesn't think anyone can drive through the ditch. I don't know what Tom's going to do, but if he doesn't open that gate, I don't have any other option but to try for the ditch. I will not let him take Bear back.

The Jeep is too new to me, for me to really understand its capabilities. I've never had one before, but it's a *Jeep*. Isn't this what they're made for? To climb over obstacles and go where other cars can't? I wipe the sweat from my brow, saying a silent prayer. Then Tom moves. He turns around and for a flash, I'm relieved. I believe he's going to open the gate for us and let us go home in peace.

But in an instant the relief is gone. He's not going for the gate. He's going back to the truck to grab the shotgun. The moment I see him reaching in, I know what he's doing. Shifting back into drive, I hit the gas at full throttle. Left or right, left or right? I turn to the right side of the gate. We dip down, something scrapes, and there's a loud thud as we bump down, but I don't let off the accelerator. The Jeep lurches back up, and it feels like we're flying as we jump up over the other edge of the ditch.

"Yes!" I yell, as we land onto the main road.

A gunshot rings out. The sound is deafening. Adrenaline pumps through me and my foot hammers down on the gas. We shoot rocks behind us as we lurch forward. Ellie screams, her hands are covering her ears. Bear is barking. My ears are ringing, and my head is pounding, but somehow I got us the hell out of there.

CHAPTER

TEN

I fumble for my phone. *Where the hell is it?* I'm trying to keep us on the road while I look, but we're swerving all over the place. I realize we're going too fast down the gravel road, but I'm not about to slow down. It would take nothing for Tom to open his gate and follow us. Panicked, I keep glancing back to see if he's there. I keep thinking there will be another gunshot blast aimed right at us.

Finally, my fingers brush the phone. I latch onto it like it's a lifeline. Our driveway is coming up, but I keep driving past it. There's no way I want to go home right now. We live too close to our neighbor, and if he decides to come over, we would be trapped. I have officer Adrian's phone number saved to my favorites and call him.

"Adrian here," he answers.

"Officer! Tom is shooting at us!"

"What? Where are you? Are you okay?" His tone makes me want to cry. He's concerned. Yes, it's his job, but there's also a difference between someone who fakes concern because they have to at least act like they care, and someone who genuinely *does* care. Officer Adrian is a good man. I can tell.

"We're in the car," I say. "I went over there to look for

Bear. He had him!" I cry now, unable to hold back any longer.

"That was stupid, Paisley," he sighs. "Look, don't go home. Come straight to the station and I'll get your statement. I'll have a squad car sent to Tom's."

I do as he instructed, heading straight for the police station. Officer Adrian has someone analyzing the Jeep for remnants of the shotgun blast to see if anything hit us, while he takes another statement from me. He takes pictures of Bear, so we have a record of the condition he's in.

Officer Adrian, or Hank, as he's asked me to call him, gives me an earful about how reckless I've been. "You're so lucky," he says. "You could've been killed."

"I-"

"God, I can't believe how lucky you were. Tom's a great shot, even drunk as a skunk."

"He kept saying I was trespassing."

"Technically, you weren't trespassing because you were trying to leave. If he would've found you before you found Bear, and you refused to leave, then that would be a misdemeanor."

"But-"

"Even if you were trespassing, though, he has no legal right to use deadly force. He broke the law, and he's going to have to pay for that." He shudders. "I hate to think what Tom would've done if he came home any sooner."

"I had to find Bear." I look into Hank's eyes. "Don't you understand?"

He nods. "I do. It was stupid, but I do understand." Hank looks at Ellie, who's clinging to me, then he looks at Bear, who won't leave my side. "A friend of mine is a veterinarian. I'll call him and see if we can get you an emergency appointment."

I'm shocked by his kindness. "Thank you, Hank."

He blushes. "Don't thank me yet. Let's see if we can get him in first."

WHEN WE GET HOME, THERE'S A POLICE CRUISER PARKED AT the end of our driveway. He's going to stay there for the night, just to make me feel a little safer. I've been assured by Hank that Tom has already been arrested. And I do feel safer.

We were able to get Bear in to see Hank's friend. Hank went with, and thinking about how concerned he is, sends warmth through me. It's been so long since I've felt that kind of attention.

The vet gave Bear a thorough look over. "How long was he gone?" he asked.

"Almost three days."

"He's dehydrated and malnourished. It's a good thing you found him when you did. Dogs this big can't go much longer without eating." He rubs Bear gently and gives him a treat. Bear thumps his tail, happy to get the attention.

"What can I do for him?" I ask. "He seems so weak."

"That's to be expected. We'll start him on a regimen. Give him plenty of water and gradually introduce some solids back into his diet. I have a special food that will be perfect to get him up and going again. I'll have Nancy print out the instructions for you."

After our appointment, Hank followed us home to make sure we were fine. In the trailer, Charlie is already inside, asleep. I can hear his snoring from outside. I check my phone, but he hasn't texted or tried to call all day. The warmth I felt with Hank fades. I can feel the hollowness inside me pulsing. It's spreading up to my heart. I can feel its numbness taking over my body.

I have the urge to scream at the top of my lungs. I want Charlie to see me. I need him to *understand*. But he doesn't; he won't. There's nothing I can do that will be good enough. Turning to Ellie, I put on a false smile. "Well, cupcake, what should we do?"

I'M OUT OF SURGERY NOW. THERE'S AN IV DRIP WITH A cocktail of painkillers going straight into my bloodstream, but it does nothing for the pain in my heart. My body is limp, but my mind is frenzied. The doctor's words echo in my mind, unrelenting.

"There were complications," he said.

"Where's my baby?" I asked.

I saw nothing but *pity* in his eyes. It told me what I already knew. "I'm sorry, Paisley. Your baby didn't make it."

The tears came then, hot liquid scorching my cold cheeks. My voice trembled; I could barely speak. "I need to see her." He left me then, uncomfortable with facing my raw grief, claiming he would give me some time. *Like that will do me any good.* Now I'm waiting. Waiting for someone to bring her lifeless body to me.

CHAPTER
ELEVEN

Katelyn opened the shower door to test the water temperature. Steam engulfed the bathroom, fogging up the mirrors. A little too hot. She turned the handle, adjusting it just the way she liked, then she stripped down and stepped in. Halfway through washing her hair, the water shut off.

Soap was everywhere. She reached for her towel to clear her eyes. Katelyn fiddled with the handle, but water wasn't coming back out. *Shit.* "Mike!" She called for her husband. He was a pain in her ass, but handy as hell around the house.

"What?" She heard his faint reply.

"Mike!"

"What?" He was still yelling at her from across the house. She wanted to smack him. She wondered, *why won't he just come here?* "Mike! Mike! Mike!" Katelyn kept yelling for him until he finally came.

He opened her shower door. "What?"

"There's no water."

Mike sighed. This was the third time this week that the well was acting up. "I'll take a look. Hang tight."

Ten minutes later, there was still no water, and the soap was drying on Katelyn's skin. Shivering, she got out to wrap herself in a towel. Mike helped her rinse her hair out by using a five-gallon jug of water they kept for emergencies. They both agreed it was time to call a well serviceman.

Katelyn opened her social media application and went into one of the community boards. She posted a public question, "Any recommendations on a well repair company? We have no water! Thanks!"

She and Mike wrangled up the kids and made a run to the local grocery store to load up on water bottles. When they got home, Katelyn checked her phone again to see who responded to her question. The consensus said Vic's Water Works. Three people had raved about how the company had saved them and had reasonable prices. She responded, "Thanks, all! Looks like I'm calling Vic's!"

It was the weekend, and she knew a lot of service techs wouldn't come out until Monday. She was hoping she was wrong about that, but didn't think she was. When Katelyn called and their soonest appointment was Wednesday, she nearly fainted. "Wednesday! We have no water!" she cried.

"I'm sorry ma'am. It's the best we can do."

She took the appointment, and in the meantime, called around to other companies. No one had any sooner appointments. Katelyn wanted to rip her hair out. She was so frustrated. Katelyn thought, *how can this be?* She sighed, defeated.

On Monday, Mike took the kids to school before going to work. Halfway through the day, Katelyn got a phone call from a blocked number. She felt a surge of hope, thinking, *maybe it's Vic's!* She wasn't disappointed. As soon as she answered, someone claiming to be Taylor Victor said, "Hello, I'm calling regarding your appointment set for Wednesday."

"Yes?" Katelyn replied, eager for more information.

"It looks like we had a cancellation. There's an earlier appointment available if someone will be home today?"

"Yes! Yes, that sounds great. I'm home until this afternoon."

"Excellent. I should be there within twenty minutes or so."

"Thank you so much!" Katelyn hung up, breathing a sigh of relief. *Thank God,* she thought. She was dreading the family going any longer without showers and baths. Having no water was miserable. Katelyn decided not to text Mike. She wanted it to be a nice little surprise for him when he got home that evening. She walked down the driveway to block the gate open, so the service tech would have no issues driving in.

Less than twenty minutes later, an unmarked white van caked in mud pulled up the driveway. It was old and looked like it was barely running. There was a tic coming from the engine, which is what caught Katelyn's attention. She had a moment's doubt. Surely a successful repair company would invest in better, more reliable vehicles. Then she shrugged. Beggars couldn't be choosers, and right now she was definitely a beggar. They needed to get this well fixed as soon as possible, and she wasn't about to turn this company away just because they had crappy cars for their workers.

Katelyn answered the door. "I'm so glad you could squeeze us in. Thank you so much."

Taylor Victor smiled. "It's my pleasure."

MIKE GOT A PHONE CALL THAT AFTERNOON FROM HIS KIDS' school. They were still waiting for a parent to pick them up. He was confused, not understanding why his wife would have forgotten them. "She never forgets the kids," he said.

When he could not reach Katelyn on her phone, he took off work early to pick the kids up.

He was starting to worry about Katelyn. This was odd behavior; she always remembered the kids' pickup time and always answered her phone. Mike thought about calling the police, but decided to go home first. If she wasn't there, then he would call the police. That something had happened to her while she was *at* home didn't cross his mind.

As soon as he opened the front door, Mike was met with a sight that gagged him. A pool of blood, and what looked like bits of meat, were in the entryway. Blood was smeared through the house and splattered on walls. "Katy!" He called for his wife, his mind racing. She could be hurt; she could need his help. Mike was about to run inside, but then he thought about how much blood there was.

He didn't walk inside, although he was desperate to find Katelyn. Mike knew from watching CSI that he would cont-aminate any evidence. He closed the front door with a shaking hand.

"Dad, what's wrong?" Mike's kids were already worried about their mom, and now that he was acting strange, they knew something was really off.

"Nothing's wrong," he said. He couldn't hide his voice from shaking, though. "I forgot. I promised your mom I would stop by the store on the way home. Let's get back in the car."

"But we were just there."

"Don't argue." He turned to the side so they wouldn't see him wipe a tear away. "Please guys. Just get back in the car. I need to make a quick phone call, then we're off."

When the kids were in the car, Mike called 911. He told the operator everything and asked what he should do about the kids. "Keep them out of the house. Police will want to talk to you when they get there, so it's best if you can stay put." He didn't want them to be anywhere near there, but he did as he was instructed. He thought, *they're going to find out one way or another.*

When the police showed up, they entered the house, searching for Katelyn. It didn't take them long to find her. She was in the kitchen. Her bare body was dismembered; all of her pieces were lying in a row, including her head. Her uterus had been cut out of her torso and was gone.

Across the upper cabinets, there was black spray paint that read, "Fuck you."

TWELVE

It's raining again today. It's the perfect reflection of my mood. I don't hate the rain, but it's sad to me. It reminds me of tears. It reminds me of the day I came home from the hospital. When it rains like this, Ellie and I are trapped inside the trailer with Bear. It's stuffy and crowded. We're all bored, and I think about how unprepared we were for this move.

Everyone says it rains a lot in Washington, but for a California girl, who's not used to this amount of rain, no amount of explanation is good enough. I don't mind it completely. It's just different and depressing because of the memories it brings to the surface.

We came up here with umbrellas- useless. We have no ponchos or even rain jackets. We were too concerned with moving, with finding the land and the trailer to live in and having the money. It's lucky we thought to at least have some mud boots.

"Let's sit under the awning for a while," I say to Ellie. She grabs a few toys and I sit in a fold up chair outside, while she sits on the fake grass we have rolled out. It's better than nothing. As the rain falls in a steady rhythm, not pouring down and not exactly a sprinkle, I remember when we first moved here.

I WATCH THE WINDSHIELD WIPERS SWIPE ACROSS, WIPING AWAY the rain. It continues to spatter down constantly, making me grip the door handle. This is the first time we've towed our trailer, other than the day we brought it home, and that day was scary as hell.

There had been a windstorm, but Charlie insisted he knew what he was doing. He drove a semi for a living, after all, how hard could pulling a travel trailer really be? But the wind was a nightmare, making the trailer sway back and forth all over the road. The whole time, I was terrified it would flip and take us with it.

We were lucky it was only a few miles out of the city. We kept it at a storage facility while we slowly moved out of the apartment. The fear I felt then comes back now with the rain. I'm afraid. The wind was worse by far, but that doesn't stop doubt from creeping in, telling me *we can't do this.* That little voice in my head keeps showing me pictures of terrible things that the rain can do.

My fear is unfounded, though. An hour into our drive, the rain has stopped, and everything is fine. Mostly. We're over our maximum weight because we didn't account for how loaded down our trailer would be once it was full of our stuff. Another rookie mistake. We have something called a "sway bar" now, and it's been a tremendous help keeping us on the road.

Charlie takes us along nice and slow. I feel like we've been on the road for an eternity, but after two days of driving my nerves have calmed. I'm thankful he respects my need to feel safe. He never laughed when I was nervous; instead, he slowed down, no matter how slow he'd been going to begin with. When he does things like that, my anger towards him melts away. Even if it's only for a moment, the little things make a difference.

"Welcome to Washington!" Charlie cheers, clapping his hands as we pass through the border from Oregon.

"Hands!" I cry. He puts them both back on the steering wheel in a blink. Then I say, "Finally!"

We smile at each other, relieved to almost be home. The relief is replaced by cold dread when I see snow out the window. "Charlie, is that snow?"

"It'll be fine."

"It's the middle of March! *Why* is there snow?"

Charlie only shrugs. He's trying to maintain the look of calm, but I can see the beads of sweat forming on his forehead. He's nervous, and it makes me terrified.

"Have you ever driven in snow before?" I already know the answer. Neither of us has.

"Doesn't matter. Look, we're going to be fine. If you start freaking out, it's going to make me nervous."

I take a breath. He's right. I think I might lose my stomach, but I fight it. From my mirror, I see Ellie sleeping in the back seat. She's been so good for the entire ride, hardly making a sound. I feel so proud of her bravery. I want nothing to happen that will hurt her or traumatize her.

Four hours later, we're in bumper-to-bumper traffic in Tacoma. I'm thankful we already stopped for a bathroom break and to eat, but I'm aware if we don't get through this soon, we're all going to be miserable. Traffic is nothing new to us. Traffic in a snowstorm *is*.

We've gone from seeing a bit of snow on the side of the road, to light snowfall that doesn't even stick to the ground, to something that's almost a blizzard. I'm sure people in the Midwest would laugh at my description, but to me this is insane.

There's slush everywhere. The snowplows can't keep up with the snow and neither can the windshield wipers. Out the window, it looks like piles and piles of snow have accumulated. I'm so nervous I can hardly breathe. "Maybe we should just stop. Let's just pull over and go home tomorrow." *Home.* It feels so weird to be saying that.

"If we stop, we might not get back out again for a while."

"Oh." I hadn't thought of that.

"It's only another two hours. We'll be fine."

In good weather, I think, praying the pass is open. I'm silent though, because he doesn't need my negativity right now.

As soon as we take the turnoff for I90 things go from bad to worse. We're driving through a sheet of complete white, and the only thing visible through the windshield is the car in front of us. I'm clutching the sides of my seat with all my strength, and I can see Charlie's knuckles turning white on the steering wheel. We get to a flashing sign that says, "Chains required on all vehicles except 4x4."

Reading my mind, Charlie says, "We have four-wheel drive, we're fine."

"Are you sure? Maybe we should stop?" He already clarified that he wants to pull straight through, but I'm not sure how much more of this my nerves can take. In response, Charlie says nothing. He just keeps driving up the mountain at a snail's pace.

When we reach East Pass, we start going downhill. Charlie is trying to keep his slow pace, but other drivers are getting frustrated with us. A BMW flies past us in the left lane, like we're sitting still. Then, a semi follows.

The sound of the air horn as he passes makes me jump. His tires spit snow at us, covering our windshield, and there's a moment where we're blinded. Charlie flicks the wipers to go faster, but they're already maxed out and struggling to clear the glass. Then we start to rock back and forth like a baby in it's cradle. The sway caused by the semi makes us hang on for dear life, although I thought I was doing that already.

Charlie looks in the right-side mirror. "Fuck! Hang on, hang on, hang on!" he yells.

My blood runs cold. I want to clench my eyes shut until it's all over, but I can't help but look out my window. The back end of our trailer is starting to come around. I can feel its drag slowing us down as its wheels spray out snow and salt. The sight has me paralyzed with fear. Our trailer is about to either drag us into the ditch or flip us, or both.

The sound of our engine getting louder fills my ears. Charlie punched the gas, launching us forward. Somehow, he knew this would get us back into control. When I glance back out the window, the trailer is straight behind us again. Tears spring to my eyes. Charlie says, "It's okay," as he grips my hand in his. I don't ask him to put it back on the steering wheel.

Somehow, we make it to our new property alive and in one piece. Forty acres all covered in snow. My breath catches at its beauty. Nothing but snow-covered trees for as far as the eye can see. Most are pines but some are bare, their leaves long fallen. Charlie can't see the driveway because the snow is too deep, but we know it's there because it's the only path with no trees. I get out to guide him, anyway. Better to be safe and I'm sick of sitting.

When I get out of the truck, the quiet is like nothing I've ever experienced. I feel like I can hear my heartbeat. There's no wind and no movement other than the falling snowflakes. I feel like I'm in a whole new world. My lungs breathe deep, taking in the cold air. At this moment, I feel *alive*.

Charlie is backing in because there won't be enough room to turn around when we get up to our clearing. I'm using a stick to poke through the snow, in combination with sinking through it with every step. By the time we're parked, I'm soaking wet, and my feet are almost frozen. But we made it. I want to laugh, to cry, to scream at the sky. *We made it!*

"Mommy!" Ellie's cry breaks me out of my reverie. "There's a car coming."

THIRTEEN

I stand up, worried. *What is it now?* Hank's car stops in the driveway, and he walks up like he doesn't notice the rain.

"Hi," I say.

"Paisley."

"What is it?" He doesn't look happy.

"It's Tom."

My blood turns to ice at his name. "Wh- what about him?"

"He's been released on bail."

Even though I was expecting something like this to happen, the news is still a shock. I gasp, taking a step back like Hank has just slapped me. He steps toward me, holding out a hand. "There was nothing I could do," he says. Of course there wasn't.

"It's not your fault," I say.

"I can have someone parked here. Hell, I'll do it if need be."

The thought warms me, and I wonder why he cares so much. But I can't take him up on it. Having a police car here like that would just freak Ellie out, and I don't want to scare her. There's nothing to suggest Tom will come back again and if he does, Bear is with us. Bear hasn't left my side since the day I saved him. He's not going anywhere.

I shake my head at Hank. "Thank you, but I can't"

"Why not?"

"I just- I don't want to live in fear."

"Paisley." He's standing so close now I can feel his breath. I look up into his green eyes. They're dark and remind me of deep inside the forest. "I understand how you feel but it's dangerous."

"I'll call you if anything happens," I say in almost a whisper. I can tell he wants to say something else, but he leaves it at that.

I CAN'T SLEEP THAT NIGHT. THOUGHTS ABOUT MY NEIGHBOR race through my mind, making me wonder if I was stupid to decline Hank's offer. I think back to when Charlie didn't have to work nights. He used to hold me in bed; at least we had that time together. It's so different now. Maybe it would be fine if our neighbor wasn't so crazy, but I think I would still feel a little lonely.

When I can't sleep, I have a habit of watching the news. Tonight, there's a headline about another murder in the area. "Folks, it seems we might have a serial killer on our hands," the news anchor says. *A serial killer?* I think we might've moved to hell by accident. What's next? An alien invasion? Maybe Bigfoot will come and abduct me.

Suddenly I feel vulnerable and the complete opposite of safe. In little more than a fiberglass box, I realize that pretty much anyone or anything could get in if they really wanted to. Charlie still hasn't had time to install a gate on the driveway, not that it would really do much to stop anyone. We have no gun or weapon to defend ourselves; we don't even have a bat or crowbar on standby. The thought crosses my mind again, of how unprepared we really are.

In the morning, the sound of Bear's tail thumping against the floor wakes me up. Charlie is home, and I'm making a point to wake up early and finally have a much-needed discussion.

"Good morning," he greets me, surprised that I'm awake.

"Charlie, we need to talk."

He sighs. "Do we have to? I'm beat."

"You're always beat. We've been putting this off for too long. Please." He has a habit of walking away while I'm in the middle of saying something, and he's done it this time, too. It grates on my nerves that he can't stand to have a five-minute conversation with me. I want to scream at him to stop putting his things away and pay attention. I'm grinding my teeth in frustration, on the verge of tears.

Instead of giving in, letting him walk away, or continuing to get angry, I decide to take a fresh approach. I walk up to Charlie's back and jump on him, wrapping my arms around his neck. "Whoa!" he cries. Laughing, I cover his eyes with my hands, blinding him. Charlie stumbles back, waving his arms frantically, trying to keep his balance. Bear barks and I'm worried about Ellie waking up, but not worried enough to stop. I've got his attention now, and by God I'm going to keep it.

I lean forward and whisper in Charlie's ear. "This is important." I can see the gooseflesh prickle on his arms in response.

"Okay, okay," he says. "What's so important?"

For a second, I think about how he hasn't even tried to touch me in weeks. With all the hours he's putting in, our opposite sleeping hours, and different schedules, I can't remember the last time we've been intimate.

I want to talk to him about it. Not just the lack of intimacy, but that he doesn't seem to care at all. He doesn't reach for me or even try to touch me. It's like there's an invisible barrier between us. But as much as it hurts me, I say something else all-together. Something I think is probably more important.

"Hank says Tom's out on bail."

Charlie's jaw tightens. "Who's Hank?"

"Officer Adrian. Is that really all you get out of what I just said?" I can feel the anger rising to my cheeks. His jealousy is uncalled for and just plain stupid. What he should care about is our crazy neighbor coming after me.

"Why are you calling him Hank?"

I throw my hands up, exasperated. "Why don't you care that our psychotic neighbor is out of jail? He could come for us any time!"

Charlie sighs. "What do you want me to do about it? There's nothing I *can* do."

"I want you to care! I want you to make us as safe as possible! I want a gate and a gun and-"

"A what?" he interrupts. "No way in hell."

He can't be serious. I look at him, wondering how he could be so obtuse. I'm asking myself if he is really that stupid, or he just doesn't care about the safety of our family. Then I'm sad because these are not thoughts I should have about my husband. This is not what a healthy marriage looks like.

I'm contemplating if it's really worth arguing over, or if I should just drop it. Charlie's right: there's not much he could do. But it's that he seems to brush it off that bugs me so much.

"I don't need your permission," I say.

Charlie looks a little shocked and even hurt. "You would go get a gun even though I don't want one in our household?"

I want to laugh at his selfishness. "I need to be safe. I need to feel safe, Charlie," I say.

"I don't understand why you don't feel safe."

"Are you kidding me? We have no way of keeping anyone off our property, no deterrent whatsoever. The man *shot* at me! We have nothing to protect ourselves. Our 'house' is a fiberglass box that could fall apart with a strong wind."

"Are you going to fence our whole property? What's a gate really going to do? Someone could just drive around it. And we have Bear to protect us."

I want to strangle him. My fingers dig into my palms, and I relish the pain it brings. I have to fight myself to maintain control of my anger. He doesn't understand. It's about making me *feel* safer, even if it's not really going to work. It's about making the effort.

Before I can say anything else, Charlie says, "Look Paisley, you know I'm no lapdog."

"What the hell is that supposed to mean? I don't want a damn lapdog!" Charlie doesn't answer. He goes into the bedroom and closes the door, ending the conversation.

FOURTEEN

One Year Ago

"How's Bear?" Dr. Reymore asks. I'm sitting in his office for my regular bi-weekly therapy session. I wanted to stop coming ages ago, but promised Charlie I would keep it up. It's the only reason I'm here today.

"He's great," I say. "I love him so much. He's really given me a new purpose."

Dr. Reymore nods. "I'm glad to hear that, Paisley. And… are you still seeing visions?"

I cringe. He makes me sound like I'm crazy. "No."

He nods again. I wonder if he's really seeing me, or if he's just going through the routine. I wonder if he listens enough to believe me. "Have you given any thought to our last discussion?"

At my last appointment, Dr. Reymore suggested Charlie and I move. He explained how sometimes a new environment will help a person leave behind painful memories and create new ones. "It can be helpful for the healing process," he'd said.

"Yes, I've thought about it, but I'm still not sure. The

market is crazy right now. There are no apartments available, and you can forget us trying to buy a place. Prices are insane. Plus, Charlie would have to find a new job for us to spend more and-"

"Whoa-" Dr. Reymore interrupts, holding up a placating hand. "I didn't mean to cause any undue stress. I merely wanted you to consider the possibility."

I take a deep breath, nodding my understanding.

"Have you talked to Charlie about it?"

"No."

"Why not?"

"I just didn't want to put ideas into his head when I'm not sure what I want."

"That makes sense." Dr. Reymore nods again. "Perhaps you could discuss the matter together and he can help you decide what you want to do?"

Ugh. I know where he's going with this. It's all about communication. "Maybe," I say, just to get him off my back, but he sees through my one-word answer.

"Do me a favor. Just talk to Charlie about it. See if you can decide together, and if you still aren't sure, then *tell* him that, too. If another apartment is out of the question, maybe another city or another state is the answer." He shrugs.

"Another state?" My mind reels. My life is here. All my and Charlie's friends, everything is here. How can we leave it all behind?

"It would be a fresh start. I feel like it would be really beneficial for you, at this point."

"But what about our appointments?"

"We can continue virtually, or if you prefer, I can recommend another doctor wherever you choose."

I can't believe it. He's really pushing this on me. I don't understand why I need a fresh start *that* badly. I'm not one hundred percent opposed to the idea, but it's a scary thought to find a new home and start all over. There's got to be another answer.

"Do you make all your victims- I mean clients move?"

He laughs. "No. Certainly not, but yours is a special case, Paisley."

I'm conflicted. I sort of feel like he's pushing this on me, railroading me. I'm not sure if I'm ready to move. It feels too much like letting go. At the same time, I love the idea of adventure in my life. Something new might not be *so* bad. I just don't like it being pushed on me.

At night, when Charlie gets home, we sit up together in bed talking about what Dr. Reymore recommended. He's way more into the idea than I'd expected. I'm surprised at how much he actually doesn't mind. Charlie has always been supportive, but this seems like it's something more than that. "You seem almost excited about this idea," I say.

"Well, yeah. I sorta am," he admits.

"But why? You'd have to find a new job, and we'd be starting over completely. We'd know no one and nothing about the area."

"Babe, that's kinda the point. Didn't Dr. Reymore say you need a fresh start?" Charlie smiles. "I don't mind a new place; I really like the idea. And don't worry about my job. I can transfer to certain cities around the country, I'll just lose my seniority here."

"But are you sure you *want* that?"

"It's no biggie. Just means I'll have some shitty hours for a while."

"Ugh."

"But if it's for your health, it's going to be worth it."

There it is again. *My health*. Just another broken object everyone's trying to fix. My baby *died*. I don't think I'll ever be the same or *fixed* or whatever they want to call it. I want to scream at my psychiatrist, at Charlie, at everyone who thinks there's something wrong with me. How does he expect me to behave? There's a piece of my soul that's been torn away. I'm not sure if I'll ever be the same woman Charlie married.

Charlie sees my mood turning dark as I think. Eager to stop me from going to an even darker place, he says, "Besides, this is the perfect opportunity to get a bigger place." He looks around. "This place is tiny! I'm sure Bear would love to even maybe get a yard of his own."

At his name, Bear gives a yip. He's only a year old, but already a little genius. He sleeps at the foot of our bed every night. I hadn't thought about it before, but Charlie is right. A bigger place would be really nice, and a yard of our own would be heaven. I'm still worried about the cost, though. That's not all I'm worried about, but it's all I'm willing to say to Charlie.

"Okay," I say. "Let's just start looking and see what we can find. But Charlie, I swear if we can't afford it, I will not have you work yourself to death just for us to have the money for it."

Charlie looks the most excited he has in a long time. Almost as excited as the day I told him he was going to be a daddy. I choke back the emotions that want to rise. "You mean it?" he asks.

"I mean it. I'm willing to look. Let's just see what we can find. With this market, who knows."

"We could go anywhere, though. Surely the entire country isn't going through a housing crisis."

"I'm not going anywhere crazy." I laugh.

"Babe, I'm on it!" Charlie says, giving me a kiss. His excitement is transparent, which makes me smile. I'm still not entirely sure about what I want to do, but I figure it can't hurt anything to look.

FIFTEEN

A gun. The idea of owning one scares the hell out of me, but at this point, I think it's something I really might need. I've never used one before; I've never even held one. How hard could it really be, though? Point and shoot, right? Of course, there's more to it than that, but if it's a matter of life and death, I think I'd rather have one. Who knows, just waving one around might scare my crazy neighbor away. Or it might piss him off.

Charlie doesn't want me to get one. I'm sure it's because I know nothing about them, but who says I can't learn? I can take a safety course. I'm not helpless. That he didn't even want to discuss it, just said, "no," makes me want to get one more.

Yes, I'm probably being rash or immature, but I'm upset and scared. What else am I supposed to do? I *don't* need his permission, and although it's wrong to go behind his back, sometimes you have to do what it takes to feel safe. This is one of those times. No one can take better care of you than yourself.

As soon as Ellie gets up, we head for the gun shop. Bear goes with us, riding in the back seat next to Ellie. We have the top off the Jeep today, and he rides the entire way with his head in the wind. At the shop, he waits patiently.

I pick a small handgun, something lightweight, but supposedly it'll still do some damage if needed. I know nothing about it, but it feels right in my hand and the shop owner says it's a good fit, so that's the one I go with. After I fill out all the information for my background check, he tells me to come back in a week for pickup.

Relief washes over me in a comforting wave. Maybe I'm being irrational like Charlie said, but I don't care. I feel safer already. In a week, I'll be able to protect myself in a life-or-death situation, better than I can today. I'm not telling Charlie. I'm not hiding it from him, either. If he finds out about the gun, so be it, but I will not be the one telling him about it.

Charlie and I haven't spoken since our argument. We talk little anymore as it is, but somehow this seems worse. Maybe it's me. Later, I get a text from him. "Perc test scheduled." I'm torn between the joy of finally getting something done that needs to be done, and irritation with him for not acknowledging the rift between us.

He probably thinks nothing's wrong. The more I think about it, the more I think I'd be surprised if he even remembered what we talked about last night.

"When?" I text back.

His answer comes a few hours later. "Two weeks."

I send a thumb's up emoji. Two weeks and we'll be another step closer to getting our building permit. I'm so happy, I can almost forget about all the bad stuff. Almost.

Getting our percolation test is a big deal for us, not just because it's required by our county in order to get a building permit, but because it will tell us if we can get a traditional gravity fed septic system or if we're going to need to spend double the money on an engineered above ground system. It's all about the way the water flows in the ground, supposedly, and this will tell us what we need to know.

It all comes down to the money, and this little test is going to make us or break us. Not really break us, but it will put a big wrench in our budget and might mean getting a smaller house. Either way, I'm relieved that we're finally able to take this step. All of Charlie's hard work and extra hours are paying off.

In a much better mood, I take Ellie and Bear back into town to explore. It's the first time we've bothered to walk through the small town since moving. We stroll past the gun shop we visited earlier, and Ellie spots an ice cream parlor. "Pleaaaase, Mommy!" She begs and I'm helpless to resist her.

A few minutes later we're sitting outside on the patio eating our scoops while others walk past. Bear lays at our feet, enjoying the feel of the shaded cement on his tummy.

"What are we doing now?" Ellie asks me before putting a spoon full of strawberry ice cream in her mouth.

"We're exploring our new town, cupcake."

"Oh."

"You're not having fun?"

She takes another bite and is too distracted to answer. Ellie loves going on new adventures, so her question is surprising. She doesn't seem bored, but I'm also not familiar with a three-year-old who's one hundred percent proficient in expressing their feelings. "Ellie," I ask. "Do you want to do something else?"

Ellie thinks for a minute then says, "I want to see Daddy."

"Daddy is at work. You know that, silly."

"Let's go Daddy's work."

"Can't, cupcake. Daddy drives for work. He's too far away."

She already knows all this. She's missing Charlie and I

understand. I miss him too, even though I'm still mad at him. He's never spoken to me that way before, and thinking about it is unsettling. I'm not sure what's happening to our marriage, but it doesn't seem to be good.

"Daddy!" Ellie jumps up, pointing and yelling at a green Dodge that looks just like the one Charlie takes to work every day.

Bear sits up, giving a warning bark. "Shh, Ellie, don't yell like that," I say, while eyeing the truck. It looks so much like ours. I wonder if it really is him. I check the time and shrug. "Maybe Daddy's off a little earlier than normal today."

"Let's go home!" Ellie cries.

"Okay, okay," I say, laughing at her excitement. Inside though, I'm wondering if Charlie really is off early, what's he doing driving through town. He takes the highway into Seattle and does not travel through the middle of downtown like this.

When we get home, Charlie's truck is nowhere to be seen. He's not home. Seeing the crestfallen look on Ellie's little face makes me angry at Charlie all over again. No, it's not his fault we thought we saw his truck heading home, but it is his fault for never being home for his daughter. He says he's trying to support us; I get it. But there's a line that needs to be drawn and he's unwilling to draw it.

"Ellie, baby," I say as she cries. There's nothing else I can say, though. She knows already.

CHARLIE PULLS INTO THE DRIVEWAY AS I'M MAKING DINNER. He's been gone for twenty hours, but who's keeping track? I shouldn't be. Thinking about it just brings questions and anger and suspicion. He's only supposed to work a maximum of fourteen hours at a time, plus an hour commute each way, so where did the extra four hours go? That's four hours he could've spent with his family.

I push the thoughts away. I feel like I'm doing nothing but counting hours like a crazy person. It will do no good to question him. Charlie will have some kind of excuse or reason and some way of making me feel guilty for "being at home all day" while he's out working his ass off. He's making money; he's supporting us. That's what matters, right? I swallow down the questions that want to rise. It doesn't matter how long he's been gone. Charlie is home now.

Through the kitchen window, I watch him walking up the driveway. For someone who's been awake for almost an entire twenty-four-hour period, he doesn't look that tired. Looks can be deceiving, can't they? I have the chicken diced and I throw the pieces into a pan so they can fry. Bear hears Charlie's feet crunching the gravel on the driveway and he sits up to watch the door. "It's okay, Bear. Dad's home," I say. He thumps his tail, recognizing the words.

When Charlie walks through the door and proceeds to tell me he's getting ready for bed, it's no surprise. Of course he would want to sleep. He's going back in less than ten hours, which gives him just enough time to get a full eight hours of sleep. This evening isn't the first time that I've wished we lived closer to his work. The commute is eating away so much of his time. We tried so hard to get something closer, but it just wasn't feasible with our budget.

"I thought I saw your truck in town today," I blurt out. He was just walking into the bedroom and his back stiffens. When he turns around, his cheeks are red. Charlie's reaction tells me everything I need to know. It *was* him we saw. The fury I've been trying to hold back breaks past the dam. There's nothing I can do to stop it.

"What the hell, Charlie? That was hours ago!"

"I can explain." He's holding his hands out.

"Explain what?" I roar at him, knowing I'm only making things worse, but not caring. Ellie was so heartbroken today. He made us feel like fools for *nothing*.

"I was working."

"What do you mean you were working?"

"I was waiting on my load and Simone asked me to run an errand for her."

I'm staring at him now, openmouthed, speechless. He's making absolutely no sense. Charlie is a truck driver. He does nothing in his personal vehicle; he drives a semi. Why would he have to drive from Seattle all the way to our little town, an hour's drive, for an *errand*?

I don't think he's going to tell me the truth here. Something is going on with Charlie. I don't know what it is, but it's starting to worry me. The lies are adding up one by one. Charlie has the unfortunate characteristic of being a terrible liar. He can't think of a good one to save his life, and I'm not sure if I like it that way or prefer him to tell me something more believable.

"Can't you just cut the bullshit?" I ask.

Charlie turns away and walks into the bedroom. I thought he went to bed, but a few minutes later he comes back out. My chicken is done cooking now and I'm just getting ready to eat, but I set it aside. Any time Charlie wants to talk to me, I seize the opportunity.

"Look," he says, "I have to cover someone's vacation this weekend."

"Okay." That's nothing new. Why is he telling me about it?

"It's a long haul."

A long- my breath catches. A long haul. It wouldn't be so bad if I wasn't worried about our neighbor coming over to kill me. Charlie has done long haul before; I know what it's like to have him gone for a few days. It's not bad. What's bad is being alone on forty acres with no way to protect myself against my psychotic neighbor that has it in for me. I take a deep breath and Charlie says, "It's only two nights."

"Two nights?"

"It'll be fine. We're lucky I don't have to go for a week or two at a time."

Of course he would say that. He's not the one worried about the neighbor. I think about the gun I just bought. It won't be ready for me by this weekend. Just a few days shy of a week. There's nothing else I can say to Charlie. It's not like he has a choice. If his boss needs him to cover for someone, that's part of the job.

SIXTEEN

The day of Charlie's long haul comes in the blink of an eye. I've been trying not to think about it, keeping myself busy with tasks around the yard and designing a floor plan that will work for us. There's so much to do for the house, it's easy to find something to occupy my time. A lot of what I do is research—finding places to do the different reports we need, and subcontractors to do different parts of the job. Charlie and I have decided that if we sub out jobs, it's going to save us a fortune in the overall cost of the project.

When I think about Charlie leaving for two days, I tell myself it's going to be no different from having Charlie working his normal fourteen-hour days. What's the difference between having him gone or at home sleeping? *Not much.* I swallow the lie, knowing there's no other choice. If I dwell on it, I'm going to drive myself nuts.

"Mommy, let's go exploring!" Ellie is up to her usual adventures, which is a perfect distraction. It's raining again, but we throw on our ponchos (I even have one for Bear now) and mud boots, and head out. In the months we've lived here, we still haven't explored our whole property. It's seemingly endless, but right now that's not a bad thing at all.

"This way, cupcake," I call to Ellie, leading her back onto our started path. It's been slow going, clearing a narrow space for us to walk, but it's been worth the effort. Our land is mostly flat, but the farther into the forest we go, the more we find gentle sloping hills. Bear climbs them effortlessly as Ellie and I struggle. Still not used to the physical exertion required to be a true explorer, I pant, trying to catch my breath, but don't mind one bit.

It feels good to know this is *my* land. I feel pride in the ownership of something so beautiful and full of life. I'm amazed at how fortunate we were to find this property and thankful that Charlie took the initiative the way he did. I feel my city roots becoming attached to my new foundation, not just acclimating, but falling deeper in love by the day.

The silence that was once deafening, is now beautiful. I feel like I can hear for miles and miles. There are no cars, no horns, no people. At the top of a hill, I close my eyes and lean my head back, facing the sky. This is the deepest Ellie and I have gone into the forest so far, and I can't wait to go even farther. For a minute, I absorb the sounds of birds chirping and branches swaying in the breeze. But then there's something I wasn't expecting. I hear music.

My brow furrows in confusion. I focus on listening but can't make out any words. I realize it's not music. It's just beating drums, faint, but distinct enough for me to know what it is. Instinctively, I don't like it.

It's not a particularly unpleasant sound, but it gives me a strange feeling inside. I don't like that I can hear it here. It's not just that I was enjoying the silence, either. I suppose it makes sense that I would hear music even if it was really far, because it's so silent out here, but it still unsettles me.

"Ellie," I say.

"What?"

"Time to go back, baby. Are you ready?"

"No!" she yells, running away from me.

"Ellie, no!" But it's too late. She's taken off running. Lucky for me, Bear has no problem keeping up with her.

"Bear, get Ellie!" I cry, trying to keep up but failing miserably. He gives me an answer bark before pulling in front of Ellie and licking her. She stops, unable to move past his attention and seems to give up.

"Bear!" she cries, laughing and holding onto his fur.

I finally catch up to them and give Bear some love, too. "Good boy!" Ellie and I walk hand in hand back toward the trailer. As we trudge back on our trail, there's an odd feeling that overcomes me. It feels almost like something or someone is watching us.

Watching Bear closely, I notice he doesn't seem to have the same feeling as me. He's walking in front of us, nose to the ground, leading the way. His tail is wagging, and it seems he senses no danger. If he did sense something, he wouldn't appear this casual. His body language tells me so much about what he feels; I've learned to pay close attention to his signs.

Then why is this feeling of dread in the back of my mind? I'm glad Bear doesn't notice; it's somewhat reassuring, but I still can't shake my paranoia. As my heart rate speeds up, my breathing becomes shallower. I try to calm my trembling hands. Slowly, so I don't alert Bear, I look all around us and especially behind. There's nothing I can see. Maybe I'm just dehydrated.

At the trailer, I still have the feeling of being watched. "Bear, who's here?" At the practiced question, Bear perks up into alert mode. He barks three times, then scans the surrounding area, before trotting down the driveway to do it again. When he finds nothing and no one, he comes back to me, sitting at my feet. The feeling seems to be gone, for now at least, which brings an immense amount of relief. Bear will always be my number one protector.

I remember again that Charlie isn't home. He's not in Seattle either. He's two states away. At least I have Hank's- Officer Adrian's phone number if there's an emergency. Maybe Charlie is right, though. Maybe I'm getting to be a little too familiar with our local law enforcement. I probably should delete his personal phone number. I think of him as a friend- the only friend that I've made in this new place, but maybe I'm reading too much into it. He probably thinks I'm some desperate housewife full of drama.

It doesn't take long for me to be glad I didn't listen to myself- glad I kept his number.

CHAPTER
SEVENTEEN

The sound of the drums is back in the middle of the night. What was faint back in the forest is now much louder, sending anxiety down my spine. How did they get closer? I'm not the only one who is woken up by the sound. Bear is lying next to me on the bed tonight. When I lean to peek out the window, he's already alert.

There's nothing I can see outside; it's pitch black. I didn't expect to see anything anyway, and if I saw something, I think it would be a thousand times worse. I thread my fingers in Bear's fur, stroking him for comfort. I wonder if it's true what they say about dogs being able to smell fear. If it's true, I'm sure I stink pretty bad to Bear right now. *Sorry, buddy.*

The beating continues at the same volume and pace. Minutes pass while I'm waiting. I'm not sure for what, but how long can drums really go for? Finally, silence falls again. I release a breath I didn't realize I was holding. Even Bear seems to visibly relax.

I'm surprised he's been silent this whole time; I thought he would've been barking at the unexpected sound, but he hasn't. It's fine by me because his barking is too loud for inside the trailer, and I don't need him to wake up Ellie or freak me out even more than I already am.

Bear and I snuggle closer, trying to fall back asleep now that all is quiet. I'm startled awake again when the drums are back. "Again?" I moan. Bear whimpers, seeming to agree with my complaint.

Am I going crazy or are they louder now? It seems like they're close enough to be on our property and almost loud enough to wake up Ellie. "Geez," I say to myself. It's Saturday, so it makes sense that one of the neighbors might have a party, but this seems a little bizarre. What kind of party has nothing but drums beating over and over? And the rhythm is off-putting. It reminds me of a horror movie.

I glance at my phone to note the time. Almost three in the morning. Who the hell is having a party at three in the morning? *Someone who doesn't want anyone to know about it, that's who.* The thought sends shivers through me.

Why do I have to think things like that? I don't care if my neighbors are crazy enough to be rockin' it at three in the morning to some weird beats. It doesn't concern me as long as I can sleep. I shove the little voice back to the recesses of my mind that insists *it's no party music.*

I put a pillow over my head, trying to block the sound. It seems to work because I fall back asleep. When I wake up for the third time, it's pure terror that engulfs me. The steady beating drums sound like they're right outside the trailer. Bear is barking frantically at the door. I'm frozen with fear. *What the hell is going on?*

Tears come unbidden. I reach for my phone to call Hank for help. Of course, something insane would happen to us when Charlie is gone. I *knew* it would, although this wasn't what I was expecting. That thought gives me pause. Tom, is what I was expecting. Maybe the drums are Tom's doing, another way to harass me. He's doing this to keep me from getting sleep.

"Bear, it's okay," I say. He stops barking but stays by the door, alert and ready to eat anyone who tries to come in. I take a deep breath, releasing some of my pent-up anxiety, then I call Hank.

"He's doing what?" Hank asks.

"Yeah, stupid, isn't it?"

"Drums, you said?"

"Yeah. Well, I'm not sure if there's more than one. I'm not good with instruments. There could be multiple." I listen for a minute. "Yeah, okay, maybe there's more than one."

"I'm sorry to call you so late, Hank, I was just scared out of my mind and knowing he's out there trying to harass me again, I just didn't know what else to do."

"No, no. Don't be sorry. You did right." He lets out a deep breath. "Look, there's no way to prove it's him, even though we know it is. Who else would it be? It's too dark to see and there's no way you're about to go out there."

I bristle when he says this, like he's so sure of what I will not do. But I let him finish. "In a situation like this, you just have to let him play it out, tire himself out. Don't show him a reaction and he'll bore himself. Give it a couple of days."

I mull it over in my mind. *Do nothing.* I don't like it; In fact, I hate it. Hank must be able to tell what I'm thinking because he says, "I know you don't like to hear that, but our hands are tied."

"How am I supposed to sleep with him outside my door?"

"Do you have a way to defend yourself?"

I think about the gun waiting for me to pick it up at the gun shop. A few days short of a week for that background check. "No," I say. "Well, other than Bear."

I can hear him grinding his teeth. "Bear is a good dog, he'll protect you."

"I know, but I don't want it to come to that."

"Look, I can head over there and maybe scare him away, but like I said, he's going to know that he's getting to you. If you have a reaction, he's going to keep it up, hoping to break you. It's your call."

I think Hank can hear me crying now, even though I'm trying to hold back. I don't want him to hear me. I don't need his pity, but it's hard to hold back. "No. You're right. I need to just ignore it."

Before I cover my head with the pillow again, I peek outside one more time. I press a flashlight against the glass, trying to get it to light up the yard as much as possible. I swing it left and right slowly, taking in every square inch that's lit up. The drums stop. I hold my breath, waiting to see if something else will happen. Nothing does. Unable to see anything outside, I put away the flashlight and go back to bed.

EIGHTEEN

Six Months Ago

"Maybe this is a bad idea," I say.

"Nonsense," Charlie responds. "We're going to find something perfect."

We've been looking for months, trying to decide on a city to start our new lives. It's not just finding a city, but finding a place to live that's close enough for Charlie to commute. The housing market is insane. As soon as we find an area that works for us, it's hell trying to make anything else happen. There are virtually no rentals within our budget; everything has a wait list.

It's pointless to move without having something guaranteed. If we're on a waiting list, there's no way to know if we would actually get a place in time. There are so many variables to moving and after spending all this time searching, I'm losing hope. Originally, Charlie's enthusiasm was contagious, but now it's wearing off. It seems to be more trouble than it's worth.

"The problem is that we're looking for port cities," Charlie says.

"Yeah, well, that's where the jobs are."

"What if I quit? I could always go with another company."

"But I thought we agreed it was best for you to stay?" We're picking up our entire lives; the thought of Charlie starting over with a new job is one more thing on the list that terrifies me. I'm not sure if I can handle *everything* new. Is it too much for me to hold on to just one thing? But I'm being selfish. This isn't about me; it's about us.

Charlie sighs. "Right now, I don't mind looking for something new if it's what gets us a new start."

"You might have to go long haul." The thought brings dread. I know the stories about trucker's wives and how lonely they can get when their man isn't home for a week or more at a time. I don't think I'm strong enough to handle that kind of loneliness; it takes a stronger woman than I am to handle that. Plus, I worry so much about him now. I couldn't imagine the worry that comes with long-haul spouses. Yes, I'm maybe being selfish *again*, but after losing the baby, I'm just not in a place where that would be healthy for me or our marriage.

I think Charlie realizes this too because he says, "No. I won't go long haul. I promise."

We leave it at that, both continuing the search. Charlie mentions nothing else about finding a different company, but I think he's probably still looking. We're both trying to make this work. Part of me wonders if this is truly what I need; maybe Dr. Reymore is wrong. How can this much stress be helpful?

A few days later, Charlie comes home with a new idea. "Hear me out," he says, full of excitement.

I think he must've found something good because he hasn't been this hopeful in days. "What is it?" I ask.

"What if-" he starts then stops for a dramatic pause.

"What?" I cry.

"What if we build our own house?"

"What? Charlie-"

"Just hear me out." This is the craziest idea he's come up with yet, but I listen to what he has to say. "We can find some raw land. We're not really picky; it doesn't have to be very much. There's tons of open land just waiting for us."

"But we don't know anything about building a house."

"Oh, come on! How hard can it be? We'll hire professionals, of course, and we can find everything else we need to know on the internet." He's so wrapped up in the idea that he starts to walk around, pacing back and forth, waving his arms around. I've never seen him this excited about anything, not even about being a dad. Why is he so into this?

"I don't know." I don't want to keep shooting him down, but this is scary. *Raw land.* It's got to cost a fortune to start from scratch like that. Apprehension sits in the pit of my stomach and suddenly I feel sick.

"Listen," he says. He's in front of me now with both arms on my shoulders. "I have faith in us."

I look into his eyes. "Can we afford it?"

"Yes! Trust me I've spent all day looking into it." By that, I'm sure he means his thirty-minute lunch break. "If we find land cheap enough, we can get a loan for everything else. All the work we need done, everything. They call it a 'construction loan.'"

"Do we qualify for something like that?"

"Of course."

"Well, where are we going to live in the meantime?"

Charlie blushes now. I have a feeling this is the part he has to really convince me. "Well..." he says. "I was thinking...."

"What, Charlie?"

"An RV."

I furrow my brow, trying to understand. "An RV? Like a motorhome?"

"Yeah. Well, a travel trailer would be cheaper. If we bought one with our savings, we wouldn't have a payment and we could live in it until the house is built. Then we'll just sell it when we don't need it anymore."

I'm in shock. He wants me to live where? I have nothing against people with that lifestyle choice, but Charlie and I know *nothing* about RV's; we know nothing about camping! We're *city* people. I can count on one hand how many times I've been to the country. I think I've seen a cow once in my entire life. We would mess something up royally. How would we empty the poop? How would we get water? I have so many questions I want to scream.

My head is starting to ache, so I place a hand against my temple. I can feel my eyes pooling with water. I'm not crying yet, just scared and frustrated. Charlie wraps me in his arms. "Hey, don't stress about it."

"How can I not?"

"Easy. Just don't."

I laugh. "Charlie, we're so ignorant about this stuff. We know literally nothing about any of this. Probably less than nothing."

"So, let's figure it out."

I think about what life might be like if we did this. This is a huge thing. "Could you keep your job?" I ask.

Charlie grins. "Yes. I can transfer to Seattle. Even better, I already found the perfect place."

"What?" I feel like a broken record, asking what over and over.

He looks down sheepishly. "I was just browsing like normal, and I found the perfect property and that's when I had the idea and started looking into all of this." He's making it sound like he's had this idea for more than just a day. I'm wondering how long Charlie's been thinking about this without telling me about it.

Charlie pulls out his phone and brings up his real estate application. Scrolling through the choices, he comes to the one that has him so excited. Forty acres. I feel faint. "It's old logging land," he says. "They haven't touched it for years, just been letting everything regrow. Look at it. Everything is fully grown; you'd never know the difference."

"Do we need so much?" I whisper.

"No, but I mean it's perfect."

"Are we supposed to buy it without seeing it?"

"Well… It's sort of hard to walk around raw land like that. We could get a realtor and have them video chat with us or something." My mind is spinning with all this information, but Charlie keeps pushing. "In this market, babe, you know there's not much time to think. It's basically yay or nay, right now." Don't I know that all too well? How many times have we found a place that interested us, only to have it pending within a day?

"If it's so perfect," I ask, "why is it still for sale?" I point to the spot that says it's been listed for a year. Charlie's right about the market and seeing it listed for so long tells me there's got to be something wrong with it. The price is painfully low; so low it makes me hesitate. The old saying, "If it's too good to be true, it probably is," comes to mind.

Charlie shrugs it off, though. "Old logging land; who wants that?"

That's not very convincing to me. "Is it on the side of a cliff?"

He laughs. "No. Look, I've pulled up the county records. It's legit."

Looking over all the records he shows me, I start to relax. He's really done his homework on this one and it impresses me. I can't believe how much information is on public record about a piece of property. I know Charlie wants an answer now. He's giving me literal minutes to decide our fate. How can I decide something so huge at the snap of his fingers? This is all so sudden.

Seattle, I think. I've never been to Washington, but I've heard about its beauty. I close my eyes and imagine living somewhere surrounded by pine trees. The thought is peaceful. It's going to be so different. "There's nothing a little smaller? Maybe closer to where your work would be?"

Charlie shakes his head. "There's nothing closer. If you want smaller, there are some, but they're actually more money."

"How is that possible?"

"Better area, I guess. Like I said, I'm sure no one wants old logging land. I'm sure most people are like us and don't want forty acres, so it makes it cheaper."

I'm not sure if Charlie really knows what he's talking about here, but it doesn't matter. What matters is, are we going to do this or not? "Can I have a day or two to think about it? This is so spur of the moment."

"Babe." He gives me that look, the one that says *no*. "You know we need to jump on this."

"It's been for sale for a year. What's one more day to let me think?"

"Exactly! Look," he points to another spot on the screen. "They just lowered the price. There's no way this baby is going to stick around."

He's right. He must be right. The pressure is on, and I don't like it. I stand by the window, looking out at the city below. *Is this what I want?* The truth is: I have no idea what I want. I don't know, and Charlie does. He wants this bad; it's written all over his face.

"Let's do it," I say.

NINETEEN

Day two that Charlie is gone on his work run, I try keeping myself busy again. It's almost an exact repeat of the day before. Dark gray clouds cover the sky, drizzling on and off. Ellie, Bear, and I spend the day outside. Ellie and Bear play while I handle business. In the afternoon, we go exploring in the forest again, bringing our mud boots and tools to keep clearing away the path we've been working on.

We reach the peak of the same hill from yesterday. I stop to listen but this time there's no drums. What Hank said about Tom boring himself comes back to me. Maybe he's going to leave me alone tonight. I didn't react to him, so maybe Hank was right. Maybe Tom has run out of steam. I smile to myself, hopeful.

"Mommy! Butterfly!" Ellie calls to me, trying to catch an enormous yellow butterfly that's the size of her hand. It flutters around her, teasing her, before flying away.

"Wow! That was pretty!" I say. She tries to follow Bear, but we haven't extended our path any farther yet.

"Cupcake, stay behind me while I clear a little more of the path for us." We continue on for what seems like hours but couldn't possibly be that long. It's funny how slow moving we are in a forest, twisting and winding our way through the trees and foliage. We've found a game trail that seems to be pretty reliable and for the most part I've been able to clear it nicely for us.

"Who lives in that little house?" Ellie asks, pointing into the forest.

The question shocks me. I freeze, staring with wide eyes into the thick trees. "What house?" There better not be a house here, especially one we don't know about.

"The little house." She's pointing to the same spot, but I must be blind because I see nothing. Fear bombards my senses, weighing me down. It becomes hard for me to breathe. It strikes me how alone we are out here. "The house. The house. The house." Ellie is chanting now, waving her arms around.

"Ellie, I don't see a house."

"Oh." She seems to forget all about it, moving on to see what Bear has gotten into. Her nonchalance eases my worry. Ellie is always playing pretend. This must be another one of her games. I hope, anyway. Either way, I'm not really in the mood to go any farther into the woods today. We've been gone long enough, and it's time to head back for some food. We slowly wind our way back down the cleared path.

BEAR SLEEPS WITH ME ON THE BED AGAIN. I'M NOT SURE IF Tom is going to try harassing me again tonight or not, but either way, sleeping next to Bear makes me feel better. When I get up in the middle of the night to pee, I hear the faint sound of drums, like when I was in the forest yesterday. I look at Bear, but he's still asleep, seemingly not noticing the foreign sound.

I don't understand why Tom would start out so far away and end the night so close. Creepy doesn't begin to describe it and it's also just plain weird. Yes, it's scary, but it's baffling. Part of me wants to ask him what the hell he's doing just so I can understand it. Maybe that's his point. He wants me to be not just scared, but confused, too. Well, congrats Tom, you hit the nail on the head.

Lucky for me, the sound of the drums is so faint that it's no problem falling back asleep. Just like yesterday, though, I wake up to the sound of them again. This time they're much closer and Bear is growling.

"Ugh," I moan in protest. I wonder if I should call Hank to let him know it's happening again. After five minutes, the drums still haven't stopped, so I shoot hank a text. "Tom's outside again doing those stupid drums. Just keeping you updated."

There's an immediate reply. It's a thumbs up. I'm more annoyed than anything else, but I still feel fear coursing through me. There's a little voice in the back of my mind asking me, *how sure are you it's really Tom?* Hank and I *think* it's him out there harassing me, but what if it's not? I have no idea who else it would be or why there would be anyone out there at all, but *what if?*

"Stop it," I say to myself. It's Tom. He's harassing me over his stupid chickens and Bear. That's all there is to it and I'm going back to bed. He can go fall off a cliff for all I care. I put a pillow over my head, trying not to toss and turn. Bear doesn't like if I move too much, and he'll jump off the bed.

Just like last night, I wake up for a third time hearing the beat of drums. Unlike last night though, this time Bear isn't just barking; he's snarling. The sight of him with his back hairs raised, baring his teeth, drooling his anger, and ready to tear something to pieces, sends chills through me. Panic sets in and I feel like I'm suffocating. My throat is closing up and I fight against it, clawing at my neck. I turn away from Bear, trying to take deep breaths.

Something is going on outside. It can't be good, but with all the noise and lack of oxygen I can't think. Gasping for air, it takes me several minutes to calm down enough to get my breathing back under control. The drums seem like they're even closer than yesterday; they're so loud I feel like my head is pounding to their rhythm.

Suddenly, someone is banging on the door. It's not a polite knock; it's a ferocious pounding. Bear gets even more violent, now actually biting at the door. *Fuck, fuck, fuck!* I grab my phone and call Hank. "Calm down," he says. "Breathe."

"Hank, what do I do?" I cry. I feel like I'm screaming over the noise in order for Hank to hear me.

"I'll be there in fifteen minutes. Just hang tight. Don't open that door."

"I won't." But how safe is my door? It's made of styrofoam and fiberglass. If he wants to get through, the only thing in his way is Bear.

A few minutes pass, and there's more pounding on the door. I'm afraid Bear is going to be the one to rip a hole in the door just to get to the asshole on the other side. *Maybe that's what he wants.* "Bear!" I cry. He stops snarling and turns to me, but he's still in attack mode. "Bear, stop." Shaking, I pull him back into the bedroom so I can hold him close to me. There's no way I'm about to sit by the door.

When we're on the bed, the drums stop. I hear someone yelling but can't make out what's being said. The panic threatens to take over again, but I fight it, taking deep, steady breaths. I close my eyes, leaning into Bear for comfort. Bear can't stand it, though. His protective instincts win. He jumps off the bed, heading back to guard the door.

Crying, I follow him. That's when I'm able to understand what the voice outside is saying. "Hello! We're your neighbors!" It's not Tom outside. It's someone else.

TWENTY

A different voice yells, "We're your neighbors!" Magically the panic dissipates. What replaces it is cold, hard anger. I can feel the heat rising to my cheeks. It's 3:45 in the morning. *What. The. Fuck.* What are they thinking?

My mind is spinning with so much anger and confusion that I feel dizzy. I want to go out there and slap someone for scaring the shit out of me. I'm not sure if I can take whoever it is at their word- if it really is another psychotic neighbor, or if it's someone trying to fool me. I'm plagued by crazies, it would seem. My hands pull on my hair in frustration. Once again, I don't know what to do, so I wait for Hank to show up. *What a time for my husband to be gone.*

There's no more noise from outside now. No more yelling, and no more drums. I can't hear anyone moving around either, but Bear must be able to because he's still alert and ready, facing the door.

The Neighbors. Of course, we would have other neighbors besides Tom. I just didn't realize they would try to introduce themselves in the pre-dawn hours. I'm not sure which of our neighbors these are, but I already don't like them.

I pace the trailer, wired with energy. It seems like it's

taking Hank forever to get here, but true to his word, he shows up. Bear barks when the gravel crunches. At first, I think it's the neighbors back again, but when I glance out the window, I see the glow of police lights. *Thank God.*

Unable to wait another second, I swing the door open to release Bear. I follow him down the steps and run to Hank. It's probably not the smartest move to be running in the dark towards a police officer, but I don't seem to have my full thinking capacity at the moment. Hank doesn't seem to mind when I fling myself at him, clutching him and sobbing into his shoulder.

"Shh. Now, it's alright. Shh." His kindness and comfort have the opposite effect on me, and I cry even harder. *What's wrong with me?*

"I'm sorry." I try to say through the tears. I sniff, wiping the snot away and trying to clear my face as best I can.

"Don't worry about it." Hank clears his throat.

When I pull away from him, he seems almost shy and I blush, realizing how my behavior seems. I take a few steps away from him, needing the distance.

"Did you see them?"

Hank gives a small smile. "Uh, you kinda attacked me before I had the chance to look around."

My face is on fire. "I'm sorry. Of course. I'll go back inside."

"I'll knock on the door once I've had a look around."

I nod my agreement, then turn to look for Bear. "Bear!" I don't see him anywhere. "Did you see which way Bear went?" I ask.

"No. I'll go look around." He walks away and I'm torn about going back inside without Bear.

"Bear!" I call again. I strain my ears, listening for the slightest sound that might be him. There's nothing but the sounds of the night. I don't hear any people either. I think about how I heard the gravel with Hank's car and how there had been none with the neighbors. *Did they walk up?*

I look around the trailer for Bear, but it's too dark for me to see anything. The only light I have is the outside lights on the trailer, because in my haste to throw myself at Hank, I forgot to grab a flashlight. There's nothing else I can do.

Ellie is asleep inside. By some miracle she hasn't woken up, and if she *does* wake up without me there, she'll be terrified. Hoping Hank will find Bear, I go back inside the trailer to wait.

Minutes pass. I'm pacing again. There's only about fifteen feet I have to walk back and forth, but I'm making the best use of it. My palms are sweaty, and I keep wiping them on my pants to dry them off. I have a nasty habit of pulling on my hair when I'm frustrated, so I tie it up in a bun. I want to scream at Hank to hurry, but I keep silent.

Finally, an eternity later, I hear a soft knock at the door. When I open it, Hank is there with Bear. Relief fills me. The feeling is so strong I have the urge to cry again. I'm not about to do that, so I pinch myself. A little physical pain sometimes helps keep the tears at bay.

"Thank you," I say as they climb inside the trailer.

"He was at the border of the clearing," Hank says. "About to go onto your little trail."

"Oh, how do you know about the trail?"

Hank turns away, busying himself with his belt. "I saw a trailhead out there; just assumed you guys were doing some hiking."

"So, no neighbors?"

"Nope. No sign of anyone. There are a few houses down your road and even behind your property. It's going to be hard for me to pinpoint who it was, exactly."

I feel deflated. Hands are tied *again*. "Is there anything we can do?"

Hank purses his lips in thought. "Not really. I'm sorry."

"So, they're just going to keep coming back?"

"I don't know. It's the most bizarre thing. Maybe they'll come back in the morning? You did the right thing tonight, though. That's for sure."

His words don't make me feel any better. I miss the city so much right now. Is this what they want? They want to scare us away? It's starting to make sense why this property took so long to sell. Even though the price was crazy low, I'm starting to think we got ripped off.

I look at Bear, who didn't lick me when he came in, just went to lie down on the couch. There's something off with him, but I can't put my finger on it. We're sitting in the dark with only the light above the stove on. Now, I flick on more lights so I can get a better look at him.

"Bear," I say, but he doesn't look up. "Hey, buddy, what's wrong?" I kneel in front of him and turn his head to look at me. When he meets my gaze, I gasp and jerk back, almost falling backwards.

"What is it?" Hank asks, rushing to my side.

"That's not Bear."

"What?" Hank has a mixture of concern and confusion on his face. "Of course it's him. Who else would it be?"

"I don't know!" I yell. "But this dog is not Bear."

"Paisley, it's late-" he starts, but I cut him off.

"His eyes, Hank. Bear has green eyes." The dog on my couch has dark brown ones.

TWENTY-ONE

With the lights on, it's easy for me to see that even without the different eye color, this dog is definitely not my Bear. I feel the panic coming back. How could I have not seen it right away?

Hank bends down to get a good look at the dog, but I don't have the patience to wait anymore. I fumble to find a flashlight, then run outside. I don't bother to shut the door behind me. I'm running as fast as I can towards the edge of the clearing, screaming for Bear as I go. It's where Hank said he found the other dog, so maybe it's where Bear really went.

"Bear! Bear!" I scream for him until I'm hoarse, but it doesn't stop me. In the quiet of the night, I know he has to hear me. The only way he wouldn't come to me is if someone has him. *Oh, God! Not again!* "No!" I trip over a branch and fall to my knees hard. Crying, I brush myself off and keep going.

I don't know what I'm doing out here. It's pitch black, other than the stars and the beam of my flashlight. I can't see my feet or what's in front of me because I'm shining the light into the forest, looking for Bear. Terror holds me in its grip, preventing me from thinking rationally. The only thing I'm thinking of is finding my dog. How could this be happening for a second time? I trip again. This time I feel warm blood on my skin. It doesn't deter me, though.

Hank is calling for me. I can hear him clearly, which is good because that means even more noise to attract Bear's attention. When I turn to look back, Hank's beam of light is bouncing up and down. He must be running to catch up with me. I don't care what he does as long as I find my dog.

Pushing farther down the path, I try to keep from stumbling again, but it's hard to hike in the dark. The bushes move to my right. I stop dead, shining my light on the spot, but nothing else happens. "Bear?" Nothing. "Bear!" Panting, I stay still, listening to the sounds. Maybe he's responding to me and I'm too busy screaming to hear him.

The forest is silent. I'm sure I've scared all the nearby wildlife. I wait. One owl hoots, and then another. Silence. Some leaves rustle again in the distance; they're faint. I hear something else, but what is it? Was that a bark? Fear shoots down my spine, but I stay still, silent. *Come on, Bear. Come on.* The sound again. Yes, it's a bark! "Bear!" I scream as loud as I'm able.

"Bear! Bear! Bear!" I'm about to take off again, but a hand grabs my shoulder. "Ahh!" I cry out, then another hand claps over my mouth.

"Shh. Paisley, it's just me." Hank. He twists me toward him then takes his hand off my mouth.

"Don't do that!" I whisper scream at him. "You scared the crap out of me."

"I'm sorry. Listen, all this screaming in the middle of the night is pointless. We should come back in the morning when there's light. Who knows what's in these woods?"

"I heard barking. Bear is out there."

"I'm sure he is, but you're going to be no help to him with a broken leg." He gestures to the scrapes and blood on my legs.

"You're not going to stop me, Hank." I glare at him. "I'm not letting that fucker take my dog again."

"If that's what happened, then we know where to look first thing in the *morning*." He glares back at me. I huff, annoyed. I turn from him. How can I just go home and leave Bear out here all alone? I cup my hands around my nose and mouth and breathe into them, closing my eyes, thinking.

"I swear to you, we'll come back out as soon as it's light. A few hours tops."

He's right. All I'm doing out here is tripping over myself. If Bear was taken, there's nothing I can do about it right now, other than exhaust myself and be useless. Just because Hank's right, though, doesn't mean I have to say I agree with him. I head back towards the trailer, saying nothing.

I can hear Hank's footsteps as he follows behind me. The beam of his light shines next to mine, comforting me. I'm sure he can hear my sniffles even though I'm trying to hide them and be quiet.

We walk in silence. Despite my anger and despair, a part of me is relieved to have Hank here. It's been so lonely having Charlie either gone or sleeping every minute of the day. Having a friend, someone to help me and defend me, is really nice.

"Do you have a chair for me?" he asks when we're back at the trailer. "I'm staying here."

"You're going to sleep outside?"

"Yeah. I'm not going anywhere."

"Hank, you don't have to do that."

"I want to though." His look is so intense, I feel like I might catch fire from it.

Blushing, I turn away. "Okay. But not outside. I'll fold out the couch."

"No, no. Better for me to watch out here."

"In the dark?"

He smiles at my use of his own reasoning against him. "Alright. Lead the way."

The other dog, the one that's not Bear, is still inside the trailer. It feels like a betrayal to have another dog inside Bear's home, but what else can I do with him? It doesn't feel right to just turn him out. The weirdest thing about the whole situation is that this new dog has Bear's collar on.

It's not one that looks just like Bear's, it *is* Bear's. His name tag is hanging from it, with my phone number on the back. Why in the hell would this dog have Bear's name tag? I don't mention it to Hank. He's got enough going on, and the fact that he's staying with me means more than he knows.

TWENTY-TWO

I wake up to the sound of knocking on the door. I jerk up, looking around, because for a moment I don't remember what happened last night. I expect to hear Bear's bark, but it doesn't come. Then I remember. He's gone.

The other dog doesn't bark at the knocking. I'm not sure what I was expecting of him, but it's strange having a dog around who doesn't seem very protective. I guess it makes sense; he's not my dog, so why would he protect me?

"Paisley?" Hank calls for me. His voice is raspy. He must've been woken up by the knocking, too.

"Coming," I say. I walk out of the bedroom to meet him. "Do we answer it?"

"Let me, if it's okay."

"Thank you." I grip his hand in thanks, then stand back.

Hank answers the door with his left hand slowly, keeping his right hand at his holster. A woman's voice greets him. "Officer Adrian! Hi there, I wasn't expecting to find you."

His cruiser is in the driveway.

"Gladice Maubry," Hank says. "What are you doing here?"

"Oh." Gladice sounds flustered at Hank's dry tone. "I just came by to introduce myself to the new neighbor."

"Was that you with the drums last night?" Hank asks.

"Yes, yes, it was. The night before, too. I wanted to apologize for that. I think we might've scared the dog off who lives here."

At the mention of Bear, I step forward. Hank moves slightly to the side, and I stand next to him. I'm so close that I breathe in the smell of him. He smells so *good*. Like a man in the woods. I'm not expecting it and it hits me hard, making my heart beat faster. I want to turn toward him and inhale, but I resist the urge. *What's wrong with me?*

"Did you see Bear?" I ask Gladice.

"Oh, hi there," she says to me, smiling. "I'm Gladice, your neighbor behind you. We're a ways back there, but still neighbors none the less," she chuckles to herself.

"I'm Paisley." I grit my teeth, trying not to be rude, but not really caring who this lady is at the moment. "Did you see Bear?" I ask again.

"What's that? A Bear? No. I didn't see a Bear." She sounds confused.

"Bear is the name of her dog," Hank says. "Did you see a German Shepherd last night?"

"Oh, a dog! Yes, I saw one of those."

"Where was he?" I cry. Hank places a hand on my shoulder. I take it as a sign of comfort, even though he's probably trying to tell me to calm down.

"We left last night when no one answered the door," Gladice says. "Then when we were almost home, he came running after us. He didn't stop though, just passed us right by. The strangest thing."

None of this makes any sense to me; there's so many questions I have for this woman. If Bear ran after them, why would he just pass them like they weren't there? "Was there anyone else there?" I ask.

"Just my husband, Jack," she smiles.

Hank meets my gaze. "Thanks, Gladice," he says. "Now isn't a great time to visit, though. Paisley's dog is missing and we're going out to look for him."

"Oh, my," Gladice says, putting a hand against her chest. "Of course. I'm so sorry about that, Paisley. Please come have a chat anytime."

I nod, acknowledging her apology, but not ready to be friends with this woman. The list of questions I have for her is building by the second and I'm too afraid of what I might say to her at the moment, to speak. She and her husband must be nuts, just like Tom. Thankfully they seem to be far more harmless and more of a nuisance. Hank says his good-byes, waving Gladice off, then shuts the door.

"Hank, I know you must have a thousand other, more important things to be doing today. You really don't need to help me look for a dog." I smile at him. "Thank you for all you've done. Really, I'm sorry to be such a pain in your ass."

Hank smiles back, looking like he wants to pull me closer, but he keeps his distance. "Yes, there's probably a thousand other things I could be doing," he says. "But this is just as impor-tant. We don't know what really happened to Bear. There's not much we *do* know, and I'm determined to help a friend."

My chin wobbles, threatening to betray my emotions again. Hank says, "I'll step outside to give you a chance to freshen up."

I finally have the chance to glance at the clock. It's just past seven in the morning. *What the hell?* That woman was out all night banging drums and is up again before seven in the morning? Does she not sleep? Another thing- we've lived here for months now. Why are we just now finding out about these people? I can't wait to talk to Charlie about this the second he's home. *If he doesn't run to bed first,* I think grimly.

It's normal for Ellie to sleep until eight o'clock or even nine sometimes, but I can't believe she slept through all the noise last night without making a single peep. I crack her door to check on her and sure enough, she's sound asleep, snoring softly, holding her stuffed dog that looks just like Bear. I sigh, amazed but thankful she slept through it all.

Deciding she'll be fine for an hour or two alone, I take five minutes to freshen up. I set up her baby monitor to connect to my phone so I can keep an eye on her, then I step outside, taking the other dog with me to meet Hank.

"Ready?" I ask.

"Ready," he says.

We're going to find my dog.

TWENTY-THREE

The trees block us from most of the rain. Hank and I are back on the trail, where we left off last night. We have the other dog on a leash with us. I didn't want to leave him with Ellie and wasn't sure what else to do with him, so here he is for now. I'll have to take him to the vet to check for a microchip later, but that's not my primary focus at the moment.

We wind our way down the trail, calling for Bear, stopping every so often to listen for him. After an hour of searching, I'm losing hope. Last night I heard him and now there's nothing.

My fists clench in frustration. *I knew I should've kept looking last night.* I'm not blaming Hank, though. He was just trying to help me. And for him to be out here with me, I can't be anything other than grateful towards him.

When we reach the end of the existing path, Hank says, "Do you want to keep going?" He's ready to take our journey off trail if that's what I want. My throat is sore from all the yelling. I'm cold and tired, but we can't give up. It seems like we're getting nowhere though; there has to be something else we can do.

"I don't know if we're going to find him out here." I sigh, thinking about Bear hurt and helpless. What if he's dead? I shudder at the thought. "What do you think we should do?"

Hank looks around, thinking. "We haven't heard him. He might be too far off the trail to hear us."

I think about the satellite dishes Bear has on top of his head. With those ears, there's probably not much that Bear can't hear. I'm torn. "What if Tom has him locked up again?" I ask. "He would hear us but that would explain why he's not coming."

Hank nods. "That's true."

"Let's go to Tom's."

"Whoa, hold on. We can't just go over there because we think he might have Bear again."

"Why not?" I ask, throwing my hands up in frustration. "Didn't you just say last night that we could? He's out on bail, isn't he? There's got to be something in the law that says you can go over there just for the hell of it, isn't there?"

"That's not what I meant and that's not how it works." Hank shakes his head, frowning. "I want to help you, Paisley, and I'm going to, but we have to follow the rules."

"Why?" I scream, unable to control my anger. He doesn't answer. It's a rhetorical question, anyway. If there's anyone that's going to follow the rules, it's the Sheriff. "What if I go alone? You can wait for me at the end of his driveway or something. You wouldn't be breaking any rules, I would."

Still shaking his head, Hank says, "No. We're going to find another way." I'd like to know what the hell other way there could possibly be. If Tom took Bear, then we know where he's going to be. It makes sense that I would hear him last night; it makes sense that Bear isn't coming back to me. The only time he's ever *not* come back is when he was taken.

We go back to the camper and Hank makes me promise not to go to Tom's before he leaves. Grudgingly, I agree to wait for him. Again, Hank's probably right. After the last time, I hate to think what Tom would do if he saw me over there again. Hank will think of something.

When Ellie wakes up looking for Bear, my heart breaks all over again. I can't help but think that something is wrong here. Something isn't sitting right. Ellie wants to go looking for Bear, even though I explain that Hank and I have already tried. It doesn't hurt to keep trying, though. This time, I pack Ellie and the other dog in the Jeep. I'm going to pay our *other* neighbors a visit.

With the help of my GPS, I'm able to pinpoint where I think Gladice and her husband live. She said they're behind us, and we have a lot of land back there, but the map shows a dirt road. The access to that road is off our main gravel road, as far as I can tell. Hoping for the best, and praying we don't get lost, we head out.

Somehow, I'm right. Less than ten minutes later, we're on a narrow dirt lane. "Where are we?" Ellie asks from her car seat.

"The neighbor's, I think."

The lane ends at a small cabin. It feels like we're in the middle of the forest. There's barely enough land cleared for me to turn the Jeep around, but somehow I manage. I want to be ready to get the hell out of dodge if needed. "Stay here, Ellie," I say. I'm not sure if I'm even at the right house, but when I get out and shut my door, I see Gladice coming out the front door of the cabin.

"Hi, there." I wave.

"Hello! Wasn't expecting you so soon! Welcome." I can see the surprise on her face, and I feel a twinge of guilt. I would hate for someone to show up unannounced like this. I squash the feeling as quickly as it came, thinking of exactly how unexpected Gladice and her husband were in the middle of the night.

"I was hoping to ask you a few questions about what you saw last night, if you don't mind?" I ask, walking toward her. The rain has stopped, but the dirt in her front yard is all mud. I slip as I'm walking, and cry out as I fall on my butt.

"Oh, my! Are you alright?" Gladice asks. But I'm not listening. In the back, I hear barking. *Bear.*

"Bear!" I yell, getting up. Gladice looks worried. There's more barking and I know it's him. If looks could kill, Gladice would be dead from the one I'm giving her. "You have my dog!" I take off for the back of the cabin, going as fast as I can but being careful not to slip again.

"No, no, you have it all wrong!" Gladice cries behind me. I don't wait for her to explain. The only thing that matters is getting my Bear back.

Around back, my breath catches. I feel my heart in my throat with the sight that meets my eyes. Bear is in a cage. It looks like it's meant for an animal a third his size. He's crouched over because it's too small for him to sit up, and too small for him to lie down. He's squeezed in so tightly that his sides are poking through the holes. I wonder how they got him to fit.

"Bear!" I run for him now, not caring about the damn mud. "Bear, I'm here, baby!" He whimpers for me, thumping his tail against the bottom of the cage. He has something on his muzzle; I'm not sure if it's dried blood or dirt. He looks like he's been through the ringer. I want to ring someone's neck.

I pull at the door of the cage, but there's a lock. *A lock!* Unable to pull it free, I turn back toward Gladice, who's still making her way towards us. "Open this cage!" She flinches when I yell, and it gives me a pang of satisfaction.

"That's my dog," she says, looking around, like someone's going to come help her.

"The hell he is!"

"I'm sorry," she fumbles, "you're mistaken."

It hits me then. The other dog. She's the one mistaken here; she thinks Bear is hers. Somehow, they got mixed up. But why does the other dog have Bear's collar? It doesn't matter. I'm going to solve this mix-up right here and now.

"Gladice," I say, trying to sound a little less murderous. "Your dog got switched with mine, somehow. I don't know what happened, but your dog is back in my Jeep." I can see the gears turning in her head. She doesn't answer me right away; it looks like she's weighing something.

Finally, she takes a closer look at Bear. When he snarls at her, she jerks back. I notice the bandage on her arm and wonder if it's Bear's handiwork. *I hope it is.*

"I thought there was something up with him." She's trying to act casual, but there's something not right with her. How did she not realize this wasn't her dog? It's blaringly obvious. I feel guilty about giving the other dog to her if she's just going to throw him in a cage like this, but I have little choice. The look on her face when I showed up makes me think maybe she didn't want me to find Bear.

"Can you get him out for me, please?" I clench my jaw, trying to stay calm. She hems and haws, like she's trying to think of a way out of it. "Now," I say, leaving no room for further discussion. Gladice's eyes grow wide, but she finally moves to let Bear out. He jumps on me, knocking me to the ground, licking every inch of my face. I hold on to him, letting him lap up the warm tears that are falling.

I lead Bear back to the Jeep, where I let the other dog out. Guilt clenches at my heart when he doesn't look like he wants to go. "I'm sorry, buddy. This is your home," I say to him gently, swearing that I'm going to give Hank an earful.

Better yet, animal control is so happy to jump on people. This is the type of person they should go after. I'll give them an earful too. Hopefully, they can do the right thing here, since they can't seem to figure it out the rest of the time.

The dog goes with Gladice, who doesn't stop staring at me. She doesn't look happy. *Why?*

"Let's go home," I say to Ellie and Bear.

TWENTY-FOUR

Six Months Ago

Charlie slams his fist down on the armrest in his semi with bruising force. He's spending his lunch break searching for homes again. He's known all along it was going to be hard to find a place but didn't realize just *how* hard. Every time he or Paisley found something that looked like a good fit, it would be gone in a day or two.

He wants to move more than anything and he's afraid to tell Paisley just how much he *needs* this move. In Charlie's eyes, this is really for him, not as much for her. She doesn't need to know that, though. Let Paisley think this is all about her getting better. It's a bonus for sure, but Charlie has an ulterior motive.

Paisley has no idea about the problems Charlie is having at work. They've been having money problems ever since she quit her job and he's having a hell of a time keeping them afloat. Charlie doesn't blame Paisley at all; he knows none of this is her fault. He wishes she would hurry up and get better, but the loss she suffered is life changing. Charlie doesn't know if she will ever be in a mental state to work again.

Normal women probably would be. But Paisley isn't a

normal woman. She's... sensitive. Even though she's far recovered physically, mentally she hasn't been able to recover.

This is the opportunity Charlie has been wanting. A fresh start. Charlie can find a new job, a *better* job. He can get more pay, more hours. They wouldn't have to worry about money anymore. He wasn't about to tell Paisley that he was on the verge of getting fired. He'd been late *and* caught stealing product. The final nail in his casket had been when he rammed into a parked car.

There are no more options, and Charlie is desperate. How can he come home and tell Paisley he'd been fired? He doesn't need to lay this on her, too. Not after everything she's been through. He needs to find them a place to live. He also needs to find a new job without Paisley finding out.

Lunch break over. Frustrated, Charlie puts his phone away and gets back to it. He's on his last warning and the only reason he hasn't been fired yet is because his boss knows Charlie is going to be leaving anyway. He's shown mercy for now, but if there's any more screwups that's it for Charlie.

After his shift, Charlie sits in the car to do some more browsing on his phone, determined to sit there until he's got some kind of answer. There's a new website that comes up on his search engine. It looks intriguing. "Land to live on in this market, guaranteed! Prices to die for!" it says. *Another sales gimmick,* Charlie thinks, but he's so desperate that he continues to read, anyway.

"We can help you solve all of your problems. We won't just help you find a place to live, we'll help your family heal," it says.

"What?" Charlie asks himself, continuing to read.

"Society of The Trees." *It's a private community,* thinks Charlie. The more he reads about it, the more interested he becomes, until he finally decides to fill out the questionnaire. He figures it doesn't hurt to find out a little more. Maybe they really can help him.

Less than ten minutes after Charlie submits the form, his phone rings. It's a blocked number. His palms start to sweat from nerves. *Could it be these people already?* he wonders. He answers the phone. "Hello?"

"Mr. Lanson, I'm with the Society of The Trees. We received your information and have a few questions for you. Do you have a moment?" A woman's voice, silky smooth, answers Charlie.

Wow, that was fast, Charlie thinks. He says, "Yes, I do."

"We noticed on the online form you filled out that you're in need of a place to live. How would you feel about owning forty acres?"

"Forty-" Charlie laughs. "Forty acres! Wow, that's a lot of land. I mean sure, I'd take anything I could get my hands on, but I don't have much of a budget."

"Not to worry. For members of our community, we're able to negotiate special deals."

"But-" Charlie tries to protest. This talk about members has him confused; he didn't know he was signing up for anything.

"You *do* want to join our society, don't you Mr. Lanson?" The woman asks. Her tone brooks no argument.

"Yes, I think, but-"

"Excellent," she says. "Now, about your wife."

Charlie's spine stiffens at the mention of Paisley. "What about my wife?" he asks with caution.

"You mentioned she needs help. She needs to heal?" She's interested now. Her tone is less forceful, more gentle.

Charlie hesitates, unsure of how much he should say. "Um," he starts. "She's- we've lost a child."

"I see."

"It's been hard for both of us, but worse, I think, for Paisley. It's destroyed her." Charlie clears his throat. It's hard for him to talk about their loss. He's not sure why this woman needs to know about it, but if she's able to help Paisley, then it's worth telling the story.

"You'll need a sacrifice," she says. "Something or someone that Paisley is connected to emotionally. The stronger the connection, the better."

"Whoa, whoa, what?" Charlie asks. *A sacrifice? What. The. Hell?!*

"It's just a technical term," the woman says, sounding bored now. "It will be hard, but it's a requirement. If you want us to help her, that's what it takes."

"But-" Charlie has so many more questions, but the woman won't let him speak. She interrupts again.

"Now, we have a job lined up for you, of course. You'll be required to pass certain tests, too."

"Look, lady," Charlie says. "I appreciate this. I really do. But you're not making sense. I have so many questions. I didn't know I was signing up for anything. I just wanted some help for myself and my wife."

"And you'll get it, Mr. Lanson. Don't worry. You'll get it."

TWENTY-FIVE

As the days pass, I'm even more reluctant to let Bear out of my sight. He was taken from me *twice*. I don't know what the problem is with our neighbors wanting my dog, but it's driving me crazy. I'm getting paranoid. I keep Bear in my sight at all times now, too afraid to lose him again. He just wants to be a dog, but what would I do without him? This is how it has to be until the tension with the neighbors blows over.

"Just let him go play, Paisley," Charlie tells me.

"I will *not* lose him again," I say, annoyed he doesn't understand.

"It was a freak accident."

"Well, we have freak neighbors!" Charlie is annoyed with me, too. It's a brutal pattern, but I've promised myself I would do whatever it takes to keep Bear safe and that's what I'm doing.

They haven't been back with the drums, but who knows when they'll decide to take them up again. I haven't heard them out in the forest, either, but I know this can't be the end of it. It was so random, so unpredictable.

I'm too afraid to go back to Gladice's house and ask her all the questions plaguing me. There's so much I want to know, but I can't bring myself to go back over there. Part of me is afraid to leave the camper, too. What if they're watching us? What if they're just waiting for me to leave?

I try to stay as positive as possible because these people live right next to us. Thinking about being forced to avoid them for years stresses me out. Maybe they really are just weird. Some people are weird. Nothing wrong with that. Maybe we really did just have some kind of miscommunication and started off on the wrong foot. I haven't asked my questions, so of course all I can do is speculate.

I'm finally able to pick up my gun from the gun shop and I feel like a mountain has been lifted off my shoulders. I hope I'll never have to use it. In fact, I've locked it away where it will be hard to even get to it, but just having it makes me feel safer. It's still my little secret. I have told no one- not Charlie, not Hank, and not my therapist.

Dr. Reymore has tried calling and emailing several times during the months we've been up here, but I haven't had a chance to get back to him so far. It hasn't been a top priority. I was only seeing him in San Francisco to please Charlie, and now it seems continuing our sessions is moot.

But after what happened with Bear, I scheduled an emergency video session with Dr. Reymore. He talked me out of my panic, just like always. I admit to myself it makes sense why Charlie wanted me to see him. As far as he knows, I still do regularly. During our appointment, Dr. Reymore asked, "Why haven't you returned my calls or emails?" He was a little put off by my lack of communication. If I wasn't mistaken, it seemed like he was even a little worried.

"I'm sorry, Doctor," I smiled reassuringly. "You know, I never thought it would be this much work to have a house built. It's been kind of non-stop." He needed a reminder that I'm doing something with my life. It was *his* idea that we move, after all. It seemed to do the trick because he eased off.

"Of course," he said. "I'm glad you're checking in now, although I'm sorry to hear it's under such duress."

"Me too," I said, and I was being honest.

"I would like you to check in again in a couple of weeks, Paisley. Can you make that work?"

I'M AT THE GROCERY STORE NOW, WALKING THROUGH THE aisles with Ellie in the shopping cart and Bear walking next to us. With a town this small, I'm sure everyone has heard about what happened to Bear. No one tries to tell me he's not allowed inside. I'm not sure if Hank has said anything to anyone, but either way I'm thankful there's no confrontation. We're still the new people in town and it's bad enough fighting with *two* of our neighbors; I would hate to pick another fight with someone else in town.

As I'm shopping, my phone rings. It's a private number. I'm going to let it go to voicemail; I never answer private numbers, especially when I'm in public, but then I remember we have the percolation test scheduled in a few days. It might be something about our appointment. *Oh God, I hope they're not calling to cancel or reschedule us.*

"Hello?" I answer.

"Hello Ms. Lanson, I'm calling regarding your percolation test." *Dammit, I knew it!*

"Yes?" I ask. "I hope you're not calling to reschedule."

"Actually, I'm calling to let you know we had a cancellation. There's an opening for this afternoon, if that would be okay to come sooner than originally planned?"

"Oh, wonderful. Yes, that sounds great." Whew, what a

relief. Charlie will be pleasantly surprised, too. Maybe it will get us back on some solid footing with each other.

"Excellent. We can be there within about twenty minutes."

Twenty minutes is pushing it for me, but I make it work. It takes about five minutes to wrap up the rest of our shopping and check out. "Let's go home," I say to Ellie when we're in the car, all loaded up. "We have some workers coming to our land." It normally takes us about twenty minutes to get back home, but we should be there around the same time as the work crew if we hurry.

TWENTY-SIX

When we get home, the crew hasn't shown up yet. I have time to get the groceries inside the trailer and set Ellie up with some toys before they show up. It's not really a big deal for me to be home, but I like to be if there's someone coming out to our property.

The idea of them doing work without one of us being home makes me uncomfortable. What if they need to address an issue? What if there's some kind of problem? What if they have questions for us? All they're doing is digging some holes in the ground today, but I still feel better being here, just in case.

Bear barks when he hears the driveway under the weight of tires. *They're here.* "Bear, it's okay." He's been on edge, and I can't blame him. "Stay here, baby," I say to Ellie, leaving her with her toys under our awning. Bear and I walk down the driveway towards the white van. I wonder how they plan on digging. If they use shovels, it's going to take them forever.

We stand there for a minute, waiting. No one gets out of the van, and it's a little awkward. My heartbeat speeds up a little as I wonder what's taking him so long to get out. Bear is silent, standing by my side. My hand strokes the top of his head in a gentle rhythm. Finally, a man gets out of the driver's side. He looks like he's in his forties and fit. *Maybe he really does dig by hand.* He looks that muscular.

"Hi, there," I call to him and give a little wave, using my other hand, the one that's not on Bear.

"Hi," he says with a tight smile. He looks at Bear. "Is he friendly?"

Oh. That's why he didn't get out right away. He's worried about Bear. "Don't worry," I say, smiling. "He wouldn't hurt a fly." It's a bold lie, but this man doesn't need to know it. Bear will hurt no one unless they threaten us. If this guy keeps his hands to himself, he's got nothing to worry about.

I can tell he doesn't quite believe me. It makes me want to laugh, but I'm able to hold back. After a few seconds of internal debate, the man says, "My partner is coming with the tractor. He'll be here in a few." Darn. It looks like I was wrong about the shovel.

"Okay, no problem."

He looks around. "Do you have a place in mind for us to start?"

And this is why I wanted to be home. I *knew* they would have questions. Charlie and I have talked about where we would like to put the house. We have a couple of different choices picked out within our clearing, but I thought he would've mentioned it when he scheduled the appointment. "There are a couple of places we have in mind for the house. Can you choose where to dig based on that?" I ask.

"Lead the way," he says.

I look back at the trailer, where Ellie is playing quietly with her toys. She's visible from where we're standing, but once we're out in the field, she won't be. "Ellie, I'll be right back!" I call to her.

Once I hear her faint, "Okay, Mommy," I walk. Bear is next to me and every minute or so he glances back at the man who's keeping a respectable distance behind us. It's a little weird having such a large man walking behind me.

We're about three hundred feet off the existing driveway when I say, "Based on the survey, this is our favorite spot." He nods but says nothing, so I add, "I'll show you the other spot we had in mind, in case this one isn't a great choice."

We walk on, another hundred feet back, and then we cut over to the left, where I take him out about five hundred feet more. It's a lot farther than our first pick, which will raise our costs for electricity and extending the driveway, and we'd have to do a lot more tree clearing, which is why it's our *second* choice.

We're a little more uphill though, which might make drainage better. At least, that's what Charlie and I were thinking. We don't know anything about anything with septic systems, so we're hoping the information we found online is accurate enough. We're basing our picks partly on the survey that shows us the elevation of the land and the way things flow.

The man, who hasn't even introduced himself, has been silent the whole time we've been walking. *Not much for small talk.* With his longer stride, he walks a little faster than Bear and I. As we've made our way farther and farther back into the property, the distance between the man and me has shrunk considerably. My arms prickle when he's close enough for me to hear him breathing. He's too close. I try not to grimace when I smell him.

I clear my throat and try to walk faster. He's not getting the hint, though. By the time we've reached the second spot, he's practically on top of me. I'm surprised Bear has let him get this far. It's been so gradual though, and so quiet, other than the sounds of our steps and breathing, that it seems completely natural. Bear must think so too.

We stop walking, and I take a few steps away from the

man. He doesn't seem to notice my discomfort. He doesn't seem bothered by Bear anymore, either. He looks around, examining the immediate area, then nods again. That's when we hear a diesel engine. "That's my partner," the man says.

"Right," I say. "Is there anything else you need from me?"

"That should do it. We'll dig in both spots and see what comes up. Shouldn't take us too long."

We walk back to the driveway to meet his partner.

TWENTY-SEVEN

The drums are beating again. It's been days since I've last heard them and that sliver of hope that suggested it might've been a one weekend thing has vanished. I'm not sure if I'm exasperated or angry with our neighbors.

Gladice had explained nothing about the drums. Although, I really hadn't given her a chance to. Was that my fault, though? They were on my property, uninvited, in the middle of the damn night, *and* they took my dog. Whether or not by accident, it doesn't really matter.

How I see it, Gladice and her husband should've gone out of their way to apologize to me. They should've explained. They should've made more of an effort. They have done none of those things. And now, they're back.

I pull out my phone to text Hank. "Drums are back." I add in an annoyed emoji for good measure. I realize I want to tell Hank first, without even thinking of telling Charlie. Charlie doesn't seem to care one way or another what's going on, but Hank does. He's supportive and helpful. My heart warms at the memory of Hank helping me find Bear.

Heat rises to my cheeks, and I stop myself. *This is getting out of hand.* I'm a married woman. I'm making a fool out of myself. This isn't the first time I'm reminding myself to take a step back from Hank. He's been nothing but kind and professional, a genuine friend. I'm not going to read into the situation and make something out of nothing. I'm not that kind of woman; I'm not that kind of wife.

I squash the little voice in my head that says, "The way he looks at you, though, that's not the way a friend looks." *Why am I having these thoughts?* I'm lonely, that's all. I'm lonely because Charlie has been gone far too often. I let out a breath. I need to ask Charlie to call in sick. He needs to take a day off to be with me. We need to be *us* again. We haven't been the same since-

The beat of the drums stops. My phone vibrates- a reply from Hank. I wonder if he's awake at all hours of the night or if I'm waking him up with my late-night complaints. Great, now I feel guilty.

"We need to have a chat with Gladice," Hank says.

"I'm sorry if I woke you."

"You didn't."

He said *"We."* Does that mean he's going to go with me to speak with her? Maybe he has her phone number. That would be so much better; I'm really not looking forward to going back over there.

Tonight is a little different from the other nights I've heard the drums. I only wake up one time, not three, and there is no gradual progression of them growing closer to me. The one time I woke up, they were right there, outside the door.

I don't have the patience to just let it go. I don't like that they're on *my* property and I don't like that they're waking me up in the middle of the fucking night again. I climb out of bed and swing open the door, not caring if they see me in my see-through nightgown. Let them look for all I care. I just want some damn sleep.

"Go home!" I yell into the dark. I know they're there, even though the outside trailer lights don't shine on them. The drums just stopped moments ago. There's no way they're gone already. I take a step down onto the first step of the entry stairs. "You hear me, goddammit? Go home and don't come back with those fucking drums!" I scream into the night.

No one answers, but it seems they heard me. I don't hear the drums again, this night at least.

THE NEXT MORNING HANK SHOWS UP EARLY, BEFORE ELLIE IS awake. He's looking at me differently; it unsettles me. I try to ignore it. I shouldn't enjoy it the way that I do. He looks like he would like to eat me for breakfast and If I'm not careful, I'll return the look. I'm *not* going to let that happen. I won't do that to Charlie.

What's with him, anyway? There's some attraction between us, yes, but what's with this intensity suddenly? *Maybe it's not attraction at all*, I'm starting to think. Maybe he doesn't feel well or something. "How are you?" I greet him with a weak smile.

Hank clears his throat. "I'm fine. I came to take you over to Gladice's."

"This early?" I haven't even finished my coffee yet.

"She's an early riser, from what I hear."

"She's a night owl too," I say. I can't hide the irritation I feel towards her.

"She owes you an apology and explanation." He's determined to help. Again. *He's not the perfect man. He's not the perfect man.* I'm about to tell him I won't leave Ellie alone sleeping again, but I'm interrupted by the sound of a car coming up the driveway. Instinctively, Hank takes a protective stance slightly in front of me at the same time as Bear. My heart screams for mercy at the sight.

Then we see Charlie's old Dodge Ram. "It's Charlie," I say, shocked. He's home early today. Maybe he read my mind about needing him to be home with me for a little while. His absence has gone on for far too long. I'm relieved to see him. I feel saved from myself somehow.

Charlie gets out of the truck. "Hi, Charlie!" I greet him with a smile. I'm about to walk toward him, but I notice he doesn't look very happy. He looks pissed.

Instead of saying hello, Charlie asks, "Who's that?" He points at Hank. That tone. He's accusing me of something, without saying the words. My cheeks flush, making me look guilty. I realize Hank isn't in his uniform. I also realize how close we're standing to one another.

I take a step away from Hank and say, "Charlie, this is Officer Hank Adrian. Hank, this is my husband, Charlie."

Hank says, "It's nice to meet you, Mr. Lanson." He offers a hand to shake, but Charlie ignores it. He stares coldly at the both of us. I don't know what's going through his head, but he looks like he could commit murder. Without another word, he turns from us and goes into the trailer.

"I'm sorry," I whisper to Hank, tears threatening to spill.

"Don't be." He smiles to reassure me, but I can tell it's forced.

"I'm not going to be able to go to Gladice's today," I say. "Raincheck?"

TWENTY-EIGHT

A massive summer windstorm blew through Pierce, King, and surrounding counties. The damage left behind was of record-breaking proportions. Trees fell across roads and power lines, on top of houses and cars. Thousands were without power. Even more were isolated because they couldn't drive through the debris. The Governor declared a temporary state of emergency, allocating special funding to help with clean-up efforts.

Heather Reed and her family were among those who suffered from the storm. An ancient pine tree had fallen on their roof, breaking ceiling beams and crushing windows with its fall. Heather and her three children were home during the storm.

When the tree fell, it nearly scared them all to death. They'd been in the back bedroom, huddled together, reading a favorite storybook. Luckily, the tree had fallen towards the front of the house, in the living room area, and all were safe physically, even if they didn't feel it emotionally.

Two weeks after the storm, the Reeds were still waiting on repairs. The tree was still laying across their house, beams hanging, and windows shattered. Heather cleaned up the broken glass and other debris as best she could. Her husband,

James, helped hang a tarp over the holes in the roof and windows, but every day Heather worried the roof would collapse.

"It's fine," James said to her. "A hole is not going to make the whole thing cave in. Don't worry." He pulled her into his arms to comfort her. James realized experiencing the crash must've been terrible, but there was no reason to continue to worry and stress about it. The repairs would get done eventually and everything would be fine. Their biggest problem would be keeping bugs, birds, and rodents out of the house in the meantime. If there was another storm, they'd really be screwed.

Heather took comfort against his chest but didn't agree with her husband. This wasn't just some small hole in the roof. This was a gaping chasm. When beams from the rafters were broken and hanging down, yes, she was scared to death that something was terribly wrong. What did James know about roofs, anyway?

"Did the roofers say when they could squeeze us in?" she asked. James had been placed on a waiting list because every roofer around was slammed.

"Not yet," he said. "It seems everyone in the state needs their roof repaired, now."

"It's been two weeks," Heather complained.

"I know. What else can we do?" James was always the calmer of the two. So understanding of everyone, so patient.

"I'm scared, James," she whispered.

"I know. Don't be, love."

Anytime they were home, Heather insisted no one stay in the living room longer than absolutely necessary. This usually meant speed walking through it. She was so tense about the situation that if any of the kids forgot the rule and stopped to play under the hole, she would go off. Tears came along with guilt, but it didn't stop Heather from watching her family like a hawk.

Another two weeks passed, and Heather couldn't take the waiting anymore. The company that James was waiting for was absolutely ridiculous. They hadn't even been able to come out to assess the damage yet. James was in no hurry to get anything fixed. They had a claim in with their homeowners' insurance too, but the company hadn't responded either.

In Heather's eyes, the waiting game was getting old. The first company to respond was going to be the one to get her money. She was done. While two of the kids were in school and the baby was napping, she hopped on social media. Heather posted on a community page, "Anyone out there still waiting on roof repairs? We are! Anyone know of a company that's not wait listed?"

A few hours later, she had her answer. "Thanks all," she posted. "Looks like *The Roofers* are the answers to my prayers!" When Heather called to make an appointment, the soonest availability was still a week out. "It's better than nothing," she said. At least now they had an actual date. No more waiting around just to find out when they'd get an appointment.

James wasn't happy Heather went behind his back the way that she did, but like Heather, he was too relieved about getting an appointment to say anything else about it. His pride stung a bit, but he would be fine.

Two days later, Heather received a phone call from a private number while the kids were at school. She had just put the baby down after nursing. Not normally one to answer blocked calls, she was about to let it go, but then remembered their appointment with *The Roofers*. What if it was them calling about their appointment? A moment later, she answered the call.

"Hello, Ms. Reed, I'm with *The Roofers,* calling regarding your appointment next week."

"Yes?" Heather asked.

"We're aware with the storm, many have had a long wait," the voice started.

Heather barked a laugh. "Yeah. You could say that."

"Well," the voice continued, "I'm calling to let you know there's actually been a cancellation. If you're available now, I have a technician able to get out there to assess the damage within about twenty minutes."

"Twenty minutes?" Heather couldn't believe her good luck. Her heart raced with excitement. This was finally getting taken care of. "Yes," she said. "That sounds fantastic. Thank you so much."

Twenty minutes later, an old, unmarked, white van caked in mud pulled up the driveway. It had a tic coming from the engine and looked like it was barely running. When she saw it, Heather was confused. She thought a successful roofing company would own more reliable vehicles than this. It seemed to be a popular company. Surely they made enough money.

She had no more time to think about it, though. The doorbell rang, and she wasn't about to turn the tech away. Not when she'd waited this long to get someone out there. Heather answered the door. "Hello, Mrs. Reed. I'm Taylor," the technician said with a smile.

James got a phone call at work that afternoon, from the kids' school. Heather hadn't been by to pick them up.

Worry crept in. He wondered what could've happened; this wasn't like her to forget the kids.

He tried to call and text, but hadn't been able to reach Heather. Left with no other options, James left work to pick up the kids before heading home again. *She's tired from nursing all the time; maybe she's taking a nap,* he thought. When he got home, James found out how wrong he was.

TWENTY-NINE

Officer Hank Adrian received the statewide alert about the murder that took place last night. All law enforcement in the vicinity was placed on high alert, as a suspect had yet to be identified. Debris from the windstorm a few weeks ago was still everywhere, and officers were reminded to be extra cautious when looking for suspicious individuals.

Lead investigators were now asking for all hands on deck. Any officers in neighboring counties were being asked to assist with the investigation any way they were able. There was a hotline that needed to be manned, and countless interviews. Agencies were already short of manpower because of the storm. Those who were available volunteered to help cleanup efforts, even weeks later.

There weren't many left to help man the investigation. Officer Adrian was available, however. He volunteered to spend the day in Snohomish County, doing interviews and spending time at the scene of the crime, assisting in any way he could.

The victim, Heather Reed, was a thirty-four-year-old wife and mother of three. Hank's job for the day was to speak with the victim's husband, James Reed. He'd given an initial statement after finding his wife, but the goal was to speak with him again to see if there were any more details.

When Officer Adrian met Mr. Reed, he was overwhelmed with sympathy for the man. Mr. Reed was an emotional wreck. With purple bags under his eyes, he looked like he had gotten no sleep and Officer Adrian couldn't blame him. The man's entire world had been turned upside down. "I already told them everything," James said to Hank in the hotel room he was staying.

"Yes," Officer Adrian said. "I'm hoping to ask you a few questions about your statement and see if there's anything else we might've missed."

"What do you want to know?" James asked.

"I know this is hard, Mr. Reed, but please know that any information you provide is of vital importance."

"Yeah, yeah, I get it," James said, unable to meet Officer Adrian's eyes. The pain he felt was too raw. He was surprised the police didn't get enough from him the day before and couldn't believe the audacity of this asshole.

"I'd like to start with when you found your wife. Walk me through what you did. Start with when you got home from picking the kids up from school."

James turned away, wiping his eyes. He cleared his throat. "I don't think I can," he said.

"I understand it's hard-" Officer Adrian started, but James cut him off.

"You understand! How could you possibly fucking understand?" No one can understand. How many people actually came home with their kids to find their wife like *that*? James didn't think there were many. Only *those* individuals would be able to truly understand.

"I-"

"I came through the front door," James said. "There was no sign of Heather. The house was silent; she wasn't answering when I called for her. I figured the baby was taking a nap, so I didn't want to keep yelling for her."

"Where were your other kids?"

"They came into the house, like normal. Went to their rooms to drop off their school stuff."

Hank nodded. "Then what happened?"

"I walked into our bedroom, thinking I would find Heather taking a nap or in the shower or something." James gulped, swiping at his eyes again. "She was on the bed, alright. Or, I should say, her *pieces* were on the bed." He broke down then, sobbing uncontrollably.

Hank knew the story. He read the statement before coming over. Heather was cut into pieces, sliced and diced like a piece of meat. The bed was so soaked with blood that it dripped clear through the mattress, onto the floor below. Her uterus was gone without a trace. There was also spray paint on the wall, just like the other recent murders. James hadn't told him anything new, but it was worth a shot. Sometimes witnesses remembered details after the fact.

Hank wanted to hear the account for himself, see the pain in James's eyes. In a situation like this, anyone associated with the victim was a potential suspect. It was a hard truth. Hank wasn't really on the investigation, just lending a helping hand, but this case piqued his interest. He thought some fresh eyes might help; sometimes that was the trick.

He finished his discussion with Mr. Reed, then went back to the crime scene where the forensic team was still collecting evidence. Detective Stall, the lead on the case, was present. Hank reported his conversation. "Thanks, Hank, I appreciate the fresh eyes," Stall said.

"Pleasure to help. I don't think the husband is our perp, if that helps at all. I'm sure you already knew that, though."

Stall smiled. "I didn't think it was him, but you can never be too careful. I don't think any of the husbands are our perp, actually." He scratched his head, debating whether or not he should say more to Hank. Hank waited, wanting to hear more, but knowing if he pushed it would turn Stall off.

Finally Stall said, "I think we might be looking at a cult."

Hank was silent for a moment, unsure of what to say. *A cult.* "What makes you say that? I thought we were looking at a serial killer?"

"At first glance, it would seem that way," Stall nodded. "But it's in the details. The taking of the uterus for one."

"Plenty of serial killers take trophies."

"True. It could go both ways. Be either or, at this point, I'm just letting you know what's on the table here. There's more information, but I'm not at liberty to say. We haven't ruled out any possibilities, but I want you to keep an eye out for any reports of cult activity in your area, if you would."

"Of course," Hank said. A cold sweat was breaking out on his forehead. Hank waited until Stall was gone before he wiped the droplets away. *This wasn't good.*

CHAPTER

THIRTY

It's been weeks since I last saw Hank. I'm not keeping track of the days or anything. I just haven't had the guts to go talk to Gladice alone. After the tremendous windstorm, we've been cleaning up the yard and I can just imagine how busy Hank's been.

I won't go anywhere without Bear, but I'm afraid to take him with me back over to Gladice's after the way I found him over there. I'm also afraid I'll see how she's keeping her dog. Hank knows about the abuse I suspect, but I'm not sure if he's done anything about it or if there's anything he can do. I figure I'll just wait until Hank checks on me again, then remind him to take me back over there.

I've heard the drums at night again, but it's not every night. I haven't texted him about them again, though. I don't want to bug him. I feel so unwelcome. I wish I could figure this out on my own. I wish I could keep them off our land, but I've already made myself clear and they keep coming back. That's the worst part of it all. They won't stay away.

I feel bad about Charlie's behavior towards Hank and how we left things. I keep replaying it over and over in my mind. Thinking about it makes me feel weird; I don't like it but can't seem to help myself. For whatever reason, Charlie doesn't like Hank. He doesn't even know the man, though. It seems unfair and childish to me to judge a person so harshly so quickly. He's never really been jealous before.

There's an attraction between Hank and me. I'm fighting it with every fiber of my being, trying to maintain control. Maybe it's one sided. *Maybe it's not.* My loneliness is feeding it against my will. I don't want to feel this way; I'm not this type of person.

I wonder if Charlie saw it on my face. If he did, that would explain his instant dislike of Hank. I think some distance from Hank will be a good thing. I appreciate his help more than anything and even if there *is* an attraction, he's my friend.

It's my fault for allowing it to simmer. If I'm lonely, it's my own fault, not Charlie's, and I shouldn't let it affect our marriage. I can do something else with my life, I just have to set my mind to it.

"I THINK I'M READY TO GET A JOB AGAIN," I SAY TO CHARLIE at night, before he leaves for work. I think I've really shocked him because he stands frozen for a moment, mouth agape.

"Are you sure you're ready?" he asks once he's found his voice.

"I think so. At least part time, anyway."

"You remember what happened last time?"

"Of course," I snap. He always has to bring that up. The last time I tried to go back to work, I had a minor breakdown. There was a pregnant woman complaining about being pregnant. I grit my teeth at the memory. She kept going on and on about how she couldn't stand being pregnant, how *uncomfortable* it was, all the while rubbing her growing belly. She had no idea what it was like for me.

"I think I'm better now," I say, blushing.

"Have you been keeping your appointments with Dr. Reymore?"

"Yes." I'm not sure if he can tell I'm lying.

"Why don't we wait until the house is done? You've been under a lot of stress lately, especially with Tom and Bear and all that." He's getting on my nerves, worrying like a mother hen. Charlie thinks I'm going to break down again. He doesn't trust me. It's true; I might, but I have to do something with myself. I'm slowly losing my mind staying home with Ellie. I love it, don't get me wrong. But the loneliness is unbearable. I throw myself into our home building project and it provides comfort, but what am I going to do when it's all over?

"Charlie," I say. "I don't need your permission to get a job."

He looks wounded. "I know that. I just thought we were still making life decisions together."

"Of course we are. But this is something I need. I've been lonely lately. I haven't felt safe here, either, and maybe just getting away, getting a job for the day will help me. It will be good for me."

I thought confessing my feelings would make him understand, but it seems to have the opposite effect. Charlie goes from carefully tiptoeing around me to full-blown anger. His cheeks turn red, not with embarrassment but with rage. There's something in his eyes that I haven't seen before, and it scares me.

He yells at me. "You're blaming me? Everything I do-every. Single. Thing. Is for you!"

"I know-"

"You don't know, Paisley! You have no fucking clue!"

"Charlie, I didn't mean to upset you. This isn't about you."

"Isn't about me?!" He throws his arms in the air, exasperated.

"No. I'm trying to tell you how *I* feel. This is something *I* need for *me*. Don't you understand that?"

"Everything is for *you*, Paisley," he says.

Charlie isn't making any sense. I don't understand why telling him my feelings has him so upset. That he's angry makes *me* angry. This always happens to us when we try to talk about things. One of us gets mad at the other for being mad.

Part of the reason I want to go back to work is for social interaction, yes, but also because I feel like a burden. Before we moved, money was an issue, and not much has changed.

We have bills to pay, groceries to buy, and reports to pay for. Not to mention a house to build. Charlie just cemented in the fact that he works so hard to support me, so why isn't he happy that I'm ready to help out a bit. It's not like we don't need it. We *do* need it.

THIRTY-ONE

Four Months Ago

Charlie and I have scoured the internet for months looking for a travel trailer. I can't believe how hard it's been to find one. It seems with housing so hard to find, everyone is resorting to campers to live in (like us). Everyone has the same thing on their minds, apparently, so like housing and apartments, the prices of RVs are through the roof.

Our options are limited to what Charlie's truck can tow. It's a Ram, which is great, but it's over twenty years old, which means it can tow less than a newer one could. We already have the truck, thankfully, but we don't have a budget to get a newer, bigger one. There's no way we could afford the payment on top of all the other things we're going to need to buy.

The weight of the trailer isn't that big of a deal, mostly. The worst thing about it is that we don't want a tiny one, and we prefer to get a slide out because it will make our living area a little roomier. After doing research on how long this home building process is really going to take, we're probably going to be living in this RV for at least a year, and probably longer. I'd like to be as comfortable as possible. The apartment was small, but not *that* small.

With our list of requirements, we've had a hard time finding anything that fits the bill, but finally we got lucky. Now, we're standing outside of a twenty-eight-footer, about to do a walkthrough. We're dealing with a private owner, and he's got this thing listed for a steal.

Charlie makes the man an offer, not even trying to haggle. "We'll take it," he says.

"Great!" the owner replies.

"Will you take a five-hundred-dollar deposit? The banks are closed today, but on Monday I can have the rest for you."

The man thinks about it, hemming and hawing. He's not sure about a deposit; it seems to make things complicated for him. Charlie and I understand, but we're hoping he's reasonable about it. We didn't have that kind of cash on hand to pay the full amount, and it was such a short notice that there's no way we could get it in time to meet this guy.

"Yeah," he finally agrees. "That's okay with me. I'll take a deposit."

We shake hands and Charlie draws up a bill of sale. Charlie and I are ecstatic.

When we get home, Ellie is excited too, and even Bear joins in the festivity, although I'm sure he doesn't understand why we're all so happy. This trailer has everything we wanted, and it's the right weight and the right *price*.

We go out to dinner to celebrate, then we notify our landlord that we're not going to renew our lease. It's not up for another three months, but we're too excited to wait to tell her. It makes things feel so official and for the first time in a long time, I'm looking forward to a new future.

The next morning, all hell breaks loose. I have a text from the owner of our future travel trailer. He's changed his mind about accepting a deposit and is taking it to trade in at a dealer. "What!" Charlie explodes when I tell him over the phone. I feel the same, but I'm more silent about my anger. We can't believe this guy thinks he's going to flake. We have a bill of sale in hand, and he's already got our money.

I text the seller back. "Sorry. The deal is done. We have a bill of sale."

His reply is instant, like he's been waiting for me to say those exact words. "I'm taking it to the dealership this afternoon. I have my attorney on standby if needed." Is this really a can of worms I want to open? I put a hand against my aching head. My world is spinning. We already told our landlord we weren't renewing. Maybe this was fine. Maybe this was just a sign that Charlie and I were being stupid.

I try to call Charlie again to discuss things more, but he's not picking up. Then I decide to go down and see Larissa. We *just* told her about not renewing the lease last night. Maybe everything will be fine. Maybe she'll let us do a month-to-month thing until we can get our RV situation handled.

Downstairs, it's not good. "Sorry," Larissa says. "I just accepted a deposit this morning."

"What? Already?"

"It's the market." She shrugs, not really caring that we'll be homeless.

"Please, Larissa, isn't there anything I can do? This guy had a deposit from us, too."

"I'm sorry. I have a business to run and I can't afford to get sued. This guy is probably calling your bluff."

It's something I've thought about, but I don't think Charlie and I have the time to spend trying to take him to court. We don't have the money for an attorney, and we just don't have the drive. I walk away from Larissa, trying to hold back tears, but failing miserably.

Charlie and I are frantic to find something, *anything* that will work for our family. At this point, we face that we probably won't get all our criteria met and will be happy to have something that isn't falling apart. It seems like everything is either brand new and enormously overpriced, or ancient and still marginally overpriced.

A month before our move-out deadline we have still found nothing. Literally nothing that would work for us. I'm in tears every night, terrified we'll be on the streets with no place to sleep. I can see the stress in Charlie's eyes; he's afraid too. We finally break down. We have no choice.

We swore up and down that we didn't want the payment, we *couldn't* if we wanted to qualify for a house. In the end, the payment is what we got. Charlie and I sign papers at our local RV dealership. We're the proud owners of a shiny, brand spanking new travel trailer.

THIRTY-TWO

Ellie, Bear, and I are out on our hiking trail again, past the large hill where I first heard the drums, when Ellie asks, "Who lives there, Mommy?" She points into the forest. My heart beats faster at the question. *This again?* I squint, trying to focus my eyes so I can see what she sees.

The vegetation is too thick for me to make anything out. "I don't see anything, cupcake."

"The little house," she says, still pointing and now wiggling her hand around in a circle.

I stare a few minutes longer, still not seeing anything. "Where is it?"

"Mommy!" she yells in frustration. "It's there!"

"Okay, okay. Don't yell at me. I don't see it, love, I'm sorry." I'm trying not to panic. There must be something really there for her to ask me this question *again*, but why can't I see it? And why would there be a house in the back of our property? The place she's pointing isn't on our trail, it's perpendicular to it. I could just make a new branch off our existing path, so we can get closer to the area she's talking about. Maybe I'll finally see what she sees. "How far away is the house, Ellie?"

She thinks for a minute. "It's far."

My turn to think. Ellie thinks it's far, but it could be twenty feet away. We're really not aiming for anything with our path, not really going anywhere in particular, just exploring our property. It wouldn't hurt to create a branch off it. "Let's make a new path," I say. "We'll head towards the little house, okay?"

"Yay!"

I smile. "Okay, but I need you to lead the way, since I can't see it."

"Okay!" she says with pride. She's more than happy to be in charge.

We branch off, starting in the new direction. There's no animal path for us to work from like our main trail, so it's much slower going. I've only cleared for a few minutes when my phone rings. It's Hank. Ellie and Bear are ahead in the forest investigating, so I answer.

"Paisley, are you home? I really need to speak with you in person." He sounds almost panicked.

I hesitate, reminding myself of my earlier thought about putting a little distance between Hank and me. This sounds important though, not like a casual coffee date. "Paisley?" he asks when I take too long to answer.

"I'm here, sorry. I'm out on our trail."

"Do you mind if I come over?"

"Sure. I'll head back."

Ellie isn't happy about the interruption to our day, but I bribe her with the promise of some ice cream for dessert tonight. By the time we've wound our way back down the trail to our clearing, it doesn't take long for Hank to arrive. "Ellie, play under the awning for me, please, while I talk to Officer Adrian." She grabs a few of her favorites and listens to me well enough, while I walk down the driveway to greet Hank.

Something looks off with him. I'm not sure if it's the way we left things last time, or if something else is going on. "Hank, what is it?" There's concern in my voice, and he must hear it because his features smooth out a little.

"I haven't heard from you. I've been worried," he says.

Oh. "I'm okay," I say, blushing.

"It's been weeks. I was hoping you would check in by now. There's been some murders in the area. I've been worried about you." His smoldering gaze runs over me. "Have you heard the drums again at night?"

"Yeah."

"Why didn't you tell me?"

"I-" *What to say, what to say?* "I didn't want to keep bugging you."

"You what? Paisley, you're not bugging me. It's my job," he says, tapping a finger on his badge to remind me he's a cop. Like I need a reminder. I look at my feet, not knowing what else to say. "Have you gone to see Gladice?" Hank asks.

I shake my head. "No. I was too afraid to go without you."

"What about your husband?"

It takes me a moment to figure out what he means. My cheeks are scarlet when I say, "He won't go with me. He thinks I'm overreacting."

I can hear his teeth grinding. He's standing there looking at me without speaking. It's hard to judge his mood. Moments pass. I'm about to say something else, but Hank takes a step closer and suddenly my tongue is in knots. My breath catches as I look up to meet his gaze. When his eyes bore into mine, the entire world seems to melt away.

Then Hank wraps an arm around my waist before kissing me. It's not slow and gentle like I'm used to. It's urgent, passionate. He kisses me like I'm his breath and he can't get enough in. I meet his passion with my own, unable to stop myself. My body is swimming with pleasure and want. I push myself closer to him, needing to feel him against me. At the same time, Hank puts his hands beneath my shirt to feel my breasts.

A moan escapes. *Was that from me or him?* It doesn't matter. Nothing matters right now, except *this*. My mind is fogged over. The only thing I can think is, *more.* I reach for Hank's belt. I just have it unfastened when I hear, "Mommy?" *Shit!*

I take a step back from Hank so fast I almost fall. He reaches an arm out to brace me. We're both panting and smiling like the cat that got the cream. "Are you okay?" he asks. I'm about to answer, but something behind Hank catches my eye. I turn to look.

Charlie. He's standing there with wide eyes, watching us. How long has he been there? *Oh, God.* I don't want to know. Hank turns around to see what I'm looking at. I'm not ready for this. *This is not happening, this is not happening!* Why couldn't I just control myself?

We're in a three-way standoff, no one saying a word. It's not Hank's fault and not Charlie's either. I'm the one who did this. I could have set Hank down instead of returning his kiss. I don't know what to say to Charlie. He looks like he's been stabbed in the heart. How can he still be standing here? He has to be in shock.

"Charlie," I say. "I'm sorry" comes to my lips, but I don't say it. I can't. It's not true. I wanted to kiss Hank and still do. I'm not going to lie. Charlie meets my gaze, still saying nothing. "I didn't mean to hurt you," I say. It's the best I can do.

Charlie nods slowly, then walks back to his truck before driving away.

THIRTY-THREE

Charlie hasn't been back home. It's been days. I haven't tried to call him, and he hasn't tried to call me; I'm not sure where that leaves us. If he's expecting me to reach out first, he would be in the right, but it's not going to happen. I can't apologize for something I don't regret. Like I told him before, the only thing I'm sorry for is hurting him. Maybe I should reach out to tell him that again, but I can't bring myself to. Not yet.

I don't know where Charlie is staying. We don't exactly have a ton of money for him to get a nice hotel room long term. We don't have the money for him to get another place to live permanently either, not on his income, no matter how many hours he's working.

I've planned on getting a job; this is a perfect reason to go through with it. There's no way I expect him to support me forever, especially not now. I wish he would talk to me. Are we splitting up? Or is this something we're just going through? I wish I knew what I wanted.

Just thinking about Hank has butterflies in my stomach. I try to fight back the grin that won't go away. It feels so good to be wanted by someone who I want just as much. Is it just lust, though? Just loneliness? I don't think it is. Not on my part, anyway. I really like Hank; he's a good man. Is this worth throwing my marriage away for, though?

And then I think about Ellie. What about Ellie? What about the house and the land? What about, what about, what about everything? My mind is spinning. I don't want to think anymore. There's so much to think about, but all I want to do is feel. *Feel Hank.*

The day Charlie saw us kissing, Hank apologized, but I told him he had nothing to be sorry for. It's the truth. I don't blame him. If anything, he's set me free. He's been keeping a polite distance to give me space. I wish he wouldn't.

Space is the last thing I need. All I've been doing is thinking and thinking and listening to those fucking drums all night. The truth is, I miss him. More than I miss Charlie. It could be because I'm used to not having Charlie around; I'm not sure.

Tonight, I can't take it anymore. I put Ellie to bed, then text Hank. "Come over." It's not a question. If my marriage is over, it's not going to be for nothing. I'm going to get my fill of him. The need he woke in me still hasn't gone away.

"Be there in ten." Hank texts back almost immediately.

Yes. I spend the next ten minutes getting myself ready and tidying up. When I hear his car coming up the driveway, the nerves kick in. *What am I doing?* Do I go out to meet him? Do I let him come to the door? I have no idea what the right answer is; I've never done this before. I opt to meet him. I wait a minute, giving him time, too. Then I swing open the door.

He's already at the steps. I almost laugh as I think, *I guess he didn't need any time.*

"Hi," Hank says.

"Hi," I smile. "Come in."

IT TURNS OUT I WAS NERVOUS FOR NOTHING. ONCE HE'S inside, I feel like I'm home. It's the strangest feeling. Things happen fast. I don't need to think. I don't need to worry.

Hank takes control, and I'm happy to let him. We don't talk; there's nothing to say. We act. Hank takes me in his arms, kissing me, touching me. I pull his shirt off and he does the same to me. Our bare skin rubs against each other, taking in every inch of contact.

All my worries are gone. Every problem I've ever had melts into oblivion as we make love. It's been too long since I've felt this way. Too long since I've been without worry, without anger and hurt and loss. I want to cry from the peace that falls over me, but I don't. *I'm not going to get emotional on him and freak him out.* That thought makes me want to laugh. The emotions he brings out in me!

We lie together panting, smiling, still holding each other. I wonder if he's as amazed as I am. I don't want to ruin the moment by talking, so I say nothing, just enjoy the feel of his arms. We fall asleep that way.

The sound of drums wakes Hank. I'm so used to them, they don't wake me, but Hank isn't used to them. He shakes my arm. "Paisley, the drums."

"Yeah," I mumble.

"They come back like this, every night?"

"Mostly. Sometimes I sleep through them." I nuzzle into him, and he wraps his arm around me. It's so weird to not care about them. I've been so afraid, so annoyed, so angry about the situation. Right now, I couldn't care less. All I want is to stay in his arms.

"Let's go outside and say something to them. This is ridiculous. You don't have to live like this."

I look up at him and smile. It's so nice to have someone standing up for me like this. It's so nice to feel safe and protected. To be believed. *Am I falling in love with this man?*

I should take him up on his offer. What better chance to confront the neighbors than right now? Hank is here with me. He can put them in their place. Instead, I say, "Later," and reach under the covers.

When I have him in my hand, Hank takes a sharp breath. My smile widens; I surprised him. We make love again, ignoring the drums outside. I'll worry about the goddamn drums another day. I'm not letting this moment get away from me. Not right now.

Before I fall asleep in his arms for the second time, I hear him say my name again. "Paisley?" His voice sounds odd. I'm too relaxed, too sleepy, too happy to pay much attention.

"Hmm?" I ask. I don't know what he says though, because I fade into the black.

THIRTY-FOUR

Charlie felt like he'd been stabbed in the back. Not only that, but he also felt like someone had ripped out his still beating heart and tried to feed it to him. He wanted blood.

His hands were tied. There was nothing he could do, but it didn't make it hurt any less. *His wife.* This wasn't her fault. This *society* was supposed to be helping her, not tearing apart their marriage. There was more at play here than she was aware of. She was innocent in this.

"I need to speak with Charity." Charlie fumed to the guard outside the cabin. The society protected leadership with their lives, and Charity was one of their two primary leaders. She always had a guard stationed in whichever building she was in. Charlie knew where she was because she always had the same guard posted.

"She's busy."

"Tell her." Charlie wasn't in the mood to play games. Charity would know why he was there.

A few minutes later, he was allowed to enter. Charity was behind a desk, reviewing some papers. "Charity," Charlie said. "If this is the way things are run, it's bullshit."

She looked up. "Charlie." Her voice was glacial. She had

no sympathy for him whatsoever. Charlie wasn't the only one going through a hard time. She was starting to think he didn't really have a clue about what it meant to be a member of their community.

They were about helping others, not themselves. She stared at him, thinking about the best way to respond. Silence engulfed them until Charlie squirmed. He wondered if he'd been too rash. Yes, he was angry, but what would he do if these people decided he and his wife weren't worth the effort? What would he say to Paisley?

"Please don't assume that I know what you're talking about," Charity finally spoke.

"I'm talking about my wife."

"What about her?"

Charlie couldn't believe it. Was she really going to play dumb with him, like she didn't know what was happening? "My wife is fucking someone else. Hank Adrian."

Charity didn't flinch. *She knows,* Charlie thought. "I can assure you, that's false," she said.

"I can assure you, it's not." He fought to keep his anger under control. If he started yelling at her, the guard would come in and this conversation would be over.

Charity let out a deep breath, trying to keep her patience. "Charlie," she said. "Who is the one with all the information?"

He looked away. "You are."

"That's right. Me." It was true, and they both knew it, or at least thought they did. It was Charity's role in the society; it was her job to know everything. She had spies everywhere. "He's not fucking her," she said with conviction.

Charlie wasn't sure he believed it, but he felt slightly better. If Charity was this sure, maybe there was a chance he was wrong. *Unless she just wants me to chill,* he thought. "He spent the night with her," Charlie said, clenching his fists at the thought. "I saw them kissing. Touching."

"You knew ahead of time what would be involved."

"I didn't know *this*!" Charlie popped his knuckles. He tried to remember what this was all about, but was having a hard time reasoning it all out. Nothing was simple anymore. His marriage was about to be over, and it will all have been for nothing. "Look," Charlie said. "I want out."

That seemed to get Charity's attention. She wasn't expecting it. "This is part of the process, Charlie. We need to let things run their course."

"I can't." He wanted to cry, but he wasn't about to give Charity that satisfaction. "I wanted to help her. I didn't think I would lose her in the process."

"The fact is, you owe the society money. A lot of money."

Charlie looked back into Charity's cold eyes. *Bitch,* he thought, *you fucking bitch.* "Haven't I paid you back enough already?"

"Not by half," she said. Charity smiled. "Who do you think is paying your bills? Would you like to see the receipts?"

He imagined what it would feel like to have his hands wrapped around her throat, the pleasure it would bring to push his thumbs into her trachea. "No," he said.

"Perhaps we can bring this up with Paisley and get her input on the situation?"

She was pushing his buttons now. Charlie knew what she was doing and almost didn't care anymore. He wanted out. He was tired of the stupid games they played with people's lives.

Charity and the rest called it *helping,* but what it really was, was fucking everything up. He could laugh at how easy it had been for them to draw him in with the promises and how stupid he'd been to believe them.

Yes, there was a debt to pay. The society had been paying his bills; they owned his land and his RV. They owned everything. He couldn't let Paisley find out. She couldn't know what he'd done. Despite how much he wanted to be free of these people, he would do what needed to be done. They owned him as long as they could hold Paisley over his head.

"Maybe I can just take a short break," Charlie said.

Charity laughed. "A break? No. Sorry Charlie, there are no breaks."

"I can't stand to see her with him," Charlie ground out. "How can you expect it from me?"

Charity understood. She didn't show it; she couldn't show it, but she did understand how Charlie felt. It was hard work, there was no doubt about it. But it was too late for Charlie to go back now.

"She needs our help now, more than ever," Charity said.

There was no arguing with that. Charlie knew it all too well. Paisley was worse now than ever. His jaw clenched. "I don't like Hank. I want that on the record."

"Noted," she said. "He's not sleeping with her, Charlie."

"I wonder what they're doing all night. Braiding each other's hair, maybe?" There was nothing else to say. He got his point across; it was why he came to see Charity in the first place. Charlie thought there might be a chance for him to back out, but now he could see there wasn't. Even if he won the lottery, they would still own him.

Maybe it was for the best that their marriage was over. He'd never be able to face Paisley again if she knew the things he was keeping from her. His secrets were his downfall.

Before Charity could say anything else, Charlie turned around and walked out. He still belonged to the society; they both knew it.

THIRTY-FIVE

This morning, I realize I haven't had a nightmare in some time. They used to plague me almost nightly, but now I can't remember the last time I've had one. Maybe I really am getting better. Or maybe I've found a new way to release my pent-up rage.

I feel the heat rise to my cheeks as I think about Hank and what we did the night before. I feel like a teenager again. There's something irresistible about him; I can't seem to get enough. I shouldn't feel this way. I'm ashamed that I do. But it's the truth.

I don't know where these feelings came from, or how long I've been growing away from Charlie. It could be since we lost- since our loss. Or maybe it didn't start that far back. Maybe we've just been growing distant since he's never around anymore. Maybe it was the move that did it. We were supposed to start over, a new life, and maybe we really have in more ways than we planned.

I reach across the bed, expecting to feel Hank's body lying next to me, but I feel nothing but empty sheets. It's probably a good thing because I'm not sure how I would explain Hank's presence to Ellie. It still stings that he didn't say goodbye. I think he was trying to tell me something last night, and I was too tired to listen. Maybe he'll bring it up again today.

Rolling out of bed, I let Bear out to go potty, then get ready for the day. It's not until Ellie asks, "Mommy, what's this?" that I realize Hank left me a note. I didn't even think to look for one. I can't hide the smile that emerges as I realize he didn't leave without saying goodbye.

"That's for me, cupcake. Thank you." I kiss her on the forehead as I take the note from her.

My eyes scan his note faster than I can process the words. I'm so eager to know what he said I have to go back and reread a second time to take it all in.

The note reads:

Paisley, I'm sorry I had to go. Work. Call me later.

That's it? It's so short. I can't really read his emotions about this, which makes me want to pull my hair out. Does he regret last night? He's sorry he had to go. Does that mean he wishes he could've stayed for round three? I wish I knew what was going through his brain. I can't really be that upset with him, though. Not after last night. And he left a note.

"What should we do today, cupcake? We can work on our trail some more or go into town, see if there's something fun to do."

Ellie makes a big show of thinking it over. She's an introvert like me. We both prefer staying at home most of the time, although we love to get out and have fun at least a few times a week. I think she's going to opt for the trail, but she surprises me by saying, "Town." The surprise on my face makes her grin. She's starting to understand some of the things I expect, and what that means, and she loves being unexpected.

"Okay," I say, smiling back at her. "Town it is."

Our new town is sleepy; there's not much to do other than walk past the small shops and grab some lunch at the diner. The local women will spend the day gossiping, pretending not to be talking about you as you walk past. We've done that already and I know it's going to bore Ellie to tears within fifteen minutes. I'm not about to take her grocery shopping, so today I take her and Bear to Seattle.

We've spent no time in Seattle yet, despite our relatively close proximity to the city. Part of me was waiting for Charlie to take us out to have a fun day there, so we could do something fun as a family. But why wait, now? There's no reason I can't take Ellie and have a fun day with just the two of us.

The day is filled with all kinds of exciting new adventures for the both of us. We spend most of the day at the waterfront, exploring some piers, visiting the Seattle aquarium and Pike Place Market, doing everything we can that is Bear-friendly.

We ride a ferry to Bainbridge Island and back, which blows Ellie's mind. She sees a huge boat driving down the road and points to it, saying, "Mommy, what's that? What's that?" The side of the boat reads, "Ride the Ducks."

"That's a tour, cupcake."

"What tour?"

"They show people around the city."

"I go!" she yells, and I cringe. We're on our way back to the car. It's been a long day and I'm wiped. Bear is wiped too and so is Ellie, even if she won't admit it. She's a toddler; she'll never admit when she's tired.

"Let's drive past Daddy's work," I say. He won't be at the

hub, but it might be fun for Ellie to see where her Daddy clocks in every day.

"Yay!" she cries.

"We won't be able to see him, cupcake. Just the building."

"Okay," she says, still excited. Thankfully, she's forgotten all about the tour she wanted to go on a minute ago. There's always time for that another day.

I pull out my phone to bring up my maps app and I see two missed calls from Hank. *Shit.* I've been so busy with Ellie, I haven't been paying attention to my phone and I completely forgot he wanted me to call him. I hope he doesn't think I'm upset with him. I can't call him back right now. Not with Ellie in the car.

Bringing up my map app on my phone, I see how to get to Charlie's work. When I type in the name of his company, nothing comes up. I furrow my brow, confused that such a large company wouldn't be on the map. I open my notes to find the address he gave me. Once I have it entered into the GPS, we're on our way.

Following the directions, we make our way through traffic to Charlie's work. There's a problem when we get there. It isn't here. There's an enormous warehouse, *not* Charlie's company. I double check the address. I search online again. Nothing. I drive around the vicinity, thinking maybe he just got some numbers mixed up.

It's not long before I realize there's no mix up. The urge to scream is overwhelming. My husband has been lying to me for months. I don't know where he works. Does he even have a job? We're getting money somehow. What the hell is going on?

THIRTY-SIX

On our way home, I pull into the local gas station to fill up. Since I've needed to haul ass out of a few places lately, I'm hesitant to let the tank get too low. I'm tired, confused, angry, and all I want to do is go home so I can call Hank.

The card swiper isn't working. I weigh the options of leaving it and just going home, with walking into the building to pay. I want to go home, but if something happens and I don't have gas, I'm going to kick myself.

"Baby, I'm going inside to pay," I say to Ellie, talking to her through her backseat window. It's been rolled down part way and Bear is panting through the crack. "I'll be right back."

Inside the gas station, there's a blonde woman talking to the cashier. I wait behind her, trying to be patient. They're having what seems to be a deep conversation, both laughing at something funny the other has said. I pop my knuckles as I wait. It's not their fault I'm in such a pissy mood. The clock on the wall ticks. One minute passes, then two. *How patient am I supposed to be?*

I clear my throat, trying to get someone's attention.

Neither look my way nor stop talking. Finally I say, "Excuse me, the card reader outside isn't working."

They both stop talking and stare at me. An awkward silence descends. I give the cashier a moment to respond, but she seems baffled. How does she not understand that I need to buy some gas at a *gas station*? "Can I put twenty on pump three, please? I'm sorry if I interrupted your conversation." I'm trying not to be rude. I don't think I have an attitude; I just want to get gas and not stand here all day listening to them.

Both women blush. The blonde who was in front of me steps to the side, allowing me to pay for my gas. I hand my card over to the cashier, eager to get out of this awkward situation. Every day I ask myself where the hell I live. Charlie had to have found this town in a Stephen King novel. When I'm on my way out, the blonde says, "Pump three, that's the black Jeep?"

I turn back towards her. "Yes."

"I recognize it. I think we're neighbors."

Great. Another one! "Oh?"

"Yeah. You live off Sixty-Fourth, right?"

It's a little creepy that this lady knows that. I've never seen her before. I've never seen any of our neighbors out and about, but it's not like I go walking down our road. With the two crazies I've met so far, I don't expect this neighbor to be much better than the others.

Maybe I should deny living there and say she has me confused with someone else. There's probably a ton of black Jeep Wranglers in the area. I'm about to do exactly that, but it hits me that this town is too small. She's going to find out sooner or later I was lying, and what if she's not a psycho like the rest? I want to get on some good footing with *someone* in this damned area.

"That's right," I say. "I'm Paisley." I stick my hand out to shake.

She shakes with me, not too hard, but not like a limp noodle, either. "Charity," she says. "It's nice to meet you, Paisley." She smiles then, an open toothed smile that displays all her pearly whites. It sends chills down my spine.

SHORTLY AFTER PUTTING ELLIE TO BED, I CALL HANK. I'M filled with disappointment when he doesn't answer. Ellie and I had such an awesome day, but it ended on such a bad and then creepy note. All I want to do is tell Hank about everything. I decide to sit outside and get some fresh air while Bear plays for a while.

One of the nice things about living in the middle of nowhere is being able to go naked any time you want. You don't have to worry about anyone getting an eyeful. With all the people living around me who have screws loose, I'm not brave enough to go completely naked, but I'm enjoying the feel of my silk nightgown. It's cut low on top and high on the bottom, barely covering half of my breasts and ass. It's comfortable, which is all that matters right now.

I take a sip from my glass of wine, then a deep breath of fresh air, closing my eyes, trying to block out everything negative. It's not quite meditation, but the best relaxation technique I can manage. A soft breeze blows through the trees, and I feel the thin fabric of my nighty flutter.

I'm focused on my breathing, not thinking about anything else in the world. Just inhale, exhale. I feel a hand touch my bare knee, and I almost jump out of my skin. My arm jerks, spilling the wine, while my leg kicks out, coming into contact with someone and I scream. Bear's reaction is instant. He barks, running to me. "Paisley, it's me."

"Hank." I lay a hand against my beating heart. "You scared me to death."

"I'm sorry." He gives me a sheepish smile. "I thought you heard the car."

He's right. Normally I would've. "I'm glad you're here." I stand up.

I hear the hitch in his breath and suddenly I'm thrilled with my choice of clothing. I smile innocently up at him. "Is something the matter?" His gaze takes me in. All of me. Then there's no more talking, only kissing and touching.

There's so much I want to tell Hank but after his loving, my mind is like jelly. He takes the lead, saying, "I tried to call you today."

"I know, I'm sorry. I was in Seattle." That's when I remember to tell him about Charlie's work. "I drove past Charlie's work."

He seems to still at that. "He's been lying to me. His company isn't there. I'm not sure if they even exist."

"What?" He's as shocked as I am. "How can that be?"

"I don't know. I don't know how I'm just now finding out about it."

"I'm sorry," Hank says. He looks it too, so much so that I almost want to laugh. I don't know why he cares about my marriage. He should be glad my husband and I are about to split up. I guess we're split up currently, actually. Although if he was cockier about it, it would be a turnoff, so excellent play on his part, I guess.

"There's something else," I say. "I met another one of my neighbors today."

This *really* catches his interest. Hank's eyes widen and he sits up a little. "Another one?"

"It was at the gas station in town."

"Ah."

"Someone named Charity. Blonde. Didn't catch a last name. Do you know her?"

THIRTY-SEVEN

After leaving Paisley for the night, Hank debated about stopping at the bar in town for a quick drink. *Charity.* Paisley had met her. It wasn't part of the plan at all. Charity was known to surprise him, keep him on his toes, and normally he liked it, but this time was different. Paisley was different.

Hank decided against the bar. It wouldn't do to drive home drunk and if he went to the bar, that's what would happen. He drove straight home with the smell of Paisley still engulfing him. He pulled his squad car into the garage, mentally preparing himself for what was about to come.

Inside the house, Charity was on the couch, reading a book. She tried to appear casual, but it was obvious she was waiting for him. "Hank," she said. Charity stood, coming over to him. Hank hated the way she said his name. It was like nails on a chalkboard. He was about to say something, but she didn't give him a chance. She pulled his mouth down to hers and kissed him. She slid her tongue in to meet his, moaning with pleasure.

Charity rubbed herself against Hank, grinding against him with her pelvis. Hank was disgusted, but he kissed her back. He wanted to step away, but he didn't. She was necessary for now.

Hank stood there, letting her hump his leg like a dog in heat. He didn't have a choice. *Should've gone to the bar*, he thought. Charity grabbed his hands and placed them on her breasts. He had to think quickly, or he would not get out of this. Hank pulled back. "Sorry, Cherry, gotta take a piss."

He didn't wait for her to respond, just headed to the bathroom. He splashed cold water on his face, thinking about the best way to deal with Charity. If he flat out denied her, she would know of his interest in Paisley.

So far, he'd been able to hide it well enough. If Charity found out the truth, though, it would be bad news for everyone. She already suspected; she had to. Why else would she go out of her way to meet Paisley? Hank had no choice. He had to nip this in the bud.

He went back to the living room. Charity was stark naked. Hank gulped. "Charity," he said.

"Yes?" she asked, walking towards him.

"How was your day?"

Charity laughed. "Interesting." She began kissing his neck.

"Oh? How so?"

"Charlie Lanson told me he wanted out."

Hank yanked back, holding Charity at arm's length. "He what?"

Charity's eyes were wide with fear. She knew she shouldn't have mentioned it, but it was her responsibility to report things to Hank. She didn't know how he would react, but hoped he would still be down to have a little fun tonight.

"What did you say to him?"

"Don't worry, it's taken care of." Charity tried to move closer, but Hank kept her back.

"What did you say?" he asked again. His voice was stern

now, brooking no argument. His fingers gripped her shoulder harder.

Charity gulped. "I told him he owed too much money. I also threatened to tell his wife everything." She smiled at the memory of the fear in Charlie's eyes. "I saw her today, you know. I didn't plan it, she just showed up at the gas station."

Hank thought for a moment, taking it all in. "Did you make yourself known to her?" he asked. He already knew the answer, of course, but wanted to know if Charity was going to be honest with him. Charity's cheeks turned red. She felt the burn and realized if she lied like she wanted to, Hank would instantly know. "Yes," she said. "I introduced myself as her neighbor."

Good girl, Hank thought. If she would've lied, it would've been unacceptable. "Do we need to reassess the schedule?" he asked.

Charity shook her head. "No. Everything is fine."

"Good."

"How is-" Charity started, but stopped. Her face was flushed. She wanted to ask about Charlie's accusation against Hank, the one of him sleeping with his wife.

Charity didn't believe Hank would go that far; he wouldn't do that to her. But the urge to ask was overwhelming. Hank wouldn't like to be asked about it. Who would like that kind of interrogation? Instead, Charity asked, "How's work?"

Hank thought he knew where she'd been going with her question and was thankful her love for him won out on logic. He reached for Charity's waist. "Fine," he said. He moved to lay her down on the couch when his phone rang. He checked the caller ID as Charity sighed her disappointment.

"Work calls. Sorry, Cherry." He kissed her, then walked out the door, thankful his caller ID app had worked. Hank left but didn't go to work. He went to Charlie's.

Charlie answered the door, surprised and disappointed to see Hank. He wanted to shut the door on the bastard's face, but it wasn't an option. He waved him inside.

"Charity said you paid her a visit today."

"That's right."

"Getting cold feet?"

Charlie clenched his fists. "I saw the way you were kissing my *wife*." There was so much more he wanted to say. So much more he wanted to *do* to this asshole. His eyes showed his fury.

Hank saw it but didn't care. Of course the man would be angry. How could he not be? He didn't blame him at all. As long as he kept his mouth shut. That's what he was here to make sure of.

"Don't worry, Charlie. It's all according to the plan. Remember the plan you agreed to?"

Charlie's jaw clenched. "Yeah," he said. "I remember."

"Good." Hank looked around the bare room, then back at Charlie. There was no furniture other than a bed. No decorations or pictures of any kind. Nothing to suggest the room was being lived in at all, other than Charlie's bag of clothes in the corner and the sheets on the bed. "Is there anything you need in the meantime?"

"No." Charlie wanted to punch him in the throat. *That's* what he really needed.

Hank nodded. "I'm glad we're on the same page, Charlie." He placed a hand on Charlie's shoulder. "You are a valued part of this society. We're going to help your wife."

THIRTY-EIGHT

Hank says he doesn't know anyone named Charity, but I can't help questioning his reaction to the question. He looked like he wanted to throw up when I said her name. He was silent for a long time, seeming to zone out or be lost in thought, before I said his name again to pull him out of it. Why would he have that kind of reaction if he didn't know her?

Maybe he knew someone else from his past with her name. It could explain a reaction that strong, but then why wouldn't he just say that? So far, Hank hasn't lied to me, at least not that I've found out about. Either he's a master manipulator, or he's an honest and good man. I'm leaning towards the latter. I pray he's the latter.

He didn't fall asleep with me, like the other night. Instead, he made his excuses and left. I understand. It's not like he needs to spend the night with me every night. He doesn't need to coddle me.

I'm not even sure what we would call our relationship. Definitely more than friends with benefits, but I'm not sure if there's a name for us. I have this feeling he means more to me than I mean to him, but I felt that way with Charlie, too.

I'm trying not to think about it. I'm still married, and Charlie should be my main focus. What am I going to do about him?

I'm filled with guilt, but I keep thinking about his lying to me, which actually makes me feel better. I feel less in the wrong, which is wrong because I *am* wrong. I need to speak with Charlie about his job, but how do I have the right to question him after how I've behaved?

He caught me red-handed, kissing another man. Yes, his lie has been going on for longer, but is it as big? I want to say yes, but I'm not sure. Does it matter? Again, I'm not sure. I'm so confused. Charlie needs to explain where he's working and how the bills are getting paid. I suppose if there's no more *us* then maybe he really doesn't owe me an explanation, no matter how much I want one.

Charlie still hasn't tried to contact me. I'm getting a headache thinking about him. I want to think about Hank and his arms around me. I want to think about his lips on my neck and the feel of his chest beneath my fingertips. I feel like my thoughts are giving me whiplash.

Last night was another night with no nightmares. It was also a night with no drums. I didn't hear Hank say anything to the drummers, but he must've. Why else would they stop suddenly? *Why would they do it in the first place?* I'm thinking if it wasn't for Hank, I would move back to San Francisco right about now.

The sound of a car coming up the driveway pulls me away from my thoughts, bringing me back to the present. I'm filled with dread. I hate all these damn unexpected visitors. Having absolutely no idea who it could be, I wait on pins and needles to see the car come around the bend.

Trying to act casual, I sit in a lawn-chair outside, under the awning. Ellie is at my feet, playing. Bear is at my feet too, sitting alert, looking towards the driveway. Whoever it is, is taking their sweet time. Our driveway is long, but it feels like it's taking this person forever to reach us. Finally, I'm able to see who it is.

An old rusty pickup comes around the bend and parks. *Tom.* My mind races. *What do I do? What do I do?* I think about the gun that's sitting inside, waiting for me. Can I run inside to grab it? There's not enough time. If he's here to kill me, I'm done. Ellie and Bear come first. God, if he shoots at the trailer with that shotgun, we're all done, anyway.

The driver's side door opens. My heart pounds in my chest. So much blood is rushing to my head, making it hard to think rationally. With shaking hands, I send a text to Hank. "Help! Tom is here!" Even if Hank sees it right away, he won't be here for twenty minutes or more. That would be the fastest, most likely, so we're alone for now.

"Ellie," I say, "Get inside now."

"Why?" she asks.

I pick her up and rush for the door. She doesn't enjoy being hurried, but before she can throw a tantrum I say, "Cupcake, the bad neighbor is back. Go hide for me until I come and get you." It's enough to get the message across. I'm relieved when she doesn't argue, and I hear the patter of her feet as she runs into her bedroom.

Tom is walking towards me slowly. He hasn't said a word and isn't holding his shotgun. His hands are raised in the air, showing me he's unarmed. I'm not sure if he has a pistol hidden somewhere. I wouldn't put it past him. Bear is standing in front of me now, in his protective position. He barks a warning, but it doesn't deter Tom.

"That's far enough," I say, when Tom is within shouting distance. I'm too nervous to let him come any closer.

To my surprise, Tom stops walking, still holding both of his hands up. "I come in peace," he says.

"Like hell you do."

"I think there's been a misunderstanding."

"You think?"

"Listen lady, I need to talk with you." He takes a step forward. Bear growls. I let him, enjoying the look on Tom's face. He's trying to decide how well-trained Bear is. He's wondering how long he'll keep growling before he attacks. *Good.*

I'm not sure if I can trust this man, if I *should* trust him. Even though I hate him, and he's done nothing but be a pain in the ass from the first moment I saw him, he's been honest as far as I know.

He thought it was Bear who killed his chickens, but what if it was Gladice's dog? Maybe Tom has finally realized that and come to apologize. It might be worth hearing him out, at least for a minute. *Unless that's what he wants me to think.*

I place a hand on Bear to calm him. "You can take three steps," I say, letting him come a little closer so I don't have to yell across the driveway.

When he stops, Tom says, "You need to get the hell out of here."

What? "I thought you came in peace! Who the hell are you to tell me that?"

"I mean- it's-" The sound of sirens fills the air between us. I smile. Hank was damn fast. Tom has a surprised and hurt look on his face, but I don't care. Did he really think after our previous interactions I would be willing to sit here alone and chat it up? He came here uninvited, unannounced, after he attacked me. Tom's psychotic if he didn't think I'd be terrified. He's psychotic anyway.

"I think you're the one who better get the hell out of here," I say.

Tom looks like he's about to say more, but he doesn't. He runs for his truck, closing the driver's door just as Hank parks.

CHAPTER
THIRTY-NINE

Hank pulls behind Tom's truck so he can't back out. He gets out of the squad car, walking to Tom's driver window with one hand on his holster. Bear and I back up, while staring wide-eyed at the scene.

The men are having a heated discussion. Tom's arms are waving around in the cab of his truck, making me nervous. It looks like he could be reaching for something, but it doesn't seem to faze Hank.

I can't make out anything they're saying, despite straining to do so. They're too far away. Tom is inside his truck, which makes it even harder for me to hear. All I can make out is the tone of their voices. Tom is yelling something that almost sounds like, "Fucking liar," but it's hard to tell for sure.

After a few minutes, Hank moves his car to the side, allowing Tom to leave. Hank drives closer to me before getting out. He holds out his arms when I run to him with Bear right behind my heels. "Shh," he says, "I'm here now."

I nuzzle my face into his chest, taking the comfort he's offering. I look up at him. "You got here so fast. Thank you."

"My pleasure," he smiles. Then his face darkens. "That son of a bitch knows he's not supposed to come over here.

Come down to the station with me and we'll file a restraining order. Should've done that already."

I've never seen Hank look this angry. He's right, I should've already gotten a restraining order. I guess with Tom being arrested and facing court, and all the protection from Hank and the other deputies, I didn't think one would be necessary. "Does that mean you can arrest him next time?" I ask.

"You bet your ass," Hank says. "I'm sorry, Paisley."

"You have nothing to be sorry for."

"I wish I could've arrested him right here. I should've come up with something, anything. Hell, I bet his fucking tags are expired, and I didn't even check."

I laugh. "You can't arrest him for expired tags." I stand on tiptoes to kiss him. When we're both breathless, I say, "No more blaming yourself. You saved me, that's all that matters."

Hank kisses me again.

I go in the trailer to get Ellie out from hiding, then we follow Hank into town to file for a restraining order. It's just a piece of paper, but if it means Tom can get arrested next time, no questions asked, I'll spend the time trying to get it. I've been so concerned with my other neighbors and the drums that Tom slipped my mind. My mistake.

AFTER THE STATION, ELLIE, BEAR, AND I STAY IN TOWN FOR A while since I'm too flustered to go back home right away. I keep thinking about Tom's face when he saw Hank. I keep trying to figure out what was going through his mind, but I think it's pointless; I'll probably never figure it out.

We're walking to the ice cream shop when I look across

the street and see Charity. She hasn't seen us yet. I turn away fast, hoping she won't see us at all. I'm not in the mood to be friendly and if she waves me over, that's what I'm obligated to be. Although, if I'm honest with myself, I'm intrigued by her. It's only because of Hank's reaction to her name, but it's got me curious.

I think it's a little funny how we've lived here for months now and have never seen the woman until a few days ago. Now I'm seeing her again. I wonder if she's been hiding in a hole this whole time, or maybe I've seen her and not known it.

Inside the ice cream parlor, I order a scoop of strawberry for Ellie and a scoop of vanilla for myself. They have a peanut butter bone for Bear. I've just paid when I hear a voice say, "Paisley?"

Damn. I turn around, giving Charity a tight smile. "I thought that was you," she says. "How are you?"

"Fine, thank you. How are you?"

"Nonsense," she says, laughing. "None of that politeness. I mean it. How are you? I saw you and Hank enter the police station. Is everything alright?"

For a moment, I'm speechless. She knows Hank. Hank insisted he didn't know anyone named Charity. He was lying. What do I think about this? What *should* I be thinking? Maybe he doesn't really know her, and she just knows of him because he's a sheriff.

That would make a little sense. I have no clue who this woman is and even if she knows Hank, I don't really feel like telling her about my business. She can find out from someone else. "Just personal business," I say. "Everything is fine, really. It's nice to see you again."

I try to cut the conversation short by heading towards the door, but she follows us outside. "I'm glad to hear that. That ice cream looks delicious. I love trying two different flavors sometimes too." Her smile doesn't meet her eyes. She almost looks irritated, which is pissing me off. If she thinks I'm going to tell a stranger my life story, she's dead wrong. I suppose there's many people like that, but I'm not one of them.

I'm not sure what else there is to say or what else she wants me to say, so I just nod. Then she says, "I'd love to invite you over for dinner one night."

Shit. "That sounds nice. We have a lot going on with building the house and all..."

"Of course, of course."

Am I being unreasonable to this woman? "Do you mind if I ask?" I start.

"Yes?" she perks up.

"Do you know Tom Morgan?"

With a knowing look, she nods. "Yes, I know him, alright. I heard about what he did to you and your dog. I'm sorry about all that."

"Thanks. I guess I was just wondering what you know about him."

"Not much, to tell you the truth. He drinks a lot but otherwise keeps to himself as far as I know."

"I see."

"Sorry I'm not much help," she frowns.

"No, no, you are a help. Thank you, Charity." Our smiles feel more genuine this time.

FORTY

Tiffany was terrified. The toilets were backing up, and the yard was flooded. Their septic system was failing. It was going to cost a fortune to fix. She wanted to cry. There was no way their family could afford repairs this extensive. She had four kids to feed and they could barely manage that, let alone *this*. She and her husband both knew it.

Jake tried to comfort her by lying. "Maybe it's not that bad," he said. "Who knows, maybe it's just a wad of toilet paper clogging it up."

"Yeah, maybe," she said, lying right back.

The words were meant to soften the blow, but she knew. There was no way this was a clog. They'd had clogs before. Jake dug up the lids to the septic tanks, poked around with what he called his "shit stick," and bam, everything went back to normal. This was not one of those times. His shit stick wasn't working.

The problem was, they had to pay to get a septic guy out there to look at it in the first place. That alone was going to be an arm and a leg. The bill for the repairs would be all their arms and legs combined. There was no choice, though. What else could they do? They couldn't shit outside. They had to have working toilets.

"Do you know any good septic companies?" she asked Jake.

"No." He frowned. "Why don't you check your social media crap?"

"Good idea," Tiffany said. "But aren't you worried at all with those people on the news?"

"Which people?"

"You know... the murders."

Jake broke into a fit of hysterical laughter, acting like this was the funniest thing he'd heard in years. Tiffany glared at him, hating his sense of humor. When Jake's laughter abated, he wiped the tears from his eyes. "No. I'm not worried about that. And we don't exactly have a choice here, honey. We need to have a working septic tank."

Tiffany understood he was right. What were they supposed to do without a toilet? She searched online, not for the best company, but the cheapest. No one had prices for repairs like what they needed posted online. All they posted was their price to come out and look at the problem. She thought, who better to ask about pricing than people who have had this same problem?

Tiffany found a community page on social media and asked her question. "Any recommendations on the best priced septic company? And anyone willing to share what they paid? We're going to need a major repair here and hoping not to go bankrupt." She thought surely there would be someone out there willing to share; there always was.

At the end of the day, Tiffany checked the answers. There were a few different companies that came up, but only one person shared how much she paid. She had to get her leach lines completely replaced, and it was thousands of dollars. Tiffany choked back a cry as she read the information.

Most of the people who answered her question recommended a company called "Tim's." Instead of just going straight to Tim's, Tiffany called around to all the recommended septic companies. Their websites didn't have prices, but she was hoping to get better results over the phone. She spent hours calling but had few results to show for her efforts.

No one was willing to commit to a cost. No one would even give her a ballpark figure, even though she assured them she understood they would need to assess the damage in person before they committed to an official price.

Worse than not knowing the prices, everyone's schedule was a week out. They were all the same. Tiffany called Tim's, who also refused to give her an idea of pricing other than, "It could be a lot," but had availability five days out instead of seven.

"I'll take it!" Tiffany said. She didn't know how they were going to manage for that long, and that was just to get a price, not the actual repairs. She teared up as she thought about what she would tell the kids. "Guys, let's poop outside for a few days, okay?" she imagined saying.

And it wasn't just the toilets; that was just the worst of it. All the plumbing was connected, so if the toilets were backing up, so were the sinks and shower and bathtub. It meant no showers or baths, no dishes, and no washing hands. It was a nightmare.

Two days later, Tiffany felt like she was losing her mind. With the combination of the sludge in the yard and pooping in five-gallon buckets, everything smelled like shit to her. Inside the house and outside, she was constantly nauseous from the smell. When the kids came home from school was the worst. She tried to keep the family out doing stuff away from home, but it was impossible to be gone all day, every day, especially when they were about to spend their last pennies on repairs.

Tiffany was nursing the baby when her phone rang. It was a blocked number. She was about to ignore it, but then thought it could be the septic company. With shaking fingers, she answered the call. "Ms. Goode, I'm calling from Tim's Septic, about your appointment next week."

"Yes?" Tiffany said, terrified her appointment was about to be pushed back.

"We've had a cancellation in today's schedule, and it looks like we can actually come out sooner than planned, if you'll be available."

Tears sprang to Tiffany's eyes. This was unbelievable. She thought it was going to be another three days before anyone showed up. "Yes," she choked out. "That works for me. I'll be home."

"Great. Someone will be there within about twenty minutes."

Tiffany finished with the baby, then laid him down for a nap before tidying up the house. She wasn't sure if a septic person needed to come inside at all, or just look around outside, but she'd make damn sure he could access anything he needed.

Twenty minutes after hanging up, Tiffany saw an old white van caked in mud pulling up the driveway. She heard a tick coming from its engine and to Tiffany, it looked like it was barely running. Tiffany felt hope swell through her chest. She thought if the company van was this crappy, maybe it was because their prices were so cheap.

When the doorbell rang, she was surprised to see a woman at the door. She'd been expecting a man, but then felt ashamed for making assumptions. It didn't matter who was there, as long as it was a human being capable of doing what needed to be done. "Hello, are you with Tim's?" Tiffany asked.

"Yes, ma'am. I'm Taylor," the woman said.

"Hi Taylor, please come in."

AT FOUR O'CLOCK IN THE AFTERNOON, THE SCHOOL BUS stopped outside the Goode's home, dropping off Tiffany's three eldest children. Shane, ten years old and the eldest, made the phone call to 911 shortly after entering his home.

"Please," he cried. "It's my mommy!" The 911 operator could barely make out what he was saying through his crying and screaming.

"What's wrong with your mommy?" she asked. She could hear his siblings crying in the background, too. The operator tried in vain to comfort him and calm him down so she could get more information out of him, but Shane was too afraid and heartbroken.

The only thing she could make out was Shane saying, "She's hurt."

"Police officers and an ambulance are on the way," she told Shane, but didn't think he heard.

When the police arrived, they found Shane's hurt mommy. Her body had been chopped into pieces, scattered throughout the house. Her limbs were spread to the four corners, while her head was placed on the kitchen counter with an apple in her mouth. The baby was peacefully asleep in his crib; it seemed he slept through the whole thing.

FORTY-ONE

I finally bite the bullet and call Charlie. It's not something I want to do. I don't really want to speak with him at all, but for Ellie's sake, it's a necessity. After dialing his number, I walk back and forth in the driveway, waiting for him to answer.

The phone rings and rings and rings before sending me to voicemail. He doesn't pick up. I'm relieved because like I said, I really don't want to talk to him. But I'm annoyed too. He's up to something, and it's not the job he doesn't have.

"Charlie," I say on the voicemail. "We need to talk. I know you probably don't want to. I don't really either, but we need to. Please call me." Hanging up, I head back inside to get on the laptop. It's time I finally started applying for jobs.

Ellie and I are playing hide and seek in the yard when my phone rings. I rush to answer without looking at the caller ID first, thinking it's Charlie. So far, he hasn't answered any of the three calls I've made to him today.

On the third try, his phone was completely shut off. Texts haven't worked either, although I've only sent two. I'm not trying to blow him up. I've been spacing them out by a few hours, but it seems like it might be what I've been doing, anyway.

When I answer, it's not Charlie on the other end of the line; it's Charity. "Hi Paisley, I hope you don't mind me calling," she says.

"Not at all," I lie, unsure how she got my number. I don't remember giving it to her, and it's not something I would normally do.

"I just wanted to be neighborly and bring a plate of treats by if you're home. I hate showing up unannounced."

You're not the only one. "That's kind of you, Charity. Thank you for asking first. Yes, I'm home now."

"Excellent, I'll be over in a few."

I can't believe there's someone around here who doesn't just show up unannounced. I'm so surprised, I feel like I might be dreaming. Hope rushes through me as I think about the possibilities with this woman.

Maybe she's actually a normal human being and a *real* neighbor. There's so much I want to know about her still. Like, *does* she know Hank? And how did she get my phone number? I got a creepy vibe from her at first, but maybe that was just because I was in a bad mood. I'm thinking if she's normal, maybe I can even be friends with her one day. It would be great to have a friend close by.

When she shows up, there's a moment of awkwardness when she asks about my daughter. Ellie is standing right in front of Charity, but Charity looks right through her to talk to me. She looks around, like she's searching for where Ellie might be, instead of seeing her right in front of her face.

The air is full of tension, so I say, "Would you like to

share these with us?" I hold up the plate of brownies that she brought.

"Oh, no, thank you," she says. "I made a batch for us and just thought I'd be neighborly." Charity grins. "I haven't met your husband yet. Is he home today, too?"

What's with all the questions about my family? It's my turn to flush, now. I'm not really ready to tell this woman about my marriage problems. It's probably not a good idea to tell her he's moved out and we haven't spoken in days. "N-no. He's not home today."

"Ah, ok."

Is it me, or did her smile get bigger?

"Well, I better get going." Charity gives me a hug before leaving. I'm not sure what it is about the exchange, but suddenly I'm not interested in being Charity's friend anymore. There's nothing she said wrong, but the way she was smiling at me when she asked about Charlie made it seem like she knew more than she was letting on. I think my initial gut instincts were right about her. My hopes of her being normal have been thrown out the window.

What if she does know? What if *he's* the one who's been having an affair with *her* this whole time? No, no, no. That's insane. How would it have even happened? No, that can't be. *Can it?* No. I pull out my phone to call Charlie again. No answer. It's still turned off.

I sniff the plate of brownies, unsure if I can trust them. Why am I being like this? "Can I have one, Mommy?" Ellie asks. I eyeball the brownies again, then hand one to her. I take the rest of them and toss into the trash.

The next time my phone goes off, I rush to look at it again, again thinking it's Charlie. This time it's a text. Not Charlie. When I see it's Hank, my stomach does a somersault. He wants to come over again tonight. I don't want to seem too eager, so I wait a few minutes before responding. "Ok," is all I say.

"I'll bring dinner," he says, adding a kiss emoji.

Ellie and I continue playing in the yard for a while until my excitement gets the better of me. We go inside so I can make myself look presentable for Hank and pick up a little.

I'm reading too much into it. I'm sure it's not a big deal to him either way. He's not going to be offended if I'm still in a mom bun, but it makes me feel better to put in a little effort.

One thing is for sure, Ellie's going to bed right on time tonight. My stomach flutters again at the thought of what Hank and I are going to do to each other.

HE'S RIGHT ON TIME, AS USUAL. HANK COMES IN CARRYING bags of Chinese food that smell heavenly. My mouth is watering, but it's not for the food. We leave dinner sitting on the counter as we spend the next hour in the bedroom. Neither of us mind a cold dinner.

After Hank dishes out the food, he hovers over the garbage can for a minute. I don't like the look that comes over his face. "Something wrong?" I ask.

"What's with the plate in the garbage? And all the brownies?"

"Oh, that," I wave a hand around. "My neighbor dropped off some brownies."

He looks almost angry. "Didn't like them?"

"I hope you're not mad at me for throwing them away," I say. I'm not sure what else to say to lighten his mood. He seems dark suddenly.

"No. Of course not." He brings me my food, giving me a kiss.

"The truth is, I'm not sure if I like my neighbor. Again." I laugh at myself, but he doesn't laugh with me.

"Why not?" he asks, serious.

I look around, trying to think of the right words. I don't want to paint her in a negative light, but what's the truth here? "She seems… off somehow. She's been friendly enough and seems normal enough. Maybe she just asks too many questions or something? The way she asked about Charlie today was really weird. It was an innocent question, but just *off* somehow. I'm not sure what it is about her."

Hank finishes chewing a bite. "There are many people around here who are a little off. It's probably best to steer clear of them as much as possible."

"You're sure you don't know her? Charity?"

Hank is quiet for a long time, chewing another bite of food. "No," he says. "I don't know her."

FORTY-TWO

I sent my resume in for some more jobs today. The more I think about going back to work, the more excited I feel. It's been a long time since I've been healthy enough. I don't care that Charlie didn't think I was ready. Besides, I think our marriage is probably over, which means I need to be able to support myself and Ellie, anyway.

Charlie still isn't answering his phone. He hasn't texted me back, either. I'm not worried about him; I'm irritated. He's fine. I'm not worried about something happening to him. He's being a child, avoiding the situation instead of confronting it. We need to be adults right now, and it seems he's still unwilling to do that.

Maybe listing the property for sale will get Charlie's attention. The idea hit me when I was searching for jobs this morning. Most of the better jobs are closer to the city, which means a long commute. It would be fine if we were sticking with our original plan of being a family, but since we're not, it looks like I really don't have a reason to live in the middle of nowhere anymore.

I can still start a new life here; I can still start over. It just won't be in the middle of nowhere, on forty acres. I can't fight the smile that comes when I think about living in an apartment again. It won't be nearly as peaceful, true, but I won't be nearly as alone, either. I won't have psychotic neighbors pounding on drums all night long outside my door, or trying to steal my dog, or trying to shoot me. I won't have to lose an ounce of sleep wondering if there's a bear or cougar or fucking big foot outside.

When I think about moving, I look forward to the future. But then I think about Hank. I'm not sure what's going on with us, and if I move, how it'll play out. I really like Hank. I might even love him, but I can't stay here just for him. I have to do what's best for Ellie and me. I think Hank will understand that, too. I've resolved to talk to him about it soon, before I do anything like listing the property for sale.

Ellie and I are spending the day at home again, exploring per our usual. It's her favorite pastime and excellent exercise, so I can't complain. Bear leads the way down our path, all the way to where we started the new split, towards the cabin that Ellie sees but I don't. When we've gone as far as the existing path goes, I bring out my clippers and continue clearing.

After a few minutes, I hear a noise nearby. It sounds like a branch breaking- loud enough for me to hear over my clippers. I stop moving. Bear stands at attention. We wait for the noise to come again. There's nothing but silence. I realize there's *no* sound, not even birds chirping. I can feel my pulse starting to race. My palms grow sweaty as the feeling of being watched descends.

Peering into the foliage, I try to get a glimpse of what might've made the noise. There's got to be so many kinds of animals that live out here. I just hope it's a friendly one nearby, and not one that wants to eat us for lunch. Bear sniffs the air. He knows there's something here too, but he hasn't barked yet.

I see nothing. Right when I'm about to resume clearing, a pair of glowing yellow eyes appear. I jump back, terrified.

They look so malevolent I'm shocked to my core. Before I have a chance to cry out for Bear, a dark grey cat comes walking out, tail in the air, like it hasn't a care in the world. It saunters right to me and circles my legs, rubbing its face against me. My leg vibrates from the purring.

When I glance at Bear, his ears are tucked. "Bear?" He sits down. I bend over to pet the cat. His name tag reads, "Shadow." It's the perfect name for him because that's exactly what he looks like- a dark shadow. He allows me a minute to scratch his back, then he walks into the trees. "Bye!" I call after him, relieved it was him and not someone or something else. As soon as he's gone, Bear stands back up and comes to me, whimpering. It's the oddest behavior I've ever seen from him. Thinking he's jealous, I give him plenty of love before resuming my cutting.

"How much longer?" Ellie asks. She's impatient to keep moving forward, but the forest is thick here, since we're not on the game trail anymore. I clip as much as I can, but I should've brought a chainsaw too. Low-lying branches force me to duck down constantly and they're too thick to cut with the branch clippers.

"I'm going as fast as I can," I say. "Ellie, you wanted to find the little house, remember? We don't have to go this way if you don't want to."

"I want to."

I huff a breath, then continue, trying to clear the path. As I work, Ellie looks into the thick trees. She sees whatever little house this is clearly, but I still can't see it. "Who lives there?" she asks.

"I don't know, cupcake, I hope no one."

"Why?"

"Because it's on our land."

"Why?"

"Because it is." She doesn't understand how creepy it is

for this to exist at all. Not only creepy, but how wrong it would be for someone to be living on our property without our knowledge or consent. She's too young, of course, but her "whys" are grating.

TWO HOURS LATER, I'M FINALLY AT A POINT WHERE I SEE what Ellie has been seeing. She called it a little house because that's exactly what it looks like. Sitting between two large pines, is what looks like a tiny home, not much bigger than a garden shed. Now that I'm able to see it, it's as clear as day.

I'm not sure why I wasn't able to notice it before. It might be the color- it's a hunter green that blends in perfectly with the surrounding forest. Or it could be because it's so worn and broken in. Moss is on the roof, branches and leaves lay against the walls and front window. It completely blends in. How was Ellie able to see it so clearly, so far away? It's blended in so well; it almost seems like it's been camouflaged on purpose.

"There," Ellie says. She waves her arms and jumps up and down with excitement now that we're so close. Her antics set Bear on edge.

"Shh, now, cupcake. Don't scare Bear. Should we keep our path going?"

"Yeah!"

Although the little house is clearly visible now, it takes another twenty minutes, at least, for us to clear our way to it. The vegetation is thicker here than anything we've gone through so far, making me sweat with the effort it's taking to clear it. I've thought about not bothering with clearing and just making our way in there, but I wanted us to have trails, anyway.

If we're going to bother with fighting our way back here, we may as well have something of a path to be able to walk on for next time. It's worth the effort to me.

Finally, we're at the cabin. Up close, somehow it doesn't seem quite as worn and falling apart or as small as I originally thought. It's narrow but long and from my vantage point before, I couldn't see its rectangular shape. I peek through the little window to see it's bare, besides a rectangular table with eight chairs.

"Should we go inside to eat our snack?" I ask Ellie.

It's dark inside, since the only light is coming from the single window and the open door. I shine my phone's light, but it's not much help. I was expecting the cabin to be musky smelling and dusty, but it's not. It looks *fresh*. A feeling of dread grows at the pit of my stomach. *What the hell is going on here?*

I want to leave. I don't like this little house; I don't like how clean it is or how lived in it feels. My palms are growing sweaty again as my nerves take over. What if there's someone actually living here? What would they do if they came home to find me? I need to call Hank. I need to tell him about this. I need to tell Charlie, too.

That's when I have the thought. *Charlie!* What if it's Charlie living back here? How could that be, though? He doesn't have a driveway or electricity, and his truck is nowhere to be seen. Although he could have a way of getting here that I don't know about. Ellie interrupts my train of thought. "Mommy, I'm hungry."

"Sorry, cupcake, let's eat."

I'm a little less afraid now that I'm thinking it could be Charlie living here. It would make sense, since we don't have the money for him to be renting a place or even staying in a hotel for very long. I don't understand the table with eight chairs, though. There's no bed, no nothing but a place to eat. I'm so confused.

Ellie and I unpack our snacks and enjoy a few minutes of peace together. We even remembered to bring some treats for Bear to enjoy, too. He doesn't like the little house at all. His hair was raised as soon as he was within sniffing distance, and he's refused to go inside at all.

His reaction has me more worried than anything else. His instincts are never wrong. Bear sits outside munching his treats while I sit at the table, and Ellie dances around inside.

Then my phone rings. This time when I check the caller ID, it's Charlie.

CHAPTER
FORTY-THREE

I step outside by Bear to take the call.

"Paisley, where are you?"

"I've been trying to get ahold of you for days-"

"It doesn't matter. Where are you?" He's insistent, demanding. Him not seeming to give a damn about confronting me about kissing another man, grabs my attention more than his tone. Something is wrong.

"I'm out back on our trail. We found a small cabin-"

"We?"

"Who's we?"

I stay silent. I've said too much already.

"Fuck, Paisley!"

"What? What is it?" He's scaring me now. His tone has gone from urgent to shocked to pure rage.

"Is Ellie there with you?"

I'm silent again for a long time. Finally, I say, "Yes."

I can hear the gears in Charlie's head turning through the phone. I don't think he's going to answer me, so I say, "Charlie, she's missed you. She needs you to be a part of her life still."

"My God, I can't believe this!"

I ignore his outburst. "We drove by your work and low and behold it doesn't exist! Something is going on here, Charlie, and you need to tell me what the hell it is."

Charlie mutters to himself. He sounds so distraught I can barely make out anything he's saying. "Charlie?"

"I'm here," he says. "Head back to the trailer and I'll meet you in a few minutes."

"Okay."

"And Paisley, don't go back to that cabin. It's not safe."

When I go back inside to get Ellie, I can't find her. The cabin is bare besides the sparse furniture. It's too dark for me to see clearly, but it's also a small space. It's not like there are many places for her to hide. "Ellie?" She's not inside. I go back outside to call for her again. "Ellie!"

No answer.

My heart beats faster as terror sets in. *No, no, no! Not now, please!* "Bear, go get Ellie."

He tilts his head sideways like he's trying to figure out what I'm saying.

"Bear!"

He stands up but doesn't move.

"Go. Find. Ellie."

He tilts his head again but doesn't take a step.

Shit. "Ellie!" I'm about to go into full-blown panic mode when Ellie takes a step out of the cabin. I run to her and hold her in my arms. "Didn't you hear me calling for you?"

WHEN WE GET BACK TO THE TRAILER, CHARLIE IS ALREADY there waiting. It makes me wonder where he was when he called for him to arrive so fast. I thought he sounded angry on the phone, but his face shows nothing but worry. He looks at me and pets Bear.

"Paisley."

"Charlie."

He takes a step forward but doesn't try to touch me. "We need to talk."

"No shit."

"About Ellie-" he starts.

"Ellie? No, no. Let's talk about that little cabin in the back. The one you know about. You told me it's not safe, Charlie. What the hell is a cabin like that doing on our property? And let's talk about your job. You know... the one you don't have!"

He puts his hands up in a placating gesture, trying to calm me down. He hasn't said it, but he's right. We shouldn't be having this conversation in front of Ellie. I take a deep breath to steady myself, then turn to her. She's clinging to my leg, halfway hiding her face while peeking out at Charlie. "Ellie, go play with your toys please, while Mommy and Daddy have a grownup talk."

I'm four feet away from Charlie, but I can still hear him grinding his teeth together when I say this. She nods her head before running to her toy box under the awning. Turning back to Charlie, I say, "Tom came back."

Charlie's brow creases. "I'm sorry."

"I don't need an apology. I need an explanation. You haven't been here. Our marriage is over. Why have we gone through all of this? What was it all for?" I wipe the tears from my cheeks. I don't want his sympathy; I just want answers.

He stands there, looking at me in silence. I can see him thinking. It's good he's here now, willing to talk. But it's infuriating it's taken him so long. I'm not sure if I can trust whatever comes out of his mouth now, but at least he's here. I suppose that counts for something.

Finally, Charlie speaks, but what he says doesn't answer any of my questions. Instead of answering me, he asks me his own question. "Paisley, how long have you been seeing Ellie?"

"Don't change the subject. I want answers Charlie."

Charlie runs his hands through his hair in frustration. He sighs. "You told me it was over. Ellie is dead. She died, Paisley. It's been over three years now, almost four."

I feel dizzy. An overwhelming anger threatens to take over. I feel myself losing control by the second. "You're wrong," I say. "She might be dead to you, but she's here. She won't let go of me and I won't let go of her!"

"No." He reaches out for me now, but I slap his arm away. "Please, Paisley," he breathes.

"You remember what happened. I know you do."

"Of course, I remember!" I yell. Why does he feel the need to bring up the past? Why can't he just leave me alone and let it be? "You can't just let me be happy, can you?"

Charlie looks around. He leans to look directly at the awning where Ellie is supposed to be playing. "Happy? She's not here, Paisley. Don't turn this into something it's not. This is about reality. You need help. I know you haven't been talking to Dr. Reymore like you should be."

"She's right there!" I yell, pointing at her. I can see Ellie clear as day, sitting with her legs crossed, playing with her toys. She's humming to herself, playing pretend with her animals. The image is so vivid, so *real*, it brings tears to my eyes. I look back at Charlie with wide eyes full of tears, waiting for his response. I already know what he's going to say before he says it.

"No, she's not."

"Look!" I scream, waving my arm at her, desperate to

make him see the child I see. Charlie won't look anymore. Instead, he stares at me. I know he can't see her. Only I can. It's my gift and my curse.

A tear falls from one of Charlie's eyes. "She's gone, Paisley. She's been gone for a long time."

FORTY-FOUR

Three Years Ago

The pain that rips through me is excruciating. There's no way to know what normal pain feels like when you're in labor for the first time. "Be prepared to feel like you're dying," they tell you. It's true, but how do you know if there's something wrong?

On a scale of one to ten, everyone's perception of pain is different. Some have a higher threshold than others, so if you're *supposed* to be at ten during labor, how would you know if it's not right? I read all the pregnancy books and websites, everything I could get my hands on to prepare myself for the big day, always worried about the complications.

Now, I feel like my lower spine is being ripped out of my body while my uterus has cramps from hell. I scream for Charlie when my contractions get worse, but I'm all alone. When I look down and see the blood, I'm so afraid I can barely breathe. I *know* something is wrong.

I'm too afraid to drive myself to the hospital; I don't think I can do it, so I call 911. The operator talks to me while the ambulance is on the way. "Blood can be normal during labor," she says. "There's nothing to worry about. Everything is going to be fine." She means well, but she's wrong.

As I'm being rolled through the hospital, nurses and doctors surround me. They've given me a sedative of some kind, to try and ease my pain, but it's done nothing but make me loopy. The pain is still there, as bad as ever. Every single one of them has pity written all over their faces. Why would they look that way if this was normal?

When I look down at myself, I see the blood that's still gushing from between my legs. I cry out for Charlie again, forgetting he isn't with me. I'm still alone. "Is the baby okay?" I ask no one in particular. No one answers me. They're too busy rushing me into an operating room. I'm so out of it I can barely see straight but the pain won't stop. "My baby!" I cry.

Moments later, I black out from the medication that was given to me through an IV. If anyone explained what was happening, I didn't hear. If I heard, I didn't understand. Because when I wake up, I'm absolutely clueless about my situation. Laying in the hospital bed, I look around the room for my baby. I'm not sure if they would have her in a portable basinet or if there's a nursery in the hospital where the babies sleep.

She's not in the room with me, so she must be in the nursery. I look around for Charlie, but he's not here either. When I see the IV connected to my arm, I try to remember what happened, but my memory is blank after being rolled through the hospital on a gurney. I press the call button on the side of my hospital bed, eager to see my baby.

Seconds later, a nurse comes into the room. "Can I help you?" she asks.

"Yes, I'd like to see my baby, please."

Her brow furrows. "Your baby?" she asks.

Her confusion scares me. The blip on the blood pressure

machine beeps faster, reflecting my increasing heart rate. "Yes. My baby," I say. "Ellie Lanson. Where is she?"

The nurse's eyes grow wide at my tone. She looks more surprised and confused than anything else. I think she suspects I'm about to lose it if someone doesn't bring my baby in here in the next two minutes. "I'll be right back," she says before scurrying out the door.

My heart rate monitor hasn't slowed back down yet. I wonder why I'm even connected to one. I don't remember any of my literature mentioning that requirement after childbirth. I wince when I stretch too far, the soreness in my abdomen hitting me.

I wonder if Charlie is somewhere in the hospital waiting for me to wake up. He could be downstairs getting a snack or something. He's probably visiting our baby in the nursery. That would make sense. Any minute he'll come strolling in holding her. I smile, picturing the image of him holding our little bundle in his arms.

The door to my room opens. It's not Charlie. It's a doctor and two nurses. *Why is there a medical team here and not my baby?* The doctor asks, "How are you feeling?"

"A little confused. I asked the nurse to see my baby, and she hasn't brought her." I nod toward the nurse I spoke with earlier.

The doctor has a grim expression on his face. "Paisley, I'm sorry. I have some unfortunate news." He fidgets with his clipboard, clearly nervous and not looking forward to this conversation. Whatever he has to say to me isn't going to be good.

I start to cry before he says anything else. I'm too hormonal still, too afraid, and too confused to hold back. The doctor is understanding. He gives me time to stop crying as much as I can before he continues. "Your baby didn't make it," he says.

I squeeze my eyes shut, trying to block out reality. My head is pounding, my stomach is throbbing, I feel my heartbeat in my throat. The heart monitor is going crazy, and a nurse presses the button to silence it. The doctor continues. "Your uterus was hemorrhaging. We had no choice but to do an emergency hysterectomy. It was the only way to stop the bleeding. Without it, you would've died."

"A-" I can't even say the word. *Hysterectomy.* I'm inconsolable. The doctor mumbles something else about giving me time before leaving. One of the nurses sits next to me, holding my hand, saying soothing words in my ear. The other injects something into my IV.

My world is shattered. I can't think, can't breathe, can't live. How can I go on? Not only did my baby die, my chance of *ever* having another died with her. I hyperventilate while I shiver from the adrenaline. I feel more alone now than I've ever felt in my entire life. My baby is dead, and my husband isn't here. How is he *still* not here? Does he even know what has happened?

The nurse asks, "Do you have any family you'd like me to call for you?" Guess that answers that question. How is Charlie going to react to this? I lost our child. Not only that, but I can never give him another now. What use am I to him? He wanted a family so badly, we both did. How is he going to look at me when he learns what's happened?

The nurse drones on about how it will be okay and how much help there is for women like me, how adoption is always a possibility, how my baby is with God. She talks about a counselor and how someone will come by to talk to me. I wish she would just shut up. I wonder if she really cares or if she's just giving me the spiel. How many cases like mine has she seen?

I want to scream at her to shut up. I want to yell, cuss, throw things, break something. I want to cut myself, cause some kind of physical pain. Any pain at all besides this. What would her face look like if I became violent?

I want to die. Before I can open my mouth, the medicine that's been injected into my IV takes effect. I feel the drowsiness take over and I give into the darkness without a fight.

FORTY-FIVE

Three Years Ago

I haven't been handling her loss very well. "Very well," according to *them.* I'm not sure what the *right* way is. It takes everything I have just to get out of bed and some days I don't even do that. It's been a month since my baby died. Ellie. I didn't even get to say goodbye to her.

Charlie has been discussing my condition with my doctors. I'd rather he deal with them than me. He wants me to see a psychiatrist to get some more help. I scoffed when he suggested it. It's like he thinks it's all in my head and a little psychotherapy will make everything all better. It will *never* be better.

He's worried because of my violent outbursts at work. I had to go back right away, of course. There's no maternity leave for a woman whose child is dead and I only had one week of sick pay available. What else was there to do? I'll admit I probably wasn't ready to go back, but there were no other options.

My first week back was a nightmare. What am I supposed to do when a pregnant woman *complains* about being pregnant, when she's lucky enough to be *able* to carry a child? They didn't fire me, but basically, I was forced to resign.

I probably shouldn't have screamed at her. It was too embarrassing for my company; they couldn't excuse that behavior, even for me. It's too bad she fell down the stairwell after I left. So sad. Unfortunate, too, that no one was there to see how she fell or help her up. I wonder if she's feeling better now that she's no longer pregnant.

There's a secret I'm keeping from Charlie. If he knew, he'd really think I was crazy. There's no way I'm going to tell him I see her. Ellie. She's perfect, just like I've envisioned her. Ellie nurses from me, cries, poops, nuzzles into the crook of my arm. She's alive. Charlie doesn't hear her or see her, but she's here with me and it's the only thing keeping me going.

Deep down, I know it's not right. I *know* there's something wrong, but whatever it is, I don't want to fix it. Why would I? I decide to go see this doctor that Charlie has lined up for me, just to shut him up. If I must lie, then so be it, but I *won't* give Ellie up. I can't.

"WHAT WOULD YOU LIKE TO DISCUSS TODAY?" DR. REYMORE asks. I'm sitting on a sofa in his office while he's in a wing-back chair next to a window. I always pictured a psychiatrist with some kind of notebook and pen, but Dr. Reymore has nothing to take notes. Maybe he has an excellent memory.

"I lost my baby," I say. As the words leave my mouth, my throat closes up. I want to say, "I'm here because my husband asked me to come," but I can't get the words out. I don't want to cry already. I hate that. But it seems I'm not going to be able to control myself here.

Dr. Reymore hands me a box of tissues before saying, "I'm sorry for your loss."

Lord, not that. Those words. They're the right thing to say, the *polite* thing, but how they make the tears worse. I'm crying like a fool, ready to get up and leave. Why am I even here? I'm so embarrassed to be breaking down in front of this man and *already!* One question out of his mouth is all it took for me to lose my resolve.

I take deep, calming breaths and think about Ellie. She's next to me on the couch. When I came into the office, I tried to act casual, carrying her in my bundled-up sweatshirt. I placed it next to me on the couch, trying to seem as normal as possible.

It's so hard for me to ignore her laying there, though. I want to hold her. But If I reach for her, there's going to be a whole new level of discussion in here that I'm not ready for.

Seeing her out of the corner of my eye helps calm me. I ask myself why I'm so worked up about losing her when she's right here next to me. It helps me get my emotions back under control.

When Dr. Reymore sees I'm calm again, he asks, "Is she here with you?"

"What?" I'm shocked. How does he know? I guess I wasn't acting as casually as I thought.

"I haven't met many people who carry a sweatshirt in their arms that way. And you seem to be watching it extremely carefully."

"I-" I don't finish my sentence. There's nothing to say. I look down at my hands in my lap, ashamed.

"Also," Dr. Reymore adds, "your husband told me he suspected you were seeing visions of your daughter."

I look up at that. Charlie knew too. How could he? "How is it so obvious?" I ask.

"You're seeing someone who isn't there. It would be

difficult to interact with that person and *not* be obvious. Even intentionally trying to hide it would probably make it seem apparent."

His words sting. Saying she's not there stings. I feel a burning rage growing and I fight to keep it in check. When I don't answer him, he says nothing else, just looks at me. It's uncomfortable, making me fidget with my hands. I can't stand the silence, so finally I reach to pick up Ellie.

She's asleep, and I rock her gently back and forth in my arms. "I don't want to stop seeing her," I say.

"Perfectly normal to feel that way, especially after your loss."

"Will I ever feel normal again?"

"No, probably not. But that's not the goal, here. The goal is to learn how to cope with the pain. You may not want to let her go, but when you are well enough, you *will*. It's part of the healing process.

That's when it hits me. Every single move I make from now on, I'll have to watch my step. I'll make sure Charlie thinks I'm healing like he wants, so he doesn't have me committed.

I won't have to fake my grief. There's nothing about showing it that will be hard for me. The hard part will be pretending to be fine in the end. Pretending that all is well and normal.

When I think about it, I think maybe it won't be so hard after all. Ellie is here with me to get me through. I'm so thankful she's come back to me. I'm so thankful I get to hold her and love her still. As long as I can convince this doctor that I've stopped seeing Ellie at some point, I think everyone will get off my back and just leave me alone to be with her.

FORTY-SIX

Charlie wanted to stay the night with me. I didn't let him. After his confrontation, I could barely stand to be around him. He wasn't trying to sleep with me; I realize that, but I still couldn't bear to be around him anymore.

He still hasn't explained a thing. I was too worked up from talking about Ellie to fight with him about the rest. I still don't know where we stand. I still don't even know if we're going to continue building this damn house or sell the property and move on.

Hank wanted to come over again too, but I told him no as well. I needed to be alone. Damn Charlie for seeing things clearly and damn me for opening my big mouth. I've been living in a world with my daughter and it's like my husband wants to take her away from me. I'm not sure if I'll be able to forgive him for that.

I don't want to drag Hank into this craziness between me and Charlie any more than I already have. I hope Charlie won't talk to him. I don't think he will, but what if he got it in his head that it was the right thing to do? He's always been so worried about helping me, I don't want him to butt in where he's not wanted.

After Charlie leaves, I spend the night alone, just like I wanted. I thought it would be good for me, but I wake up in a sweat. Another nightmare. This time, I saw myself waking up on the operating table while the doctor was cutting out my uterus. A nurse held Ellie, who was crying. "I'm sorry. She's dead," the nurse said.

Panting, trying to catch my breath, the pain from the nightmare still lingers. I wipe the tears from my cheeks and get out of bed. "Come on, Bear." I dig the gun out of my closet. We're going outside for some fresh air, but I'm not going empty-handed this time.

Gun in hand, I grab a flashlight and lead the way outside. I'm expecting to hear owls and crickets. Instead, I hear the beating of drums. *Not again!*

Unable to take anymore, I put the gun in my back pocket and start running. Bear runs beside me as we head into the forest towards the sound of the drums.

Running helps me clear my mind from all the pain and confusion. I focus on breathing and putting one foot in front of the other without killing myself. Once we're on the trail, we slow to a steady walk, winding our way through the trees. I'm going to confront the neighbors once and for all.

As we follow the trail, the sound of the drums grows steadily louder. It seems like it might be coming from the direction of the little cabin that Ellie and I found. I feel the icy hands of fear creeping in when I think about someone *in* that cabin and what they might be doing. I'm done avoiding it, though. If my crazy neighbors are out on my property beating their drums, I'm going to lose my shit. It'll be *them* that's afraid of *me*.

I try to focus on the anger to block out the pain. The pain is still too great and after my conversation with Charlie, too raw. I think about being at the cabin yesterday with Bear and Ellie. At the moment I couldn't find her, I was so afraid she was really gone forever.

I don't want to be well enough for her to go away. According to Dr. Reymore, once my mind is able to process the grief, my visions should gradually go away on their own. Well, if my mind needs to rot inside my skull, then that's what I'm going to make it do. I *won't* give her up.

My vision is blurry from the tears that flow freely down my face. Bear turns to me, concern in his eyes. I bend down to hug him and rub him down, then we continue on our way.

Finally, we're close to the cabin, and it seems we're right on top of the drums. I shut my flashlight off, not wanting to be noticed. Wiping the tears from my eyes, I see there's a light shining through the window of the cabin. My blood runs cold as I think about confronting whoever's in there.

Bear is starting to growl, but I shush him, wanting to keep the element of surprise on our side. We need to observe first, then confront. Trying to be as quiet as possible, I lead Bear around the back side of the cabin. When we're in place, the drums stop. My eyes grow wide with fear. It feels like they know I'm out here. I stand still, holding my breath, praying Bear won't make a sound.

For a moment, everything is so silent, I can hear the pounding of my heart. After an eternity, there are voices that start talking inside. I press my ear against the wooden planks to hear better.

"She knows," a man's voice says.

"No, she doesn't." That sounded like-

"Don't worry, she's clueless," a woman's voice says.

"Then how do you explain the trail?" another woman asks.

I'm feeling dizzy as the blood rushes to my head. These people are talking about *me*! What is it they think I know? Oh God, I'm so afraid. My breath is coming fast, but I force myself to breathe as quietly as possible. I *need* to hear what these people are saying.

As I press my ear flat against the wood, movement catches the corner of my eye. I realize I'm able to see through the gaps in-between some boards. I can see the table and chairs, same as before, only now there are eight people inside the cabin. Their figures are outlined by the glow of candlelight.

I wish I could see their faces. I can't wait to tell Hank about this. I don't know people in town well enough to identify their voices just by sound, but I swear a couple of these people sounded familiar. If I could just see their faces.

"She's been exploring back here for months. It's just been a matter of time and we've always known that."

"Why didn't anyone tell us she's gone this far?"

"Does it really matter? There's no evidence here. It looks like an old, abandoned cabin."

"If the ritual is going to work, we need to know everything."

Ritual! What in the hell is going on here? With shaking hands, I wipe my sweaty palms on my pants, then place them back against the back of the cabin to steady myself as I continue to look.

"Enough. I'm tired of the bickering. Everything is going according to the plan." A man's voice says. It sounds authoritative, like he's someone in charge. It's also a voice I recognize. I know it well, in fact. Hank.

FORTY-SEVEN

There's no denying it's him. One hundred percent, I'm sure. The knife in my gut twists deeper when someone holding a candle moves. With the candle right in front of her face, I can see it's Charity. When she moves to Hank, the candle lights up their faces together. I see them kissing. I see her tongue lick his neck. She whispers something in his ear that makes him smile.

I feel nauseous. I'm so disgusted I could scream. I'd love to see the look on their faces when they realize they've been caught red-handed. Would they be embarrassed? Or instead, would they have looks of satisfaction?

If these people have gone through this kind of trouble to fool me, they have to be dangerous. I wouldn't be surprised if the other members of this little party were my neighbors, including Tom Morgan.

I feel like such an idiot. Tears fall again, this time full of anger and hatred. I fell in love with this asshole. I trusted him. For what? If I would've let him spend the night tonight, he would've been fucking me instead of here at this— whatever *this* is. Would I have ever found out the truth about him? I'm not so sure.

There's nothing else I want to see here. I'm about to

back away from the wall but someone says, "We need to kill the dog."

What?

"Not necessary," Hank says.

"Why not?" a woman's voice, probably Charity, asks.

"The dog trusts me. He can be easily delt with, without hurting him."

"What of the sacrifice?" another asks. "All of our efforts to get him will have been in vain."

Silence. I hold my breath. These people are not seriously going to try killing my dog. If I think about it though, it makes sense. All these times Bear has gone missing- first Tom taking him, then Gladice. I *knew* it couldn't be a coincidence. This has been planned from the beginning.

"Very well," Hank says.

What?! No, no, no! I back away. I have to do something. These people are insane. I have to call Charlie. He'll help me. He'll do something. Even if he thinks I'm crazy, it doesn't matter. He'll do something to protect Bear.

I take one step back and then another. I'm at the front end of the cabin when I hear the loud crack of the branch I've just stepped on. The voices inside the cabin go silent. *Fuck!* Do I run or do I stay quiet? Do I run or do I stay quiet? All the figures in the front window turn in my direction. When the glow of the candles goes out and the drums start beating again, it's clear. It's time to run.

Panic takes over. "Bear, come," I say, taking off as fast as I dare. I keep the flashlight off so I'm not a beacon of light in the night. We've hiked this trail so many times by now, I'm familiar with the twists and turns but it's still the middle of the night. I'm not sure how fast I could hike this thing in the daylight, let alone in the pitch black.

My hands reach for my phone, feeling in my pockets, but I can't find it. I either left it at the trailer or it dropped out when I was crouched by the cabin. There's no time to go back and look for it. The gun is still heavy in my pocket. At least I still have that. I can hear footsteps and the drums growing closer.

I have to make it to the trailer to call for help. If I call 911, is dispatch just going to call Hank again? I'm not sure if anyone in this town is trustworthy or not. There were only eight of them there in the cabin. Maybe that's all who's in on whatever cracked thing they're up to, but maybe there are more of them.

There's no way for me to know for sure. I have no idea and I don't really want to spend the time to find out. The first person I'm calling is Charlie, then I'm looking up every police department I can find. One of these places around here has to be for real.

When I look over my shoulder, the cabin is no longer visible. It's pure black behind me, and the drums have stopped again. I have no clue if they're behind me or how close they might be. I turn back around, and something hits me hard, knocking me to the ground. My cry of pain sets Bear off, barking. "No, Bear!" I cry.

It's what they want. They want him to come to them. "Bear, go home!" I say. He doesn't listen. My loyal protector, standing by my side, defending me against the unseen enemy. I don't know what hit me. It was hard, but not hard enough to keep me down.

Warm blood trickles down the side of my face as I get to my feet to continue moving. I take a few steps, pulling Bear along with me. He's staring into the dark woods, barking still. "Come on, boy. Keep moving."

I hold the gun in a tight grip, pointing it into the darkness. I fire off three shots. I'm as good as blind, shooting into a sheet of black. I might not hit anything or anyone, but maybe I'll scare them a little.

Something hits me on the back of the head. I drop again, the corners of my vision darken. From the ground, I see Bear snarling, attacking someone. I can't see who it is, just a dark figure. The others' footsteps are closing in on us. I try to get up again, but I'm too disoriented.

I lift the gun, trying to aim at someone, but I'm afraid to hit Bear. Bear thinks he's fighting for me, but if he loses, it's him who's going to suffer the most. "Please Bear," I croak.

Another figure stands over me. They take my gun from me with ease. It's the last thing I'm aware of before passing out.

FORTY-EIGHT

My eyes spring open the second I regain consciousness. *Bear.* I have to find him. The darkness leaves me disoriented. For a moment, I think I'm still in the forest. They've taken Bear and left me here alone. I'm lying on my back, on the hard ground.

After a moment, I realize how wrong I am. When I try to get up, my hand touches cold plywood instead of the dirt of a forest floor. Unable to see, I feel my way around to get a better idea of where I am. Instead of standing up, I stay on my hands and knees. It's easier to feel around this way.

I count the "steps" I take forward until I bump into a wall. From there, I count my steps again until I bump into another. I'm in some kind of cell. At five steps one way and four another, it's far too small to be considered a room. I feel my way up the walls, searching for a handle or lever to get out. There's nothing. I'm locked in here.

"Hello!" I call. "Let me out!" I pound my fists against the wall, making as much noise as I can. These people will not get away with this. I grind my teeth together, imagining what I'm going to do to them. What I'm going to do to Charity. To Hank. To any damn one of them I can get my hands on. My fingernails dig into my palms, drawing beads of warm blood.

"Bear?" He's obviously not in here with me, but maybe he can still hear my voice. I stop making noise so I can listen for him. I'm hoping to hear his familiar bark or even a whimper to let me know he's here. There's nothing, no sounds to indicate he's heard me.

"Bear! Bear!" I don't know what else to do but scream for him. I scream until my voice is raw, hoping he hears me even if I can't hear him. I hope my voice urges him on. I hope he gets freed and devours anyone in his path.

When I've exhausted myself to the point I can barely swallow my spit anymore from the burning in my throat, I lay back down in silence. There's nothing else to do but wait. Occasionally, I bang on the walls again, but I'm not sure if it's really doing anything other than hurting myself. I tell myself it's better than nothing. At least I'm trying.

"Mommy?" Her voice brings tears to my eyes.

"Cupcake, what are you doing here?" I whisper.

"I want to help."

"No, baby girl. You stay away from these bad people."

"Bear," she says. The tears are steady now. I don't know what else to say. My throat hurts too much to say anything else, anyway.

Sometime later, I fall asleep. I'm awoken by the sound of the thick door swinging open. A bright ray of light shines through, blinding me. I hold my hand to cover my eyes against the light. Someone is standing in the doorway. I can barely make out the trees behind them.

Outside. I must be in another tiny cabin. The person standing there hasn't said anything yet; they're just watching me.

If I wasn't so angry, it would be terrifying. But right now, I'm not worried about myself. I'm worried about Bear. He's innocent in all of this. He's just a dog. These psychopaths have no right to bring him into their crazy games. I don't know why I'm on their radar at all, but there's no reason they should be after Bear.

"Paisley." When I hear his voice, I think I'm dreaming. It's not possible for him to be here. I close my eyes and turn away from the light. *It's all in my head.*

"Paisley, please," he says. The anguish in his voice assures me I'm not dreaming. This is real.

"Charlie." He watches me stand up on wobbly legs. I walk to him with a look of gratitude, acting like I'm glad he's here to rescue me. But when I'm within reach, I slap him across the face with all the force I can muster. His head swings back and I relish the look of shock on his face.

"If they kill Bear, Charlie, it's *you* that's responsible. I'll *never* forgive you."

Charlie winces. *Good.* He looks regretful. "I never meant for it to be like this."

"What the hell is going on? I heard them talking about killing Bear. Tell me I'm wrong. Tell me it's all a misunderstanding."

"I- I can't. You need help, Paisley. These people are here to help."

It's obvious to me now what's been going on. *Charlie* is the reason I'm on these people's radar. He must've come to them with his warped sense of needing to help me. But I still don't understand why Bear is involved. Why would anyone think killing my dog would be helpful?

"I'm seeing Dr. Reymore for help! What can these people do for me that he can't?"

"He's not helping you."

"Yes, he is. I-"

"No! Stop lying to me, Paisley." He looks around the room. "She's probably here now, isn't she?"

I flush, giving away the truth. From the corner of my

eye, Ellie sits in the corner with her arms wrapped around her knees that are tucked up against her chest.

"It's been almost four years," Charlie says.

"Who are you to think you have any right to interfere? This is *my* health. You aren't my fucking doctor, Charlie! You're not God! And don't talk to me about lying. You're the biggest liar of all."

Charlie turns away, unable to look me in the face. "It's for the best."

"What's for the best?" My pulse quickens as my fear increases, threatening to overpower the rage that's been keeping me going. My mind fills with possibilities, reasons for me being here, none of them good.

"This is a community that helps people. You'll be staying here for a while. They'll help you heal."

"I don't want to stay here, Charlie."

Another figure comes to stand behind Charlie. "I'm sorry. You don't have a choice," Charlie says, turning to go.

"Charlie, please!"

He walks away, leaving me with Hank. "Don't worry, Paisley, we're going to take great care of you."

CHAPTER
FORTY-NINE

Charlie allowed himself the weekend to set up the trailer and get Paisley situated. Traveling in the snowstorm had been a nightmare. Charlie prided himself on his driving skills, but even he had been a little scared going down that mountain pass. He needed a couple of days to calm his heart rate back down to normal.

Looking around his new property, Charlie couldn't believe this was their home now. He felt like one of the luckiest men in the world. He'd been leery about trusting them, but The Society of The Trees was turning out to be great. They'd given him a job and a new home, and they were going to help his wife. It was the best opportunity he could've imagined.

Monday morning, Charlie was expected to check-in with his new community. When Paisley kissed him before saying, "Have a great first day," he felt the familiar twinge of guilt twist his gut. She believed Charlie had transferred his job to a new city within the same company. It's what he'd led her to believe. It was all part of the plan, but lying to her didn't sit well in his stomach.

Technically, the land wasn't legally theirs. Charlie led her to believe that one, too. The deal was, they had a legal tenancy, but the land wasn't owned by Charlie and Paisley. The Society granted Charlie use of the land to live on. Any house built on the land would be the property of The Society because *they* would be paying for it.

The Society of The Trees wasn't going to just give the land away to Charlie for nothing. Not even for a nice big discount. They were a helping community, but not a charity. You had to be willing to work with them in exchange. In Charlie's case, he was. Charlie was too desperate to pass up the deal they'd offered.

Paisley didn't know about any of it.

Charlie left home with the pretense of driving to Seattle for his new job. Instead of turning left, towards town and the highway, he turned right, toward the neighbors. Jack and Gladice lived directly behind Charlie's forty acres and had access to his back forest. Charlie parked his truck in their driveway before making his way to their front door.

"Welcome, friend," a short, plump, older woman greeted him, gripping his hands and pulling him inside the small house. "I'm Gladice and this is my husband, Jack." She pointed to a man sitting in a recliner in the living room.

"Hi, there. I'm Charlie." Charlie hated introducing himself to strangers. He felt nothing but awkward.

"We've been looking forward to your arrival, Charlie," Gladice said. "Isn't that right, Jack?"

"Uh, huh."

The way he was laying back with his eyes closed, Charlie thought he was half asleep or would be soon. "I've been looking forward to meeting everyone in the community. I'm so thankful for everything," Charlie said.

Gladice pinched his cheek. "We'll head out to the cabin.

Everyone won't be there today, but leadership will be and some others."

The threesome left the house, walking straight into the forest from the driveway. A few feet in, there was a clear path that they followed. As they walked, Charlie realized it was essentially taking them straight into his backyard. The realization of how close these people would be sent a chill down his spine.

"Do you all come out here often?" he asked, trying to make conversation as they walked.

Gladice laughed. "You could say that."

IN ORDER TO KEEP THE CABIN HIDDEN FROM NOTICE FOR AS long as possible, steps were taken to cover the end of the trail each time it was used. Charlie wondered who was going to notice it in the middle of the woods, but didn't argue with their logic. He was there to work, not ask questions.

The cabin looked smaller from the outside than it really was on the inside. Three people were inside having a discussion when Charlie, Gladice, and Jack arrived. Charlie noticed there were eight chairs set up to a long table, leaving enough room for two more. The three sitting up to the table stopped talking to greet the newcomer. "Welcome," they said in unison, each looking more eager than the last to have Charlie as part of their community.

Gladice introduced them as Mark, Kevin, and Charity. "Pleasure to meet you all," Charlie said, nodding to each.

"Any word from Hank?" Jack asked the room.

"He'll be here any minute," Charity said. Charlie stared at Charity after she spoke. Her voice seemed so familiar, but he couldn't quite place it. She smiled, noticing his reaction. "We spoke on the phone," she said.

"Ah. I thought I recognized your voice."

Charity was about to say something else, but the door to the cabin swung open. Hank Adrian walked through in his Sheriff's uniform. "Hank," Charity greeted him with a kiss. "This is Charlie."

"Hi, Charlie," Hank said, holding his hand out to shake. "It's nice to finally meet you. We're all excited for you to join the community. We're all looking forward to helping you and your wife as much as we can."

The others in the room beamed at Hank, holding onto his every word. It didn't take a genius to figure out Hank was their leader. Charlie wasn't sure if there was some kind of official title for him, but it was clear as day that everyone looked to him for leadership.

Because Charlie had spoken to Charity on the phone and recognized her voice, he felt a little more comfortable asking her questions. He started to ask, "About my job-" but Charity cut him off.

"Hank has all the details for you." Smiling, Charity turned to Hank.

Even without the kiss, Charlie could tell there was something between the two of them from the smoldering look Hank gave Charity. Hank looked back at Charlie. "Your job will be to complete various duties pertaining to the support of our community." He grinned at the look on Charlie's face. "Not very specific, is it?"

Charlie laughed along with the others. "Not really."

"You're going to play a star role in helping your wife. Don't worry my friend, surrender your problems to us and we'll take care of everything. Your job is to follow the plan, exactly as instructed."

No longer smiling, Charlie wasn't sure he liked the look

on Hank's face. In the short time he's known the man, he already realized how Hank could be charming one second and terrifying the next.

It normally took a lot for Charlie to get freaked out, let alone *scared* of someone. In fact, he couldn't ever remember being afraid of anyone. But within minutes, he understood this was not someone he ever looked forward to crossing.

"The goal here, is to keep Paisley in the dark. We're going to keep the pretense that you're working in Seattle and it's going to seem like you're working very long hours," Hank said.

"She's not going to like that."

"That's to be expected, but it's part of the plan. To help her, she has to *be* alone. She has to let go of everything. Isolation is the first and most important step."

"What am I supposed to do all day while I'm supposed to be working? And what about the paychecks? If I'm not bringing in the kind of money I should be, working all those hours, she's going to know something is going on. She's not an idiot. She's going to figure this out, eventually. What am I supposed to do then?"

"We'll handle the paychecks. Don't worry about finding something to do. You *are* working for us, after all. There will be plenty to keep your day occupied. This is just one cabin in our community. There are others hidden throughout this land close by. Paisley isn't the only one we're helping, and it takes all hands on deck. We'll explain more as we go. As for her finding out about your job- the goal is to put her off for as long as possible. We know it can't be forever, but just long enough to get the rest of the plan in place."

Charlie nodded. This was making sense to him so far and he liked that Hank seemed to be smart. He had this all figured out, which gave Charlie the confidence to trust him. "What's the next step of the plan? After isolation?" he asked.

"The sacrifice." Everyone in the room spoke at the same time, staring at Charlie. It sent chills down his spine, along with a feeling of dread. *That was creepy as shit!* he thought. Unexpectedly, he was nervous around these people. *What am I getting us into?* he asked himself. The confidence and well thought out plan that seemed to comfort Charlie moments ago, now scared the shit out of him.

He remembered Charity speaking about a sacrifice on the phone and still wasn't clear of what it entailed. With wide eyes, he looked in her direction. The mood in the room shifted from a friendly welcoming to that of a dead seriousness. "We spoke of the sacrifice on the phone," Charity said to Hank.

"I remember," Charlie said. "You said it was a technical term. What kind of sacrifice are we talking about here?"

"The sacrifice is vital. Without it, there can be no healing," Hank said. "The sacrifice must be something or someone she loves dearly."

Charlie couldn't believe what he was hearing. This was insane. Paisley had already lost more than anyone should lose in a lifetime, and they wanted her to suffer *more?* "I apologize, but that makes no sense. How is that supposed to help her heal?"

A hush came over the room. Apparently questioning the way things were done, was not done.

Hank smiled. Looking around the room, he said, "It's okay. It's perfectly normal for our new friend to want to understand." He turned his attention back to Charlie.

"Paisley is too focused on her loss still. She's been unable to let go of it even after several years. She needs to experience another loss to make her forget about the first. It will be a smaller loss but significant enough to make her grieve."

Charlie frowned. "I still don't understand. Why would

we do this to her? You're saying it will help her, but I don't understand how that can be."

"If you've broken your arm, you're in terrible physical pain. But what happens if you then smash your foot in a door?"

Charlie thought about it for a moment. "I'm not sure."

"Your brain focuses on the most recent pain. If you've smashed your foot, that's the pain it's going to concentrate on. The pain in your arm nearly disappears, at least temporarily, because of the *fresh pain*."

"Okay… so what's your point?"

"My point," Hank said, losing his patience, "is that this is what we're applying to Paisley. She's got this old pain and we're going to give her brain a new pain to focus on. It will allow her a chance to forget about the old and move on. The fresh pain won't be as great, so the idea is that she'll recover from it fairly quickly."

Charlie wasn't sure what to say. He saw the logic Hank was using, but he didn't know if it was right. He didn't have any knowledge about psychology.

Part of him wanted to consult Paisley's therapist about it, just to ask if it was accurate information. That wasn't an option here, though. Charlie had the feeling that what Hank said went and that was final. He was starting to think he should've asked more questions earlier on.

He nodded his understanding. "Okay, so do you know what or who it's going to be?" A shudder went through Charlie. He hoped he wouldn't have to kill anyone. He had a feeling though, with all they were doing for him, it might come to that.

"Her dog."

"Bear? What's he got to do with anything?"

Hank was tired of the questions. There was only so much patience a man had. He'd explained it in the simplest way he could imagine. "I think I've made myself clear already." His tone was ice. He didn't raise his voice. He didn't have to.

Charlie nodded. The message was clear.

"Only when she's let go of *everyone,* can she heal," Hank said.

FIFTY

*H*ank. I thought it was bad enough seeing him making out with Charity in the cabin. But that he's here now, wherever *here* is, tells me there's more to the story, still. It would seem he's playing a major part with these people.

"Hank, what's going on? Where am I? And why are you here with these people?"

"You're with The Society of The Trees." He's *actually* grinning at me.

"That doesn't tell me anything. Why are you smiling like that? Get me out of here."

He laughs. "I'm smiling like this because I've been looking forward to this day for a very long time."

My eyebrows furrow as I narrow my eyes at him. "I wish you would speak plainly. You're scaring me."

Hank nods, no longer grinning. He has a sympathetic look on his face now. "Of course. I'm with these people because we all want to help you. I've always wanted to help you, from the beginning. I-" He flushes. "I love you, Paisley."

Disappointment settles in my gut. I love him too, but how can I now? He's not the person I thought. I believed Hank was a good man, an honest man, and the moment I saw him in that cabin, I realized it was all a lie. Not just kissing another woman, but that he was there at all.

"You love me? Then why are you making out with Charity? I would bet every last dollar to my name you're doing more than that with her, too. And why are you talking about killing my dog? You know how much he means to me."

Hank is angry now, like I've poked a lion. His reaction is so surprising it makes me take a step back. "You weren't supposed to see that."

I could laugh at the irony. "Oh? I'm so sorry."

"It's not what it looked like." He clenches his fists at his side. "I have my reasons for keeping Charity close. But it's not the same with her. *You* are who matters to me."

"It doesn't matter now. I just want out of here. Whatever this *society* is, I don't want a part of it. I want to go home with Bear."

"I'm sorry, Paisley. That can't happen." He takes a step towards me to hold my shoulders.

"Hank. I'm serious. I want to go home."

"I am too, love. Don't you see? We're going to be together now." He grins at me again, anger instantly gone, like the flip of a switch.

"And what about Bear?" I ask.

Hank is sober now. *Switch flipped again.* "There has to be a sacrifice. It's the only way you can fully heal."

"No. Not him. Sacrifice something else. Please, Hank. Not Bear." I let the tears fall freely, hoping they'll buy his sympathy.

Hank purses his lips, thinking. "There has to be a sacrifice. There's no way around it. But… if it's not Bear, there's only one other possibility."

"Yes! Anything! What is it?"

"Charlie."

"What?"

"You would have to sacrifice Charlie." Hank shrugs. "Not an easy choice, I know."

"What do you mean by 'sacrifice?' Can I just give him up? Divorce him? Done. I'll sign the papers right now."

I must be a comedian because Hank laughs again, doubling over, holding his side. He wipes a tear from his eye. "No, no. That's not a sacrifice. What I mean by 'sacrifice,' is he must *die*. Divorce would be too easy. It must cause significant pain. Your brain has to recognize it as a trauma."

"Hank! This is crazy! *You're* crazy! I never asked for help. I don't *want* help. There's nothing *to* help with! Whatever Charlie said about me, he's lying. There's some kind of misunderstanding here. Just let me go. Let me out of this place and we can have a rational discussion like adults."

"Don't bullshit me, Paisley." He opens the door to leave. "Think about it. You won't have much time to decide. The timeline has been moved up because of your curiosity. Bear is fine for now, but if you don't decide, a decision will be made for you."

Hank closes the door, leaving me in my dark cell again. My mind reels. There's so much to think about and it would seem so little time. Hank's not just playing a role, he's calling the shots. He wants to be with me for whatever sick reason, and it's obvious that's why he suggested sacrificing Charlie.

This is a sick, *sick* group of people. I can't even call them that. Cult. A sick, sick *cult*. God, how did I wind up in the middle of a fucking *cult?* I'm shaking with fear. Someone isn't making it out of here alive. Hell, how do I know they won't sacrifice me right along with whoever else they choose?

Hank is crazy enough to believe he's helping me. Helping me is the *last* thing he's doing. Terror doesn't begin to describe what's running through my veins. It's just the tip of the iceberg. I can't stop shaking. My throat is dry from all the yelling earlier and then talking to Hank. I can barely swallow my spit.

Hank wants an answer from me. He wants me to give him *permission* to kill my husband. There has to be a way out of this. My marriage with Charlie is over, yes, but I don't want him *dead.* I run my fingers through my hair, thinking of anything that might give me a fighting chance.

"Mommy?" Her small voice comes from the corner where she's been sitting this whole time. She's been silent, observing.

"It's okay, cupcake. I'll get us out of this."

We sit together in silence, waiting for Hank to return. I don't know how much time passes, but it feels like an eternity. When the door opens, I'm groggy from falling in and out of sleep again.

"Have you decided?" Hank asks.

"Yes," I say. After a pause I add, "Let Charlie be the sacrifice."

Hank beams. I've said exactly what he wanted to hear.

"I'd like to speak with him alone, first."

"Of course." He leaves me alone again to wait for Charlie. I'm not sure if it's my tired eyes or if there is a spring in his step when he walks away.

FIFTY-ONE

Charlie enters the room with a grim expression. I wonder what Hank has told him and if Charlie is dumb enough to believe him. It seems he is. He's gotten us into this situation, after all.

"Listen, Charlie," I say, stepping toward him. "Hank wants to kill you. You have to let me out of here. We have to get the hell out!"

Instead of a look of surprise, Charlie just shakes his head. "He said you would say anything to get out. I knew you were desperate to save Bear, but you could've come up with something better than that."

"I'm not lying! How can you believe him over me? Charlie!"

"Paisley, we're going to sacrifice Bear at dawn. If you'd like to stop bull shitting me, I can bring him here for you to say your last goodbyes."

"Yes! Bring him here!" The thought of having Bear with me gives me so much hope I can barely stand it. I don't want to show Charlie how excited I am, how much power he's about to hand over to me, but it's hard to contain myself.

"First, admit the lie," he says.

"I told you, I'm not lying." I look him directly in the eyes.

"I am not lying to you, Charlie. Hank told me if I wanted to save Bear, the only other sacrifice would be *you*."

He analyzes my face, searching for something that tells him I'm lying. He *wants* it to be a lie. Of course he does. Because if I'm not lying, it means he's chosen to trust a nut job. *I* already know this, but it hasn't registered for Charlie yet.

He frowns. Charlie seems to be having an internal debate. I don't have time for him to try figuring it out. I've spent enough of my life waiting for him. "Charlie, bring me my dog. I wanted to warn you. I don't want you to die. I don't want either of you to die. Please, let's get the hell out of here! But if you won't believe me, at least bring me Bear."

Charlie leaves without another word. As I wait for him to return, I think about the hell we can raise together. If Bear got his teeth around *one* person, he could rip them apart. I clench my fists, imagining the destruction and blood once I set him free. Even in this locked cell, we'll provide each other strength. That's all that matters. Together, we can take them on.

"Bear's coming back to us, cupcake. Just a few more minutes now."

I FALL TO MY KNEES, SOBBING AT THE SIGHT OF HIM. I thought he had it bad before, when he was in Tom's barn, and then in Gladice's cage. Those times were nothing compared to now. With blood caked in his fur, he's been badly beaten and can barely walk to me. He's so weak that when he recognizes me, he doesn't even try to wag his tail. Bear looks like he's already half dead. A muzzle is over his face and when I look into his eyes, it's obvious he's been drugged. Someone had a hell of a time beating him.

"Charlie!" I scream.

He winces. "I know. I didn't know they were going to do this to him. I'm sorry. He wreaked havoc when they grabbed you in the forest. Bit three fingers clear off Troy."

I glare at him. "I hope he did more than that to those fuckers."

"Yeah well, this is what he gets."

"How can you not care? Look at him!" Bear is so weak he can't stay standing. His breath comes in pants, and he whimpers with every step he takes. He doesn't lie down in the room, he falls down. When he does, I lay next to him, holding him next to me as gently as I can.

My tears fall into his fur. "I'm so sorry," I whisper.

"Paisley, I- of course I care. I-" Charlie suddenly stops talking. He's interrupted by someone hitting him over the head with a wooden baseball bat. The sickening crack against his skull is so loud it makes my head hurt too.

The first thing I do is remove the muzzle. I stand up, ready to escape. Bear is going to be heavy as hell, but by God, I'm getting him out of here with me. I stop dead in my tracks when I see who my rescuer is. It's Tom Morgan. My neighbor. My mouth drops open. I look like a gaping fish.

"No time to explain," he says. "Hurry the hell up."

He's right. No time for questions. We need to get the hell out of dodge. I nod to Bear. "Help me with him."

"Leave the dog," he says.

"Not a chance. He comes with me."

Tom looks furious, but surely he knows by now I can't leave my dog behind. He, of all people, should know that. Tom looks behind, then steps inside, pulling Charlie with him. He bends down to pick up Bear.

For a moment, Tom struggles to pick up the nearly one

hundred pounds of dead weight. I think he might break his back with the effort. But Tom stands up, holding Bear in a firm grip. Bear only growls once from the effort, surprising us both that he would let Tom hold him this way. He's so weak though, there seems to be no fight left in him.

Once Tom has him up, we're off, locking Charlie in the cabin behind us. "This way," Tom says, leading the way. He's far stronger than he looks. Even holding Bear in his arms, he walks at a breakneck speed. I'm glad. The sooner we get out of here the better.

There are so many questions I'm dying to ask, but now isn't the time. I follow his lead in silence. Tom leads me out of the cabin, into the forest. Outside, there are two other cabins nearby that I'm able to make out. There are no people I can see.

It's pitch black. The only light comes from solar lights that have been placed in the ground to mark a path between cabins. They must've kept Bear in a cage, like at Gladice's house.

We're in the middle of the forest. There are no vehicles within sight. I don't know how Tom would've even found me. I look at him, questions in my eyes, but he keeps walking.

A feeling of dread is creeping up my spine, making me wonder if I should trust Tom right now, or if he's about to stab me in the back. This could all be a part of Hank's plan. What if he and Tom are in on this together?

Hank could have easily orchestrated this little getaway. He has so much influence with these people. How do I know Tom isn't one of them? I want to stop and demand answers, but he's holding Bear. "Tom," I say. He doesn't turn. "Tom, stop."

"No time," he says.

FIFTY-TWO

om is tiring from Bear's weight. He slows his pace while he adjusts Bear in his arms. I *hope* it's him tiring and not leading me into a setup. I'm not sure what the point of all this would be if it *was*, but I'm feeling paranoid. I feel like Hank could be waiting for me to walk right into his lap.

"Where are we going?" I demand.

"Out of the damn way. We have to go."

"Tom," I hiss. "Where the hell are we going? The path is *that* way." I point to the clearly marked path with solar lights on each side. It probably leads back to the road, or at least the vehicles.

"That's the first place they'll look. Now shut up and follow or I'm gonna drop this fucking dog and get out of here *without* you."

I have little choice but to follow his lead. It doesn't matter what I think right now. Tom's the one with Bear. Where he goes, I go.

It's hard to be sure in the dark, but it seems we're on a hidden path. It's not marked like the other one was. It might just be a game trail, but it seems to lead directly back to my property.

After a few minutes, Tom stops walking to set Bear down. Bear gets up. He wobbles but stays up. It looks like he's willing to give walking a shot.

"Are you sure he can?" I ask.

Tom is panting, out of breath. "Just for a while. I need a break. Unless you want to hold him?"

I sure would if I was strong enough. We both know I'm not, though. I nod my understanding to Tom, and he continues his lead, Bear and I behind. We walk by the light of the moon and stars that peek through the treetops. No flashlights. By now, my eyes have adjusted as much as they can to the darkness. It's still hard to see, but the moonlight helps.

When we reach the little cabin that Ellie first saw, I know exactly where we are. Anger floods through me. It's been so easy for them. They've been here all along. I feel like a fool all over again for trusting Hank. He's a police officer. I wonder how many others he's fooled, too.

When I think about my misplaced trust in Hank, I'm reminded that I could be doing the same thing all over again with Tom. Although being at the cabin I recognize brings relief with the anger. I think if there was going to be an ambush, surely it would be *here*. Wouldn't it? No, I decide. Tom isn't here to trick me. He's really trying to help.

Behind us the entire time, is Ellie. She ambles, looking up at the stars as she walks, reaching out to touch the vegetation that grows alongside the trail. I don't think I'm too obvious, constantly looking behind me. It makes sense I would be worried about being followed at a time like this. I'm not sure if Tom even notices me looking back.

I can tell Bear is tired. He's barely able to keep up the pace. We're near the end of the trail, where it meets our clearing, when Bear stops walking altogether. I think it's from exhaustion, but when he starts growling, I realize it's something else.

Bear isn't stopping because he's tired. He's stopping because there's danger. Even beaten and broken, he's still my protector. He stands his ground, hackles raised, stiff tail and growling in the direction of our clearing.

"Let's turn back," I say to Tom.

Tom shakes his head. "It's too late."

The sound of beating drums starts. "Boom. Boom. Boom." A steady rhythm that sends dread straight to the pit of my stomach. The sound is closer than it's ever been before. Closer even than when they were right outside the trailer door.

I turn to look at Tom. "Did you do this?"

He laughs. "That man of yours. He's one smart devil."

"That's not an answer!"

Tom shakes his head, saying nothing else. I turn to go back the way we came. "Come on, Bear!" We only make it a few feet before I realize we're surrounded.

People are coming out of the forest from behind trees and shrubs, others stand on the beaten path, blocking our way. I swing back around again, ready to run into my clearing to take my chances at getting to the driveway, but Hank is there, blocking the way.

"I applaud your efforts," Hank says with a grim smile. He nods to Tom. "The one person we couldn't help in this town."

"You're not helping anyone!" I say.

"Oh, but we are, Paisley. You'll see. We are." Hank turns towards Tom. "We had Paisley so convinced that you were trouble. We had *you* so convinced that *she* was trouble." Hank shakes his head in disbelief. "How did you figure it out?" He turns back to me. "What made you trust him?"

The others surrounding us have been moving in steadily closer, waiting for Hank's signal to grab us. Bear's still at my side, ready to protect me to the death. My throat tightens as I fight back tears. This was our last chance to escape. I can't imagine how I'm going to get us out of this now. The hope drains from me, leaving me feeling drained and empty. *Poor Bear. I'm so sorry, boy.*

I can keep Hank talking to buy us time. He's obviously curious. But what's the point? More time for what? To extend our deaths by a few minutes? Tom answers Hank first. Speaking loudly enough for all to hear. "I knew something was going on when I found out you was fuckin' her behind Charity's back."

A gasp goes through the others. Hank turns bright red. In a flash, he slaps Tom across the face. Tom stumbles backward laughing. He's thrilled that he's pissed off Hank. "Oops. Was I not supposed to say that?" Tom asks, nearly doubling over from his laughter.

"It's a lie!" Hank declares for all to hear.

"What?" I ask. I'm confused that he would be worried about admitting our relationship. He told me he wanted to be with me. Wouldn't that mean he was prepared for the world to know about us?

Hank turns to me, giving me a pointed look. He really doesn't want the others to know. *Why not?*

"He's obviously trying to stir things up between us." Hank speaks to someone behind me. When I turn around, I see the devastated look on Charity's face. It makes me feel like the other woman and I realize that's exactly what I *am*. Suddenly I'm furious with him all over again. He's been lying to *both* of us, not just me.

"You *bastard*," I whisper. Hank flinches. Only he and Tom are close enough to have heard.

When Charity says nothing, Hank says, "Cherry, we'll discuss this further, tomorrow." He gives a nod, and the others make their move. As they swarm, Bear's Barking and snarling rings in my ears. Even in his weakened state, he's a force to be reckoned with. This time they're prepared, though. I see a red dart fly into his side. He quiets before stumbling and falling.

"NO! Bear!"

"It's just a tranquilizer. He's fine for now," Hank says.

"Charity! He's lying! He's a lying bastard!" I scream at her, wanting to flip his world upside down any way I can.

Hank clenches my arm in his fist. "You better pray she doesn't believe you. You have no idea what she'll do to you." He grounds out in my ear. I expect to see fury in his eyes, but there's only worry.

There's a hush in the struggle as everyone stills to let Charity through to where Hank and I stand. The moment she reaches us, she grips my other arm even harder than Hank. "Shut your lying mouth, you bitch," she says. There's a loud crack and my world goes dark.

FIFTY-THREE

When I open my eyes, I'm lying on the ground in our clearing, bound by my wrists and ankles. Bear is lying beside me, asleep. I look around for Tom, expecting him to be right next to us, but he's not. My breath catches when I find him.

Like me, Tom is tied up. But unlike me, He's ten feet in the air, tied to a massive wooden cross. His head is slumped forward. I can't tell if he's asleep or has just given up.

From the corner of my eye, I make out Hank and Charity having a heated discussion at the edge of the clearing. Everyone else seems to be at the base of Tom's cross. They're throwing log after log onto a pile, building up a pyre.

A few feet from Tom, a second pyre is being built without a cross. I can only assume it's for Bear, unless they've gone back to grab Charlie. At this point, I'm not sure who's being sacrificed. Charity could plan on throwing me on there too, for all I know.

I pull at the rope tied around me, trying to wiggle myself free. It's tied so tight I'm going numb in my fingers and toes. "Bear," I whisper. I nudge into him, trying to wake him up. "Bear," I say again, this time a little louder. His eyes open, but he doesn't move. He's so groggy he can barely hold his eyelids open.

"Bear," I repeat when his eyelids close. They pop back open. He's trying to stay with me. They must've given him one hell of a tranquilizer. "Bear, let's go." He tries to get up but is still too weak. I'm so frustrated I could scream.

He can't get up yet, but he might be able to help me with this rope. I push my bound wrists in front of his mouth. Slowly, he sticks his tongue out to lick the rope. "Get it, Bear," I say. He looks up at me with confused eyes. "Get it." I'm using the same tone as when he's chasing after a toy. I wave my wrists around a little, trying to get him to bite.

At my tone, Bear thumps his tail. He's waking up a little more. *Yes!* He licks at the rope again, giving a playful whimper. "Get it, Bear," I urge. He opens his mouth a little, and in my eagerness, I shove my wrists towards him. It's a mistake. Bear backs off, confused. He doesn't understand what I want from him.

I look around for something that might help. *Anything* that might help. It seems everyone has a job to do and is so focused on it that, for once, Bear and I don't seem to matter much. We've been left alone in the shadows. A blessing, really. I inch my way across the grass, trying to be discreet. Bear seems to catch on, inching forward to follow me.

We're far from the driveway and the cover of the trees, but it's better than laying still and waiting for them to come back. Sweating with the effort of crawling while tied up, we've only made it a few feet before Hank makes an announcement to the group. "May I have your attention, please?"

We haven't had enough time to go anywhere. There's no choice but to stop moving while he speaks to the others, so we're not noticed.

Everyone stops what they're doing. They gravitate

towards Hank, giving him their full attention. It would be the perfect opportunity to continue our getaway efforts if Hank wasn't staring directly at us.

"We've all worked extremely hard for this moment," Hank says. The group of onlookers claps, agreeing that it's been an effort.

"Mr. Lanson reached out to our community for our help, and we were glad to answer the call. It's up to us to see this through. Without our help, Mrs. Lanson would be lost." The group cheers, growing more excited with each word Hank speaks.

"We must help her," they chant. Hank lets them have their say for a few seconds before quieting them again.

"Now, there's been some recent developments tonight. Highly unusual." He looks around the group, eyeing each individual. It's so quiet I think I could hear a pinprick in the grass.

"Mr. Lanson has volunteered to sacrifice himself for his wife."

Gasps go all around. Many are shocked, disbelieving that he would do such a thing. "Does he know what comes?" someone in the crowd asks.

Hank holds out placating hands. "Of course, he knows. I tried to talk him out of it myself. This is what he wants, folks. This is what will heal his family."

He's so believable, he makes me second guess the truth. I wonder if Charlie really did volunteer. He could have after he was hit by Tom. The others murmur amongst themselves, amazed that a man would do such a thing. "There's something else," Hank says.

The crowd quiets again, hanging on to Hank's every word. "That man," Hank points to Tom. "He's been trying to hurt Paisley!"

There's an uproar. The crowd boos and chants, "Punish." Some throw things up at Tom, trying to shame him.

"This man has been whispering lies in her ear. He has been trying to undo all of our hard work. He is *evil*. What must we do?"

"PUNISH HIM!" the crowd cries in unison. There are so many people here, it seems like the entire town has turned up for a concert. If I wasn't afraid for our lives, I would be completely amazed at how Hank has accomplished this kind of organization. *Everyone* is in on it.

There are faces from all over town that I recognize. The woman at the checkout in the grocery store. The woman at the gas station. The man at the ice cream parlor. The man at the post office. I wonder how they've never been caught. How has their group grown this far?

Hank is standing in front of the crowd, looking from face to face. He seems to revel in controlling them. He seems to love having that kind of power. The others seem to be blind to the fact that he's feeding them exactly what they need, to react how *he* wants. They're blind to the fact that half of what he says is a lie. Probably more than half.

When Hank's eyes land on mine, I hope he sees how horrified I am. Even if he's not killing me and Bear, I have to get us out of here. It seems I must get us out of this town and maybe even the entire state. Hell, if I make it out of this I'm moving to the opposite end of the country.

FIFTY-FOUR

With the crowd full of excitement and rage, demanding Tom's punishment, Hank gives the signal. The moment he does, the drums start beating. "Boom… Boom… Boom…" I try to look around for Charlie, but he's still nowhere to be seen. It's probably a strategy. If he saw what was about to happen to Tom, he might be harder to control.

As the drums beat, two people bring out containers of gasoline. They circle Tom, splashing it all over him and his pyre. Tom hangs from his cross, pleading for them to stop. "Please!" he cries. "Please, don't do this!"

Seeing this hardened man, who once showed up on my driveway with a shotgun, in such a humbled and humiliating position, breaks my heart. I wanted him to come down a peg or two, but not like this.

There's no love lost between us. I don't even like the man. But I still feel for him. He's being drenched in gasoline, about to be burned alive. Terror is written all over his face.

Even from this distance, I can see his face is soaked in tears and running snot. They ignore his pleas as they continue spreading the accelerant. Once they finish, a third person lights a match. In an instant, Tom is engulfed in flames. His screams of agony fill the night air. I cry, laying helpless, listening to his wails.

The flames calm the onlookers, who are silent now as they watch Tom burn to death. No one makes any effort to help him or save him. Black smoke fills the air, along with the stench of burning flesh. I gag, almost throwing up from the smell.

Bear whimpers in fear at my side. He's the only one keeping me going. There's no possible way to know what's to become of him. If I don't get him out of here, Hank's bound to have his way with him. I use my shoulder to wipe some tears from my face, then with Hank's and everyone's attention on Tom, I continue my slow crawl across the grass.

Eventually Tom's screaming stops. The fire crackles with the sound of burning wood and charred bone. Bear and I have gained several more feet towards freedom. I'm aiming us toward the driveway. It's full of cars blocking us in, but that doesn't bother me. If I can reach the Jeep, I can get us the hell out of here.

The first thing I'm going to do is call for help for Charlie. I'm not stupid enough to think I'll be able to do anything for him myself. I'll call anyone who will listen and get them out here. I just hope there's enough time.

As soon as the thought runs through my head, I hear the beating drums again. Panic explodes in my chest. *Charlie. No, no!* It's too late. The crowd chants "Sacrifice. Noble sacrifice. Sacrifice. Noble sacrifice..." It's enough to make me vomit. My stomach lets go, unable to take any more torment. With an empty stomach, the only thing that comes up is bile.

I see Charlie now. Someone is leading him to the second pyre. He's looking down at his feet, swaying as if he's been drugged. He probably has been. It wouldn't surprise me.

Unlike Tom, Charlie looks at peace. He doesn't have the look of a man about to be burned alive.

There's an internal debate that goes on in my mind for a split second. I have to *do* something. My plans of running for help have been thrown out the window. There's no time for that now. Yes, it's Charlie's fault we're here, but how can I just leave him like this? I can either *try* to get away unnoticed still, or I can *try* to help Charlie. I probably can't get him out of here, but maybe I can make it less painful for him.

"Charlie!" I scream as loud as I can.

Dazed, Charlie looks up, scanning the crowd for me. He doesn't find me because I'm not in the crowd. I'm still tied up on the grass, much farther away than the others.

They haven't reached his pyre yet. "Charlie, run!" I scream again.

"Please bring Paisley forward," Hank says. "If the dog gives you trouble, give him another sedative."

Two people break away from the crowd, heading my way.

"Bear, it's okay," I whisper in his ear. I don't want him to protect me this time. If they give him another sedative, he'll be out like a light, and I need him awake. I look into his eyes, silently pleading for him to understand. "No, Bear. It's *okay*," I say again. "Stay, boy." I give him a kiss on his nose.

When one man scoops me up into his arms, I don't fight him. I smile at Bear, showing him everything is okay. He looks up at me, waiting. I can see his muscles tense and mine are tense too. *Please, Bear.* The other man watches Bear for a moment, waiting to see if he's going to cause problems.

We all let out a breath when we walk away, and Bear stays put. The crowd parts, allowing us through to Hank, where I'm set down. Hank gives me a grim smile. He whispers, "I'm sorry for this. It's tradition. There's no way out of it." I meet his eyes. He looks so sincere. How can I trust him? What does it matter if he's sorry, anyway? *He's* the one doing this.

Hank addresses the crowd. "The sacrifice is ready."

"A NOBLE SACRIFICE," the crowd chants back.

"Let she who is to be healed make the sacrifice."

"A NOBLE SACRIFICE."

Hank takes out a dagger, holding it up for the crowd to see. A large red ruby is at the hilt and the handle is wrapped in leather. He flips the dagger upside down so the handle is pointing up. He pushes a button, and the end of the handle flips up. It's a built in lighter.

"Let it be done," Hank says.

"A NOBLE SACRIFICE!" the crowd roars.

Hank turns to me. He bends down to slice the rope away from my ankles. He holds me by my shoulders and looks into my eyes. "*You* are the one who has to do it."

I shake my head. "You're insane! You can't make me, Hank. No. I won't!" I start to back away from him, but there's nowhere to go. The crowd is surrounding us. The crazed look on everyone's faces tells me I'm better off here, next to Hank. "You can't make me," I say again. "Can't we kill him another way? Why does it have to be fire?"

"It's tradition, like I said. And I *can* make you." He nods toward Bear. I look to see a man standing over him with a pistol in his hands.

"No! What then? Kill my dog. Then who will light Charlie on fire? I still won't do it!"

"I'll do it myself," Charlie says.

"Charlie, no! This is deranged!" I cry. "Charlie, please!" I'm screaming at him, pleading for him to stop this insanity but nothing is getting through to him.

"It must be done!" he screams back at me.

The light from Tom's fire illuminates Charlie's face. I can see the tears glistening on his cheeks and I realize he's as heartbroken as I am. He's hiding it so well, trying to be stoic. I look around, desperate, panicked. There's no way out of this.

FIFTY-FIVE

Panic. I can't think, I can barely breathe. My palms are sweaty. My whole body is shaking. They have me in checkmate. There's no escaping this hell. With eyes full of tears, I look at Hank, pleading one last time. "Please don't do this."

"Are you going to do it or make poor Charlie do it himself?" he asks.

I can't let Charlie do this to himself. I can't. If I do, they might take it out on Bear, too, and then where would I be? "I'll do it," I say.

"Good girl."

Hank is about to hand the dagger over but stops short. "Slice his palm open to spill his blood first. Spread it across your face, then light the pyre. Try anything," he whispers, "and it's the end of your dog. And I mean *anything!*"

I nod my understanding. I hold my hands out, expecting him to cut the rope from around my wrists too. He smiles as he slices me free.

I take the dagger and turn towards Charlie. With each step I take towards him, I feel like the dagger is driving into my heart. My breath comes in quick gasps. I look up at the sky. Black smoke is still billowing out of Tom's pyre, blending in with the night sky. The smell is so strong; I gag from my proximity to it. I wonder how far scent like that can travel.

I look back at Charlie. He's watching me as I am him. He doesn't blame me, but it doesn't matter. How can I live with myself after this? How is this supposed to be *helping* me? If I wasn't so miserable, I could laugh at the stupidity. In the end, I guess I deserve this. It must be true what they say about karma. This is my payback for all the people I've hurt.

"It's okay," Charlie says as I stand in front of him.

"I'm so sorry," I choke out.

"No. I am. I should've been there for you. What you went through, losing Ellie all alone. I should've been there."

I wipe the tears from my cheeks and then his. I lean to kiss him one last time. "Yes, you should have."

Charlie holds out one of his hands to me. He already knows what I'm supposed to do. Taking his hand in my left, I hold the dagger in my right. Our eyes meet. We share a silent moment of acknowledgment. It's hard to see through the tears, but I know what I must do.

I spare a quick glance at the crowd, where I see the man still standing over Bear. I turn to see Hank, waiting impatiently to get this show on the road. When I look back at Charlie, he nods, giving me permission. I take the dagger and slice Charlie's palm.

Instead of starting at the base of his palm, near his wrist, and cutting towards his fingers, I cut in the opposite direction. The blade touches the center of his palm and slices up towards his wrist. I push the blade down as hard as I can, dragging it past the bottom of his hand, through the veins in his wrist.

Charlie is silent through the pain as blood spills out of him. He holds his hand to his chest, trying to hide it as much as possible. Charlie knows as well as I that If Hank knew what I'd done, it would be the end of Bear.

It's the last thing he does for me on this earth-protecting Bear. From his distance, Hank sees I've completed the cut, but he doesn't know I've cut into Charlie's wrist.

It won't take long for Charlie to bleed out. He'll be dead before the fire can claim him. I couldn't let him burn the way Tom did. I dip my fingers into Charlie's blood and wipe it across my face the way Hank instructed. Stepping away from Charlie, I take a small stick and light it on fire with the other end of the dagger. I toss it, lighting up my sacrifice.

The drums beat again, making my skin crawl in revulsion. As they pound, the crowd of onlookers chants, "Noble sacrifice. Noble sacrifice," over and over. All I want is to lie back down in the grass, next to Bear. I'm not allowed, though. Someone leads me back to stand next to Hank and Charity.

They're holding hands now. Hank looks on, watching Charlie burn, but Charity turns to me. "Well done," she says.

I don't acknowledge her. I turn away, looking for Bear. While I'm searching, I see Ellie in the crowd. She's staring up at her daddy burning. Guilt clenches my lungs, suffocating me. I feel dazed and light-headed from the smoke and stench of burning flesh.

"When can we leave?" I ask Hank.

"Unfortunately, it will be a while, yet," Charity says. "There will be one more sacrifice tonight."

"Oh? Another poor soul you're trying to help?" I ask.

Charity laughs with delight. "No. Only you, dear."

"You already helped me. Charlie was my sacrifice. Hank?" I'm looking right at him as I speak to Charity, but he doesn't turn to look at me. He can't. Even though his face is turned, I can see the guilty look. "*Hank?*" I ask again.

"Charity feels-" he starts. Charity clears her throat and moves her hand slowly up his arm.

"*We* feel," he continues. "It's strange how Charlie doesn't cry out in pain from the flames."

I feel a guilty blush creeping to my cheeks. "He was out of it," I say. "Resigned to die. He seemed drugged to me. Didn't you give him something?"

"No. No one gave him anything. He should be screaming in agony right now, just like Tom," Charity sneers. "Look at him! He's already dead," she hisses.

"How can that be?" I'm hoping I'm a good enough actress to at least convince Hank, if not the witch.

"Enough." Hank finally turns to me. "Bear will be sacrificed next."

"No!" When I scream, the onlookers change their focus from the burning pyres to me. Hank directs his followers.

"We will be building a third pyre tonight. Another noble sacrifice is to be made."

The crowd disperses, following his direction. As they do, I attack Charity, clawing at her face. "You bitch!" I scream. I grab a fistful of her hair and yank back with all my might. She shrieks in pain, flailing her arms around, trying to grab hold of me.

Hank's eyes are wide with shock when he sees my attack. He's so surprised that he doesn't immediately move to help her. Charity is moving around, trying to get out from under my grip, but I'm holding onto her hair like it's a lifeline, pulling on it with all my weight. I use my other hand to hit her. I'm punching at her back and sides, clawing at her face. My fingernails drag across her sensitive skin, bringing flesh and blood with them. Then I realize I still have the dagger.

I reach for it, ready to commit murder.

FIFTY-SIX

I grab the leather handle tight in my right hand, ready to either plunge it into her heart or slice it across her neck. I clench my teeth, imagining the satisfaction that will come with this bitch paying for all this suffering. "You fucked with the wrong woman," I whisper in her ear.

I reach back, but then I feel Hank's firm grip on my arm. He pulls me away from Charity and yanks the dagger from my hand. "No!" I yell. He almost looks like he wants to let me do it, too. I don't understand why he interfered if he feels that way.

Charity is panting, holding her hands against her injured face. "You'll pay for that!" she screams. I don't doubt she means it.

Looking into Hank's eyes, I plead with him. "Don't let her take this out on Bear. I already made my sacrifice. Please, Hank."

He looks between me and Charity, weighing the decision. There's something between them that's powerful enough for him to not want to cross her. "We sacrifice the dog," Hank says.

"No! Aren't you supposed to be the leader here?"

Charity has a smug look of satisfaction. Hank ignores

me. He walks away, taking Charity with him. "Stay here," he says without turning back.

I look around. Everyone is busy again, building a third pyre for Bear. I'm standing alone. He just expects me to obey. There's nothing stopping me from running. *Nothing.* Except Bear. I can't leave him. Frantic to find him now, I leave my spot to look everywhere in the yard.

Bear isn't in the spot I left him. Of course, he wouldn't be. I look through the crowd to see if he's between them. He's not. I look around the edges of the yard, in all the shadows I can get to. He's nowhere. I could yank my hair out with frustration. I look up at the sky, watching the smoke rising into the stars.

Where would they have him? I look towards the trailhead leading through the forest, back to the cabin. I wonder if he's there. I take off in a sprint.

"Hey! Grab her!" I hear someone yell behind me.

My desperation feeds the adrenaline coursing through me. I run faster than I knew I was capable of. Back in the dark forest, the trees block out most of the moonlight. I run blind. "Bear!" I scream. "Bear! Bear!"

There are voices up ahead. I stop running, unsure of my next move. The decision is made for me when I see Hank leading the group of people he's with. They're carrying a wooden dog crate. Inside, is my Bear. Hank sees me at the same time I see them. He doesn't look surprised that I'm here.

I'm the one who's surprised when Bear starts growling and snarling. He has a muzzle on again, but it doesn't deter him. He's working at getting it off and doing a good job of it, too. They haven't given him any more sedatives. Charity wants him to suffer to the fullest extent possible. With Bear wide awake and aware now, he's putting up a good fight, even through the cage. The men carrying him eye the crate skeptically.

"Bear!" I run to him. "Bear, I'm here!"

"Get her, please," Hank says.

As they grab my arms, I say, "You don't have to grab me. I'm staying next to Bear." They ignore me, escorting me behind Hank and the rest of the group.

"How are you going to make me stay when Bear's gone?" I ask Hank. He keeps walking, ignoring me. I hound him with questions, not expecting him to really answer, just wanting to annoy the shit out of him and everyone else. "Is this part of the *tradition*? Are there normally two sacrifices? You'll have no hold over me. How are you going to make me do this? How do you think you're going to get away with this?"

At the end of the trail now, we look into the clearing. Hank is fed up. He turns around to say something, but I'm looking past him, to the view. My eyes are wide with amazement, shock, and disbelief at what's going on in the clearing. Hank sees the look on my face. He turns back around, curious to see what I see.

The night is lit up by red and blue lights. The road and driveway are filled with cop cars and police. Police are in every square inch of the yard.

Those who were building the third pyre are scattered across the yard, running from police officers who are chasing them down. A fire truck is spraying the still burning pyres. Spotlights scan the area. One shines directly toward our group.

Hank is frozen. I look at him, waiting to see what he'll do. The gears are turning in his brain. He's weighing the options carefully, deciding on which route to take for self-preservation. It only takes a moment for his instincts to kick in. He grabs Gladice's arm. "I need backup!" he yells, waving his other hand in the air to get noticed. "Backup, I need backup! I'm an undercover officer!"

"Liar!" I yell. The others in our group look at Hank with disbelief.

"How can you do this?" Gladice asks. The look of betrayal on her face is so ironic I could almost laugh. Did she really trust him? I suppose I'm as much of a fool as she is because I trusted him, too.

The two men who are holding Bear, drop the wooden crate to run back through the forest. Those who are holding me let go and follow the others.

I drop next to Bear, trying to pry his cage open. He almost has his muzzle off. I'm able to reach my fingers through the slats and free his face completely. There's a padlock keeping the door sealed shut. I look around for something to hit it, *anything* that will help. I grab a large rock and pound it against the lock. It accomplishes nothing but smashing my own fingers. I reach for a branch to try prying between some of the wood slats, but I'm not strong enough to break them.

"Dammit!" I scream, kicking the ground.

"Hank! Please! It's over now. Let him out. I won't say a word, just let him out."

Hank looks me up and down, realizing how much I know, how much I can say about him. It's a matter of who's word they'll believe over who. He's with the Sheriff's department. I'm a lonely housewife. Who will they believe? I can see he's leaning towards silencing me.

"You said you wanted to be with me," I say.

"I did," he says. "I do, Paisley." He pulls out the dagger. With it, he twists around so his back is to the commotion. No one sees when he slits Gladice's throat. I gasp as her body falls to the ground. "Don't you see? It's Charity in the way. She's crazy. She'll hurt you."

"It's over now. She can't hurt me anymore."

"She can. She will." He steps towards me. There's no one left but the two of us and Bear.

"Hank. You're undercover, remember? You can just get her arrested."

He cackles. "If only it were that simple." He flips the dagger over. Flipping the handle up, he ignites the lighter.

"Never mind. Forget the dog," I say. "Let's get out of here. Together. Let someone else deal with him." I reach for Hank, urging him to come with me, to get his mind off Bear.

"She'll come after him, anyway. It's better it was by me." He tries to move past me to Bear. Before Hank takes two steps, I pull him back toward me. I throw myself at him in an embrace. I hold him to me in one of the most passionate kisses we've shared.

He drops his guard, closing the lighter and holding me in his arms, meeting every stroke of my tongue. Breathless, we both lose track of ourselves. It's a necessary evil. I'll do anything to buy more time.

Hank hasn't noticed the gnawing sound coming from Bear's cage. He's been chewing away at the wooden slats, and it's only a matter of time before he gets free. There are also police everywhere. How long can it possibly take for them to reach us?

Hank pulls away from me. His eyes go wide with shock, but he's not looking at me. He's looking behind me. I turn my head to see Charity.

FIFTY-SEVEN

From the look on her face, she's heard and seen enough to realize she's been lied to. *Welcome to the club, bitch.* "Don't let me interrupt," she says. She holds a pistol up. *My gun.* Hank and I are standing so close, I'm not sure who she's aiming at. Probably me.

Hank must think the same thing because he pushes me out of the way. "Cherry."

She cocks the gun. "No more lies."

Hank throws the dagger at Charity as she pulls the trigger. I hear the thud of the knife hitting its mark. The jolt from the impact throws her hand. "BOOM!" The explosion of the gun makes my ears ring. I still don't have my footing after Hank's push. I stumble over my own feet, trying to steady myself.

I look at Hank. He's staring at me. The look on his face scares me. He looks… *scared.* The sound of Bear's barking fills my ears, along with the ringing of the gun. There's a deafening crack and for a moment, I think Charity has shot the gun again. It's not Charity, though. It's Bear breaking through the wooden planks of his cage.

He leaps out, running straight for Hank. Now unarmed,

Hank has no other option but to try running away. He turns. The opening is only a few feet away. If he can make it out of the trees, there might be hope of some help. But Bear is too fast now that the drugs are worn off. Hank makes it two feet before Bear leaps onto his back, knocking him to the ground.

"Get him, Bear! Kill him!" I scream. I hear Bear's snarling and the sound of his teeth ripping into flesh. I hear Hank's screams of agony. A smile spreads across my face as I listen.

I'm seeing black in the corners of my vision. It makes little sense. What's wrong with me? I look down at myself, patting my body. Then I see the blood pooling out of my shoulder, near my bra strap. Seeing the wound seems to make the pain register in my brain.

The pain is so intense I feel like I'm on fire. My fingertips are tingling from the lack of blood flowing to them. I try to wiggle them, but moving my arm in any way sends bolts of pain through me. I fall to the ground from weakness. The dark corners are creeping in. I can barely keep my eyes open.

"Bear," I whisper. That's all I know before my world goes black.

I HEAR THE BEEPING OF A HEART RATE MONITOR BEFORE I open my eyes. For a moment, I imagine I've just given birth to Ellie. A nurse walks through the door, carrying my precious bundle in a soft pink blanket. Ellie opens her big eyes, looking right into my soul. "Hi baby girl," I say.

The nurse gently places her in my arms. I hold her close to my chest, nuzzling my face against her soft skin. Peace envelopes me like a warm blanket as I close my eyes, enjoying the best feeling in the world. The feeling I've waited so long for.

"Mommy?"

Ellie's voice pulls me out of my fantasy. She's sitting in the chair next to my hospital bed. I'm hooked up to all kinds of monitors and sensors. My arm is wrapped up so stiffly I can't move it.

An IV drip is connected with what I assume is morphine. There's a little red button connected to the cord that I press without thinking. When I do, I watch the dose of medicine drip down before flowing through the cord into my vein. To my right, a table on wheels holds a cup and pitcher of water. It's almost the same scene as when I lost her, in a different place and time.

"Cupcake, where's Bear?" I ask.

"Don't know," she says.

I press the call button on the side of my bed. Within moments, a nurse comes into the room. "How do you feel?" she asks.

"My arm hurts like hell. Is there a cop or someone I can talk to about what happened?"

"Of course. The doctor would like to see you first."

"Please," I say. "Please, I need to find out about my dog."

The nurse looks at me with eyes full of sympathy. I'm not sure what she knows or what she's thinking, but when she says, "Detective Stall left his number. I'll give him a call." I feel nothing but relief.

A few minutes later, the doctor comes in to examine me. He asks me some questions before checking my arm. It's not long before he leaves to check on other patients. Soon after he leaves, the detective arrives.

He knocks on the door before entering. "Paisley, I'm Detective Stall. I'd like to have a discussion if you feel up to it."

"Yes, please come in. Please, do you know where my dog is?"

"Was your dog the German Shepherd?"

"Yes. His name is Bear."

"Right. Well, Bear was taken by animal control. He mauled a law enforcement officer nearly to death."

Nearly. That means Hank is still alive. "He was protecting my life." I clench my fist on my good arm. It's excruciatingly hard to keep my temper under control, but yelling at this man will not get me anywhere. "That *law enforcement officer* had my husband burned at the stake."

"I saw." Stall frowns. "It's not up to me, about the dog. Don't shoot the messenger, here. Animal control has him in custody until they run their investigation. Someone will contact you, have no fear. I'm here to talk about what happened."

"Can you put in a word with them? Please, there's nothing I'm worried about *more* right now. He's all I have left!" I swallow the lump in my throat as tears fall down my face.

Stall hands me a tissue. "I'll see what I can do." He clears his throat. "I have an idea of what you must've gone through, but I'd love to hear your side of things and not just make a bunch of guesses and assumptions. You fill me in, and I'll see what I can do to help Bear out."

"Deal." I start at the beginning, relaying every detail to Detective Stall. I include the altercation with Tom, the affair with Hank, the drums at night, the cabin in back, everything I can think of. I explain how Charlie was part of this group and lured me to the property with the guise of building a new home. I end by explaining how Bear was the next in line to be burned on a pyre.

"He was trying to protect me from Hank and Charity, don't you see now?"

Stall nods. "You were tremendously lucky to get out of there alive."

I nod to my shoulder. "Almost didn't."

He gives me a tight smile. "We have reason to believe this cult had more in mind for you and weren't going to let you go. They're suspected of the murders of several women in the area. All of them were butchered beyond recognition."

I gasp. I hold my hand over my mouth in disbelief. "You mean the women with the missing uteruses?"

For a moment, Stall looks confused. "That's not public information."

"I heard it on Channel 5 news," I say.

His confusion changes to anger. "Goddamn Shirley Black. She can't keep her mouth shut for anything." He shakes his head. "I'm sorry. I wasn't informed she aired that information yet. We had an agreement that it would be kept confidential for now. Anyway, yes. The women were all missing their uteruses."

"How terrible. I'm so thankful the police came when they did." I shudder. "How did they know?"

"Tom Morgan called us."

THE DAY AFTER I SPOKE WITH DETECTIVE STALL, SOMEONE from animal control shows up at the hospital. It is not the same officer as before- Gonzales. This is someone different. She tries to shame me over what Bear did to Hank, without listening to a word I say in his defense. In her eyes, Bear is guilty as sin and should be euthanized.

Detective Stall was true to his word, however. I'm not sure who he spoke with, but it kept this heartless bitch from killing my dog. "You're lucky," she says. "If I had my way, that dog would be toast. An assault on a human," she shakes her head. "Unacceptable. That dog is *dangerous.*"

"He was protecting me! The man was trying to kill both of us."

"Stop blaming the victim."

"I'm not-"

"It's out of my hands. The investigation is closed. He will be returned to you as soon as you're released from the hospital."

"I suggest you keep your fucking mouth closed if it's out of your hands. I don't need or want your opinion," I say. "You know nothing, and you're not willing to listen. I want my dog *now.* Not when I'm released. Now."

She looks shocked to be spoken to this way. It's hard to imagine anyone *liking* an animal control officer. These people are way too full of themselves. Glorified mall cops is all they are.

They have too much power from the county and should be stripped of it. If it hadn't been for Detective Stall, this woman would've murdered my dog without a second thought. It makes my blood boil to know she could've had that kind of power over him.

This *officer* should find animal abusers. She should be worried about *protecting* animals, making sure they have good homes, not killing them. Even if Bear was in the wrong, it should be *my* responsibility to correct the behavior or take better care of him. It shouldn't result in Bear being declared *dangerous* or *euthanized.* Owners should be held liable, not a dog for just being a dog.

I can see the hatred in her eyes. I hope she can see it reflecting from mine, too. I'm disgusted by this woman, who has the legal authority to kill innocent animals just because *she* deems them worth killing. It's insanity. And I've seen enough of it to recognize it well.

She fumbles over her words, but I don't want to hear anything else she has to say. "I want my dog you fucking bitch," I say. "Now. Or do I need to call my attorney?" She leaves the room without another word.

FIFTY-EIGHT

One Year Later

Waves crash down one after another. "Run!" I shriek as the tide rolls in, wetting Bear's paws and our feet. He follows my lead as I walk along the beach, Ellie close behind. After splashing through the water, we turn inland for the trail that leads over a dune and through the beach grass.

At the end of the trail is a row of houses. Each one looks out onto the ocean. Ellie walks ahead of me as I dig into my pocket for the key to our front door. "Come on Mommy," she says.

"Slow down, turbo," I laugh.

Inside, we rinse the sand off our feet and legs before getting lunch. As I make Ellie a peanut butter and jelly sandwich, I look out the picture window, watching the ocean waves crash down. I think about how much I love our new home and smile.

Charlie had a life insurance policy that paid for our new home. When I tried to list the land for sale, I was informed it wasn't in my or Charlie's names. Surprise, surprise. It was the property of *The Society of The Trees*. One more twist of the knife. I'm just glad to be free of it now.

I'm glad to be back in town again, too. It's not the city, but it's just right. We have the best of both worlds now, with the added bonus of the Atlantic Ocean. Town-life with a large private yard for Bear is just what the doctor ordered.

Speaking of doctor, Dr. Reymore nearly had a meltdown when he found out about Charlie and the cult. Out of all the details, his takeaway was, "You're still seeing her?" Why is *that* the only thing that matters?

"No," I said. "Charlie was imagining it. He didn't even talk to me about it, he *assumed*." Not a lie.

"I want you to see a therapist in person. No more video chats," he said.

"I don't feel comfortable with another therapist."

"Paisley, it's for the best. I'm worried about you. *Especially* after this. Do you realize the gravity? Your husband was in a cult without your knowledge."

"I realize," I said. After a pause, I added, "Okay. Who do you want me to see?"

He sent over his referral, and I've been seeing Dr. Cliffe once a month ever since. I'm not sure why I continue to see her. It's such a waste of time. Although, I have to admit, I love being able to fool a therapist. There's something so powerful in the act of lying when I know she'll believe every word that comes out of my mouth.

These people are supposed to understand the inner workings of the mind, supposed to be able to identify mental illness and treat it. And yet, they take me at face value. How can they be so blind when they know of my history? It baffles me.

It makes sense in a way. They're not investigators. It's not their job to figure out if I'm lying or not. But surely they would be able to easily tell if they just paid attention?

At my last appointment, Dr. Cliffe updated me on Hank's trial. We've talked about my involvement in detail. Besides giving sworn testimony, Dr. Cliffe feels it's best for me to stay completely out of it and I agree.

I don't *want* to be involved. It's one reason I moved across the country, just like I swore I would. So, she keeps me updated with any pertinent news that's not in the media and unavoidable, and it's good enough for me.

"Hank has been sentenced," she said during our session.

"Finally."

"He's not going to jail. He's going to an institution for the criminally insane."

"What?" I was so shocked I shot up from my chair.

"Why does that upset you?" she asked.

I pace. "It upsets me because he's not insane. Hank deserves to be in jail."

"He's not free."

"I know that. It's just disturbing."

When I saw her watching me clench and unclench my fists, I stopped moving and sat back down.

"Detective Stall was upset as well."

"I'm sure he was."

The way she looked at me was uncomfortable. Dr. Cliffe has this way of staring at me with wide eyes like she's shocked, but it's *all* the time. It's just her normal look.

"What of the others they arrested?" I asked. "Please tell me *someone* went to jail."

"Yes. Some others were sent to jail, some made deals with the DA for their testimony."

I cried, thinking about Charlie burning on the pyre. Everything that happened to us and poor Bear. "It feels like there's very little justice being done," I said.

"I'm sure some of the other victim's families feel the same."

Other victims? What other victims? For a moment, I was confused, totally forgetting about the other women. The ones who'd been chopped up. How could I forget Hank and his cult killed them, too? I hope Dr. Cliffe didn't see the confusion on my face. What she might think.

"Yes," I said.

"G OODNIGHT, M OMMY," E LLIE SAYS WHEN I TUCK HER IN FOR the night. Many nights we snuggle together in my bed, but tonight she's in her own. Tonight, I'm feeling nostalgic. It's taken me a long time to heal. A long time to get to the point where I can truly be free.

"Goodnight, cupcake," I say. I give her a kiss on the forehead, then head into my own room.

As I lay in bed, I stare at my computer screen, scrolling through social media. A picture of the woman I met at work today, Emily Davis, stares back at me on the monitor.

I've finally gone back to work, just like I wanted. It's been good for me. Working in a library is like a dream come true. It's much better than my old job in sales. I feel no stress whatsoever, which is amazingly freeing.

The best part of my new job is when women come in with their children. Some mothers are so great with their kids, so patient and loving. Some are not so much.

Those are the ones I like the most. I like them because they give me an opportunity. The opportunity to help their children. Emily Davis is one of those women.

I look over at my open closet, smiling at the uniform hanging front and center. It wasn't hard to snag one from the gas company. I even have my own name tag that reads, *Taylor.*

After moving to this new area, I had to change tactics a little. Turns out, forty acres of forest is the perfect place to hide an old beat-up van. I've had to get rid of it, of course. Since *The Society of The Trees* has taken credit for all those brutal murders in Washington, it wouldn't do having a link left that didn't add up to what police *think* happened.

I have a different van now, but not the land to hide it. I've had to get more creative. I really should thank Charlie. I hold no grudge against him for what he did to our family. It was actually blind luck on my part that he was stupid enough to join a cult the way he did. I couldn't have planned a better scapegoat if I'd tried.

For years, I've had so many emotions towards Charlie. I've felt betrayed, burning rage, heartbreak, guilt for blaming him, and an all-consuming emptiness. I've cycled through these feelings so many times, it's been hard to keep track of exactly *what* I'm feeling sometimes.

Charlie wasn't there for me. He wasn't there when I needed him the most. He wasn't there when our child was dying in my womb. We needed him. He *promised* and look what happened.

There's one thing that's helped me. One thing in my life that's allowed me to release the pent-up fury. Helping children. Helping those children whose mothers aren't good enough for them.

I look back at Emily's profile on my screen. Tomorrow she'll be getting a call from the gas company. Everything is ready. I'm going to help her children.

Closing my laptop, I get up to tuck it away inside my closet. At the bottom of my closet, beneath the carpet, the floorboards lift. It's my special space. A secret even from Ellie.

I come in here to remember. When I run into a woman who complains about being pregnant, who complains about her children, who wishes she wasn't a mother, I come in here. When I run into a woman like Emily Davis, I come here.

Pulling back the carpet, I lift the loose boards. What started out as a small section of closet floor, now spans half the length of my closet. Beneath the floorboards lie rows of glass jars. I reach down to select one.

The jar feels cold in my hand. I grit my teeth, remembering. The uterus sits preserved inside its jar to remind me. It reminds me of what I've lost. It reminds me I *can* make those who are ungrateful pay. I *can* help their children be free of them.

THANK YOU FOR READING!

Enjoyed The Neighbors? Please consider leaving a review

Reviews help authors more than you might think. Even just a few words make a difference and are greatly appreciated. You never know if your words might inspire the next reader to pick up this story!

ACKNOWLEDGEMENTS

First, I'd like to thank my husband and son. Thank you for all you do and have done to support and encourage me through this journey. Thank you for every moment you've been there, watching me learn and grow as an author. Every milestone, big or small, you've cheered me on. Thank you for believing in me and thank you for giving me the most amazing life, the one I grew up dreaming of. I'm so blessed to have both of you. I love you to infinity and beyond.

My husband, Michael, is not a reader by any means, and yet he still reads snippets of scenes for me when I need quick feedback. He listens if I want to read something back to him or ask his opinion on characters. Michael knows how important my writing is to me and even though it's not his cup of tea, he stands by me every step of the way. His support and help mean the world. Thank you, dear, with all my heart.

I want to thank my amazing beta readers, especially Karen, Chrissie, and Terence, for taking the time to read this book and give me valuable insight. You are invaluable to the writing process, and I sincerely thank you for your help and feedback.

Finally, last but certainly not least, thank you dear reader, for showing your support in my writing by reading this book. Whether you are new to my work or are coming back for more, I truly hope you enjoyed the read.

K. LUCAS

The Wrong Stranger

He's always enjoyed the darker things in life, finding that the thrill of the hunt and the kill are the only aspects of life he truly loves...

Bill Wright has spent years building a successful career that allows him ample time to work on his favorite hobby, all while blending in with the rest of society. After a tragedy hits home, Bill's marriage to a woman nearly half his age teeters on the edge, threatening his way of life.

He begins to see another side to his wife that recaptures his attention. Bill invites Ashley to join him in his interests, hoping to reignite some passion in their relationship.

Holding on to a secret she isn't aware of keeping, Ashley struggles against the void that comes with each agonizing headache as she discovers who her husband really is… and who truly lies within herself.

… but will his wife's secret be all that it takes to undo him?

K. Lucas is an author who lives for the unexpected twist. Originally from California, she now lives in the Pacific Northwest with her husband, son, three dogs, cat, chickens, and ducks. After earning a bachelor's degree in information technology, she became a homeschool mom and then a full-time author. She loves all things thrilling & chilling, and her favorite pastimes include reading, watching scary movies, and exploring nature.

CONNECT WITH THE AUTHOR

Website:
www.klucasauthor.com

Sign up for updates:
www.klucasauthor.com/newslettersignup

amazon.com/author/klucas
goodreads.com/klucas
instagram.com/author_klucas
facebook.com/author.klucas
twitter.com/AuthorKLucas
tiktok.com/@klucasauthor
pinterest.com/klucasauthor
BookBub.com/authors/k-lucas